Jesse's DIY Mint Brownies

2 boxes of any kind of chocolate-chunk brownie mix
1 column of chocolate-covered mint cookies (If there are 2 in a box)
Water, oil and eggs
(as directed on the packages)
1 cup of chopped nuts (optional)

1. Crush mint cookies.
2. Follow directions on the brownie packages.
3. Add crushed cookies and nuts.
4. Bake as directed on the packages.

SUSAN MALLERY

Sweet Trouble

HQN™

ISBN-13: 978-0-373-77305-3
ISBN-10:   0-373-77305-6

SWEET TROUBLE

www.HQNBooks.com

Printed in U.S.A.

To Lee—who keeps me sane. You are a gift and I would be lost without you. Thank you.

Sweet Trouble

CHAPTER ONE

"THEY'RE CALLING YOU a ruthless bastard," Diane said as she scanned the article in the business magazine. "You must be happy."

Matthew Fenner looked at his secretary, but didn't speak. Eventually she glanced up and smiled.

"You like being called a ruthless bastard," she reminded him.

"I like respect," he corrected.

"Or fear."

He nodded. "Fear works."

Diana dropped the open magazine on his desk. "Don't you ever want someone to think you're nice?" she asked.

"No."

Being the nice guy meant getting screwed. He'd learned that a long time ago. He picked up one of the messages by his phone. Ironically, the woman who had taught him every aspect of that lesson had just called.

His secretary sighed. "I worry about you."

"You're wasting your time."

"Don't panic. I only do it on my off hours."

He scowled at his fifty-something assistant, but she ignored him. While he would never admit it, the fact that he didn't intimidate her was one of the reasons she'd lasted so long. Although he had a reputation for being the kind of businessman who left his competition bleeding on the side of the road, he didn't enjoy watching his staff cower. At least not all the time.

"Did you have anything else?" he asked, then looked pointedly at the door.

She rose. "Jesse called again. That makes three calls in three days. Are you calling her back?"

"Does it matter?"

"Yes. If you're going to continue to ignore her, I'd like to just tell her and put her out of her misery." Diane frowned. "You're usually more clear with your BGFs. They rarely phone after you dump them."

"I've asked you not to call them that."

Diane blinked innocently. "Have you? I'm sorry. I keep forgetting."

She was lying, but he didn't call her on it. Referring to the women he dated as BGFs—short for bimbo girlfriends—was her way of showing disapproval. She complained his women were interchangeable—like fashion dolls. All physically similar, unnaturally beautiful and lacking in heart and brains. She wasn't wrong.

What Diane couldn't bring herself to believe was that he dated on purpose. He wasn't looking for more.

"She's someone I used to know," he said, then

wished he hadn't. Diane didn't need the information. That part of his life had ended a long time ago.

"Really? Does she actually have a personality, or—" she waved her hands in front of her face as if to keep from fainting "—a brain? Now that you mention it, she sounded almost normal."

"I *didn't* mention it."

"Hmm. I'm sure you did. So tell me about your mysterious past with this woman."

"You can leave now."

"Why is she back in Seattle? Is she nice? Would I like her? Do you like her?"

He pointed at the door.

Diane walked across his office. "So you're saying the next time she calls to put her through, right?"

He ignored her and she left.

Matt rose, then crossed to the window. His office was at the top of an Eastside high-rise with an impressive view. His business life defined every aspect of success. He'd made it. He had everything he wanted and more—money, power, respect and no one to answer to.

Slowly, deliberately, he crumpled the note with the message from Jesse and tossed it into the trash.

DESPITE THE PROMISES of several famous poets and a couple of tear-jerker country songs, Jesse Keyes discovered it *was* possible to go home again, which was just her bad luck. Not that she could blame anyone for her current circumstances—she'd decided to return to

Seattle all on her own. Well, okay, maybe she'd had a little help from the cute guy in her life.

She glanced in the rearview mirror and smiled at her four-year-old son.

"Guess what?" she asked.

His dark eyes brightened as he grinned at her. "Are we there yet?"

"We're here!"

Gabe clapped his hands. "I like here."

They were in town for the summer or however long it took to get her past in order and her future set. Give or take a week.

Jesse put the car in Park, then got out and opened the rear passenger seat. She unbuckled Gabe from his car seat and helped him out of the car. He stood next to her and stared at the four-story building.

"We're staying here?" he asked, his voice low with awe. "Really?"

The extended-stay hotel was modest at best—a local place. Jesse didn't have the money for one of those fancy national chains. But the room came with a kitchen and the online reviews had said it was clean, which is what mattered to her. Once she had an idea of how long they were staying, she would look into renting a furnished apartment in the University District. It was summer, which meant empty rooms while the students were away and cheap rent.

But to Gabe, who'd never been in a hotel in his life, their temporary shelter was exciting and new.

"Really," she said, taking his hand. "Want me to get a room on the top floor?"

His eyes widened. "Can we?" he breathed.

It would mean more stairs for her, but she would feel safer up top. "That's what I asked for."

"Cool!"

His new favorite word. He'd picked it up at day care. It was about the four-hundredth time that day she'd heard it and it was starting to get on her nerves. Then she reminded herself that "cool" was a whole lot better than some other words he could have learned.

Thirty minutes later they were testing the bounce in the two double beds as Gabe tried to decide which one he wanted. She unpacked the single suitcase she'd carried up the three flights of stairs. She really had to think about starting to work out again. Her heart was *still* racing from the climb.

"We're going out for dinner," she said. "How about spaghetti?"

Gabe flung himself at her, wrapping both his arms around her thighs and squeezing as hard as he could. She stroked his soft brown hair.

"Thank you, Mommy," he whispered.

Because eating his favorite food in a restaurant was a rare treat.

Jesse wondered if she should feel guilty for not cooking her first night in Seattle, then decided she would beat herself up later. Right now she was tired. It had been a five-hour drive from Spokane, and she'd worked well past midnight the previous evening, wanting to earn every last tip she could. Money was going to be tight while she was in Seattle.

"You're welcome." She dropped to her knees so she was at eye level with him. "I think you'll really like this place. It's called the Old Spaghetti Factory." A perfect, kid-friendly restaurant. No one would care if Gabe made a mess and she could have a glass of wine and pretend that everything was all right.

"Do I meet my daddy tomorrow?"

Jesse's heart raced again and this time it had nothing to do with taking the stairs. "Probably not tomorrow, but soon."

Gabe bit his lower lip. "I love my daddy."

"I know you do."

Or at least the idea of having a father. Her son was the reason she'd decided to face all the ghosts in her past and come home. He'd started asking questions about his father a year ago. Why didn't he have a daddy? Where was his daddy? Why didn't his daddy want to be with him?

Jesse had debated lying, simply saying that Matt was dead. But five years ago, when she'd left Seattle, she'd vowed to live her life differently. No more lies. No more screwing up. She'd worked hard to grow up, to make a life she was proud of, to raise a son on her own, to be honest, no matter what.

Which meant telling Gabe the truth. That Matt didn't know about him, but maybe it was time to change that.

She didn't allow herself to think about meeting Matt. She couldn't. Not and keep breathing. So for now, there was only her son smiling at her and the love she felt for him. The rest would take care of itself. At least she hoped it would.

Because it wasn't just Matt she had to face. There was Claire, the older sister she'd never really known, and Nicole, the older sister who probably still hated her guts. Talk about a homecoming.

But she would deal with that tomorrow. Tonight there was the promise of spaghetti, then a rousing evening of cartoons and quality time with the best part of her life.

"Are you ready?" she asked as she grabbed her purse, then held out her arms to pick up Gabe.

He jumped into her embrace—loving and trusting—as if she would never hurt him, never let him down. Because she never would—no matter what. At least she'd gotten that part right.

JESSE CHECKED THE address on the piece of paper, then glanced at the portable nav system Bill had let her borrow. They matched.

"Someone's been moving on up," she murmured, taking in the long driveway that led to a house on the lake in the very chichi part of Kirkland.

There was a security gate for the property, but it was open. She was grateful she didn't have to explain her presence to whatever staff might be at the house. Not that she could imagine Matt with staff. They would get on his nerves. At least they would have five years ago. No doubt he'd changed. The man she remembered would never have lived in a massive, sprawling estate with a bronze sculpture on the lawn.

She raised her eyebrows at the confounding piece of modern art, then drove past it. She parked near the wide double doors, behind a BMW convertible. As she climbed out, she tried not to think about how shabby her ten-year-old Subaru looked in comparison. Still, her car was dependable and the all-wheel drive meant safer driving in the Spokane snow.

She patted the dashboard in a silent apology for noticing how pretty the BMW looked gleaming in the sunlight, then grabbed her purse and climbed out. Before heading up the stairs to the front door of the huge house, she checked to make sure her most recent pictures of Gabe were in the front pocket of her purse. She had a feeling that seeing Matt was going to make her nervous. She didn't want to have to search for the photos.

The front door seemed to soar to the sky. She would guess it was maybe fifteen or twenty feet high and solid wood. Visigoths would have trouble breaking into this house. She swallowed against the sudden tightness in her body, reminded herself to keep breathing no matter what, then pressed the bell.

Somewhere deep in the house, a chime sounded. Jesse waited, knowing it could take a while for someone to walk the length of the house. She counted to ten, then twenty. Was she supposed to ring the bell again? It was nine-thirty on a Saturday morning. She'd hoped Matt would be home. Of course, there were a thousand places he could be. The gym, the office, maybe at a friend's house. Make that a *girl* friend. She doubted he was at the grocery store because he was—

The front door opened. Jesse braced herself to see Matt again, only to find herself staring at a tall, slender redhead wearing a very short, sexy nightie and apparently nothing else.

The woman was in her early twenties and beyond beautiful. Her eyes were large, dark green and framed with incredible lashes. Her skin was the color of cream, her breasts pointed at the ceiling and her wide mouth formed a perfect pout.

"Ma—att," she whined, drawing his name out to two syllables. "It's one thing for you to keep telling me we're not exclusive. I accept that. I don't like it, but I accept it. But to have one of *them* show up here on *my* date? That's just wrong."

Jesse hadn't thought the moment through. If she had, she would have realized that a woman answering the door was entirely possible. It had been five years— of course Matt would have moved on. Probably several times.

"I'm not a date," she said quickly, wishing she'd taken more time with her appearance that morning. All she'd done was shower, slap on moisturizer and mascara, then let her long, straight hair air-dry. She'd been more focused on getting Gabe ready.

The redhead frowned. "Ma—att!"

The door opened wider and Jesse instinctively took a step back. Not that a couple of feet of distance was going to lessen the impact of seeing him again.

He was as tall as she remembered, but he'd filled out. An open, short-sleeved shirt hung over worn jeans. She could see his muscled chest and the dark hair there.

Her gaze rose to his face, to the eyes that were so like his son's. Recognition tugged in her belly, making her realize that, despite the time apart, she still missed him. Probably because with Gabe around she could never forget him.

Matt had always had potential—in the past five years he'd grown into it. He exuded power and confidence. He was the kind of man who made women wonder who he was and how they could be with him.

"Jesse."

He spoke her name calmly, as if he wasn't surprised to see her, as if they'd just run into each other last week.

"Hello, Matt."

The redhead put her hands on her hips. "Go away. Shoo."

Shoo? Jesse held in a smile. Was that the best the other woman could do?

"Wait for me in the kitchen, Electra," Matt said, never taking his gaze from Jesse. "This won't take long."

"I'm not leaving. Who is she, Matt?"

Electra? Her name was Electra? Did she have a golden lasso and a flying horse?

"Wait for me in the kitchen," he repeated, his tone stern.

The redhead stomped off. Matt waited until she'd disappeared before stepping back.

"Come in," he said.

Jesse walked into the house.

She had a brief impression of space, lots of wood and incredible views of the lake and the skyline of Seattle in the distance. Then she turned to Matt and drew in a breath.

"Sorry to drop by without any notice. I've been trying to call."

"Have you?"

His gaze was as dark as she remembered, but much more unreadable. She had no idea what he was thinking. Was he upset? Annoyed? Or was she just someone he used to know, someone who was keeping him from his morning coffee?

Seeing him was unsettling—an odd combination of familiar and strange. The last time they'd been in the same room, he'd been so angry, so hurt. He'd lashed out to destroy her and he'd succeeded.

"You didn't get my messages?" she asked, sure that he had.

"What do you want, Jesse? It's been a long time. Why now?"

So much for idle chitchat, she thought, suddenly feeling awkward and nervous. Couldn't they have started with something easier, like, "How are you?"

There were a thousand things she could say, a thousand excuses or explanations. None of them seemed to matter.

She opened her purse, pulled out the pictures, then handed them to him.

"Five years ago I told you I was pregnant and that you were the father. You didn't believe me, even when I said a DNA test would prove the truth. He's four now and he keeps asking about you. He wants to get to know you. I'm hoping enough time has passed that you want that, too."

She wanted to keep talking, explaining, defending herself. Instead she forced herself to press her lips together and stay silent.

Matt took the photos and flipped through them. At first he didn't register much more than a small boy. A boy who was laughing and smiling at the camera. Her words had meant nothing to him. A child? He knew she'd been pregnant. *His* child? Not possible. He'd refused to believe it then and he still didn't believe it. She was back because he was successful and she wanted a piece of the pie. Nothing more.

Almost against his own will, he went through the pictures a second time, then a third, noticing the way the kid looked almost familiar. There was something about his eyes that…

He saw them, then. The similarities. The curve of the chin reflected back at him every morning as he shaved. The shape of the eyes. He recognized parts of himself, hints of his mother.

"What is this?" he growled.

His child? His *child?*

"His name is Gabe," Jesse said softly. "Gabriel. He's four and a really great kid. He's smart and funny and he has a lot of friends. He's good at math, which he probably gets from you."

Matt couldn't focus on her words. They washed over him like rain, making no sense, then moving on. Anger flared, then grew into fury. She'd had his baby and never bothered to say anything?

"You should have told me," he said, his voice thick and cold with rage.

"I did. You refused to believe me, remember? Your exact words were that you didn't care if I was pregnant with your child. You didn't want a kid with me." She squared her shoulders. "He wants to get to know you, Matt. He wants to get to know his father. That's why I'm here. Because it's important to him."

But it wasn't important to her. She didn't have to say that—he already knew it was true.

He thrust the photos back at her, but she shook her head. "Keep them. I know this is a lot to take in. We need to talk and you need to meet Gabe. Assuming you want to."

He nodded because he was too enraged to speak.

"My cell number is on the back of that first picture. Call me when you're ready and we'll set something up." She hesitated. "I'm sorry about all of this. I wanted to talk to you before coming by but you weren't available. I wasn't trying to keep him from you. It's just, you made it so clear how much you didn't care."

Then she turned away. He watched her go.

Something inside of him yelled that he needed to go after her, but he didn't bother. She might run but she couldn't hide. Not from him. Not now.

He closed the front door and started for his office. Electra glided into the hallway.

"Who was that? What did she want? You're not seeing her, are you, Matt? She didn't look like your type."

He ignored her and walked into his study. After shutting the door, he crossed to his desk, where he sat down. He spread the pictures out and studied them one by one.

Electra pounded on the door, but didn't open it. He heard something about her threatening to leave. He didn't bother to respond.

He had a son. He'd had one for more than four years and he'd never known. Technically Jesse had tried to tell him the kid was his before she'd left Seattle, but she'd known he wouldn't believe her. Not after what had happened. She'd done this on purpose.

He reached for his phone and dialed a number from memory. "Heath, it's Matt. Do you have a minute?"

"Of course. We're heading out on the boat, but I have time. What's up?"

"I have a problem."

He quickly explained that an old girlfriend had shown up unexpectedly with a four-year-old she claimed was his.

"The first thing we'll need to do is establish paternity," his lawyer told him. "What are the odds you'll come back as the father?"

"He's mine." Matt stared at the pictures, hating Jesse more by the minute. How could she have kept this from him?

"So what do you want to do?" Heath asked.

"Hurt her in every way possible."

CHAPTER TWO

Five years ago...

JESSE SIPPED HER LATTE as she read the want ads in the *Seattle Times*. Technically she wasn't looking for a job. She wasn't qualified for anything she wanted to do and nothing she was qualified for was better than her crummy shift at the bakery. So what was the point in changing?

"Someone needs to work on her attitude," she murmured to herself, knowing feeling like a failure wasn't going to help her situation. Nor was feeling trapped. But both seemed to loom large in her life.

It was her most recent fight with Nicole, she thought, even though fights with her sister were nothing new. Maybe it was her entire lack of direction. She was twenty-two. Shouldn't she have goals? Plans? As it was, she just sort of drifted through her days, as if waiting for something to happen. If she'd stayed in college, she would have graduated by now. Instead, she'd lasted two weeks before dropping out.

She folded the paper, straightened in her seat and

tried to inspire herself to some kind of action. She couldn't keep drifting. It wasn't healthy and it made her crabby.

She sipped on her latte and considered possibilities. Before she could decide on one, a guy walked into the Starbucks.

Jesse was a semi-regular and knew she hadn't seen him before. He was tall and could have been kind of cute, but everything about him was off. The haircut was a disaster, his thick glasses screamed computer nerd. His short-sleeved plaid shirt was too big and— she nearly choked on her coffee—he had an honest-to-God pocket protector. Worse, his jeans were too short and he was wearing geeky tennis shoes with white socks. Poor guy—he looked like he'd been dressed by a mother who didn't like him very much.

She was about to return to her paper when she saw him square his shoulders in a gesture that spoke of determination. Ordering coffee wasn't that hard.

She turned in her seat and saw two women at a table against the far wall. They were young and beautiful— the kind of women who looked like models and probably dated rock stars. He couldn't, she thought frantically. Not them. They weren't just out of his league, they were on another plane of reality.

She'd never lived through the phrase "train wreck" before, but she did now. He walked toward them, his hands twitching slightly. His gaze seemed to zero in on the brunette on the left. Jesse knew it was going to be a catastrophe. She should probably leave and let him crash in private. But she couldn't seem to get up and walk away, so she slumped down in her seat and braced herself for disaster.

"Uh, Angie? Hi. I'm, um, ah, Matthew. Matt. I saw you last week at the photo shoot on campus. I kinda ran into you."

His voice was low and had the potential to be sexy, Jesse thought. If only he weren't mumbling. He sounded so tentative.

Angie looked at him politely as he spoke but her friend grimaced in annoyance.

"At Microsoft, you mean?" Angie asked. "That was fun."

"You were beautiful," Matt muttered, "in the light and stuff and I was wondering if maybe you'd like to get coffee or something and it doesn't have to be coffee even because we could, ah, go for a walk or ah, I don't know—"

Breathe! Jesse willed him to pause and break his conversation into sentences. Amazingly enough, Angie actually smiled. Could the geek possibly get the girl?

But Matt didn't notice because he kept on talking.

"Or do something else. If you have a hobby or you know, something with a pet, a dog, I guess, because I like dogs. Did you know that there are more cats as pets than dogs, which doesn't make sense because who likes cats, right? I'm allergic and they don't do anything but shed."

Jesse winced as Angie's expression hardened and her friend's face began to crumple.

"What's wrong with you?" Angie asked, standing and glaring at poor, quivering Matt. "My friend had to put her cat to sleep yesterday. How could you say something like that? I think you should leave us alone. Now!"

Matt stared at her, wide-eyed and totally confused. He opened his mouth, then closed it. His shoulders slumped in defeat and he walked out of the Starbucks.

Jesse watched him go. He'd been close to getting the girl, she thought sadly. If he hadn't gone on about cats. Not that it was really his fault. What were the odds?

She looked out the front window and saw him standing just outside the door. He looked stunned, as if he didn't know what had gone wrong. Points to Angie—she'd been willing to look past the sad exterior to the guy within. If only he'd stopped talking sooner. And dressed better. Basically, the guy needed a major overhaul.

As she watched, he slowly shook his head as if accepting defeat. She knew what he was thinking—that his life would never be different, that he would never get the girl. He was trapped—just like her. Only his problem was more easily solved.

Without having any idea what she was doing, Jesse jumped up, tossed her empty coffee container in the trash and went outside. She could see Matt walking up the street.

"Wait," she called.

He didn't turn around. Probably because it never occurred to him that she was talking to him.

"Matt, wait."

He stopped and glanced over his shoulder, then frowned. She hurried toward him.

"Hi," she said, still without a plan. "How are you?"

"Do I know you?"

"Not really. I just, ah—" Now it was her turn to stammer. "I saw what happened. Talk about a nightmare."

He shoved both hands into his jeans and ducked his head. "Thanks for the recap," he said and kept walking.

She went after him. "I didn't mean it like that. Obviously you're really bad with women."

He flushed. "Nice assessment. Is this what you do? Follow people around and point out their flaws? I'm clear on what's wrong."

"It's not that. I can help."

She had no idea where the words came from, but the second she spoke them, she knew they were true.

He barely slowed. "Go away."

"No. Look, you have a lot of potential, but no clue. I'm a woman. I can tell you how to dress, what to say, what topics to avoid."

He flinched. "I don't think so."

Suddenly this mattered. She wasn't sure why, except maybe worrying about someone else's problems was easier than thinking about her own. Besides, his life was fixable.

She remembered a segment she'd seen on the news a couple of weeks before. "I'm training to be a life-style coach. I need to practice on someone. You need help. And I won't charge you for my time." Mostly because she was totally making this up as she went. "I'll teach you everything you need to know. You'll get the girl."

He stopped and looked at her. Even through the glasses she could see his eyes were large and dark. Bedroom eyes. Girls would go crazy for them, if they could see them.

"You're lying," he said flatly. "You're not a life-style coach."

"I said I was in training. I can still help. I know guys. I know what works. Look, you have no reason to believe me. But you also have nothing to lose."

"What's in it for you?"

She thought about the ongoing fights with her sister, the job she hated and the lack of direction in her life. She thought about how she spent every single day feeling like the biggest failure on the planet.

"I get to do something right," she told him, speaking the truth.

He studied her for a long time. "Why should I trust you?"

"Because I'm the only one offering. What's the worst that could happen?"

"You could drug me and ship me off to some country where my dead body will wash up on the beach."

She laughed. "At least you have an imagination. That's a good thing. Say yes, Matt. Take a chance on me."

She wondered if he would. No one ever believed in her. Then he shrugged.

"What the hell."

She grinned. "Great. Okay, first thing—" Her cell phone rang. "Sorry," she murmured as she pulled it out of her purse. "Hello?"

"Hey, gorgeous. How are you?"

She wrinkled her nose. "Zeke, this isn't a good time."

"That's not what you were saying last week. We had a great time. Sex with you is—"

"Gotta go," she said and hung up, not wanting to hear what sex with her was like. She returned her attention to Matt. "Sorry about that. Where was I? Oh, yeah. The next step."

She pulled her Starbucks receipt out of her back pocket, then took one of the pens sticking out of his pocket protector. After tearing the receipt in half, she wrote down her cell number on one piece and handed it to him.

He took it. "You're giving me your number?"

"Yes. Changing you will be more challenging if we don't get together. Now give me your number."

He did.

She handed him back his pen. "Okay. I need a couple of days to get a plan together, then I'll be in touch." She smiled. "This is going to be great. Trust me."

"Do I have a choice?"

"Yes, but pretend you don't."

JESSE DROPPED HER heavy backpack on a chair at a table and set down her latte. She and Matt had agreed to meet at yet another Starbucks to discuss her plan.

She pulled out her list and dug through the material she'd brought for a pen, then shifted impatiently as she waited for him to arrive.

She was early. She was *never* early. Even more unusual, she was actually enthused about her make-over project. She couldn't remember the last time she'd been excited about anything. Not that Matt had sounded that thrilled when she'd called to set up their meeting. Still, he'd agreed.

Five minutes later he walked into the Starbucks. He was dressed just as badly as he had been the first time she'd seen him. What was with the too-short jeans? And the pocket protector? They *had* to go first.

He waved at her and walked up to the counter to order. Her cell phone rang.

She grabbed it. "Hello?"

"Babe. Andrew. Tonight?"

"Andrew, has it ever occurred to you that things would go more smoothly in your day if you used verbs?" She looked up and smiled as Matt approached. "I'll just be a sec," she whispered.

"I don't need verbs, babe. I got the goods. So we

on or what? There's a party. We go there, come back here. Everybody wins."

Wow—almost an entire conversation. "Tempting, but no," she said. For once she wasn't in the mood for Andrew and "the goods," as he referred to his penis. Which she supposed was slightly better than naming it Andrew Junior.

"Your loss."

"I'm sure I'll regret it for weeks. Bye." She hung up. "Sorry. I'm officially turning off my phone. We won't be interrupted again."

Matt sat across from her. "Not your boyfriend?"

"Are you asking or telling?"

"The guy from before was Zeke. This one is Andrew."

"You're observant. An excellent quality. And no, neither one is my boyfriend. I don't get serious like that." What was the point? She'd never really found someone she wanted to keep seeing more than a few times.

"Interesting. Why is that?"

She stared into his dark eyes. "Don't for a second think you can make me forget why we're here by asking me about myself."

He shrugged. "It was worth a try."

"Uh-huh. Moving on. We have a lot of stuff to get through today." She paused for effect. "I've come up with a plan."

Matt sipped his drink and blinked at her.

She refused to let his lack of support slow her

down. "First, I have a few questions. What do you do for a living? Something with computers?"

He nodded. "Programming. I work on games a lot. At Microsoft."

"I figured. Do you have any hobbies?"

He thought for a second. "Computers and games."

"Nothing else?"

"Movies, maybe."

Which meant no, but he'd had to come up with something quick. "Have you seen *How to Lose a Guy in Ten Days?* It opened last week."

He shook his head.

"Go see it," she told him, then tapped the table in front of him. "You should be taking notes. You're going to have homework."

"What?"

"You have a lot to learn. It's going to take effort on your part. Are you in or out?"

He hesitated for a moment. "In," he said, although he didn't sound very excited about the prospect.

She passed him a couple of pieces of paper. He dutifully wrote down the movie title.

"We'll deal with your apartment later. Today I want to talk about cultural references and your wardrobe."

"I don't have an apartment."

She blinked at him. "Excuse me?"

"I live at home. With my mom." He pushed up his glasses. "Before you say anything, it's a really nice house. A lot of guys live at home. It's convenient."

Oh, my. The situation was worse than she thought. "How old are you?"

"Twenty-four."

"It's probably time to fly free. What's the point in getting the girl if you don't have anywhere to take her?" She made a note. "Like I said, that's for the advanced half of the class."

"Where do you live?"

Jesse stared at him, then started to laugh. "With my sister."

He looked smug. "See?"

"I'm not a guy."

"So?"

"Point taken. But you have to move out first." She dug into her backpack and pulled out a stack of magazines. "*People* is weekly. Subscribe. *Cosmo* and *Car and Driver* are monthly. So is *In Style*. Read them. There *will* be a quiz."

He grimaced. "These are girl magazines, except for the car one and I'm not into cars."

"These are cultural textbooks. *In Style* has a great section on guys who dress well. There are also lots of pictures of pretty women. You'll like that. *People* will keep you up to date on celebrity news, which you may not care about but at least you'll recognize a few of the names people are talking about. The car magazine is to make you well-rounded and *Cosmo* is every twenty-something woman's companion. Think of it as the enemy's playbook." She pushed the magazines toward him.

"Next," she continued. "Television."

"I don't watch much."

"You're going to start watching *American Idol* and *Gilmore Girls*. You can find old episodes of *Gilmore Girls* on the Family Channel every day. Record them to watch when you're free. That's going to teach you how to talk to a woman, or at least how women fantasize that men will talk to them. It's fast, it's funny, it has lots of insight. *American Idol* is the most popular show on television. Get involved. Discuss it with coworkers."

"You can't learn how to talk to women by watching television," Matt told her.

"How do you know? Have you tried?"

"No."

"Okay, then." She scanned her list. "Next. We're going out to dinner. I want you to call and ask me out on a date, over and over again. Sometimes I'll say yes and sometimes I'll say no. We're going to do that every day for a couple of weeks, until you're comfortable with the process. Next up, shopping. You have got to get some new clothes."

He glanced down at himself. "What's wrong with my clothes?"

"How much time do you have? Don't worry. It's all fixable. I'm actually more concerned about the glasses."

He scowled. "I can't wear contacts."

"Have you thought about LASIK surgery?"

"No."

"Check it out online. You have great eyes. It would be nice if we could see them. So what do you think about the Mariners' chances this season?"

He looked blank. "That's baseball, right?"

She groaned. "Yes. Follow the team this season. Add it to your homework assignment."

He pushed back his chair and stood. "This is stupid. I don't know why you're bothering. Just forget it."

She rose and grabbed his arm. He was much taller than her and had plenty of muscle. That was good. "Matt, don't. I know it seems like a lot, but once we get the big things out of the way, it won't be so bad. You may like it. Don't you want to find someone special?"

"Maybe not this badly."

"You don't mean that."

"Why are you doing this?" he asked. "What do you get out of it?"

"I'm having fun," she admitted. "I like thinking about you. It's easier than thinking about me."

"Why?"

"Because I'm stuck right now." She didn't have a career or anything close to direction or a goal. She changed guys as often as most women changed panties, which wasn't anything she was proud of.

He looked surprised. "You're the one who's big on change."

"Those who can, do. Those who can't, teach."

He studied her for a second. "You're evasive."

"Sometimes."

"Why?"

Interesting question. "Because I don't always like who I am," she admitted. "Because I don't know how to change, but I can see exactly how to change you. It makes me feel better to make a difference."

"That was honest."

"I know. It surprised me, too." She waited until he sat down. "Give me a month. Do what I say for a month. If you hate the changes, you can go back to your old life and it will be like it never happened."

"Not if I have LASIK surgery."

"Is that a bad thing?"

"Maybe not."

"You have to trust me," she told him. "I want this to work for you." Because somehow, if it worked for him, maybe it would work for her, too. At least that was the theory.

TEN DAYS LATER, Jesse nearly fell off the bench at the Kirkland Olive Garden. She stood and pointed.

"Who *are* you?" she asked.

Matt grinned as he stopped in front of her. "You told me which clothes to buy. They shouldn't be a surprise."

"They look better on than I remember," she murmured, motioning for him to turn slowly.

It was amazing what a little time and a couple of grand on a credit card could do. He'd been transformed from top to bottom. An eighty-dollar haircut at an upscale Bellevue salon had only been the beginning. Gone were the too-short jeans, the tennis shoes and the geeky shirt with the pocket protector. Instead, Matt wore a pale blue dress shirt, tailored slacks that showed off his slim hips and surprisingly sexy butt. She'd teased him into buying leather loafers that cost nearly four hundred dollars but had been worth every penny.

But the real change was how he looked without glasses.

His face had masculine lines and a chiseled chin she'd never noticed before. His eyes were even better than she'd imagined, and his mouth…had it always been that sexy, with a slightly crooked smile?

"You're gorgeous," she told him, actually feeling a slight tingle inside. "Really sexy. Wow."

He flushed slightly. "You look good, too."

Jesse dismissed his compliment with a flick of her fingers. Her appearance didn't matter. This was about him.

The hostess returned and offered to seat them. Jesse noticed her checking Matt out as they were led to a table.

"Did you see that?" she asked in a low voice when they'd slid into their booth. "She was totally into you."

Matt flushed. "You're just saying that."

"I don't think so. If I were to get up right now and go to the restroom, she would be all over you."

He looked more nervous than excited. "You're not leaving, are you?"

She laughed. "Maybe next time. You'll have to get used to the attention first, then you can start to enjoy it." She ignored the menu and leaned toward him. "So, tell me. What's new at work?"

"We're brainstorming a new game. The theory behind it is really advanced, but there's a—" He paused as she dropped her head to the table and groaned. "What?"

"Do I look like I care about game theory?"

"No, but you asked."

"I asked what was new at work. That means with the people."

"Oh." He reached toward his face, as if he was going to push up his glasses, then dropped his hand to his lap. "It's different."

She straightened. "How?"

"People are talking to me."

She smiled, knowing he was already getting results. "Women, right? You mean women."

Matt grinned. "Yeah. A lot of the secretaries are saying hi to me now. And this woman in Finance asked me to help her carry some stuff to her car, only it wasn't that much and she could have done it herself."

"Did you ask her out?"

"What? No." He looked shocked. "I couldn't do that. She was, you know, older."

Jesse raised her eyebrows. "How much older?"

"Maybe five or six years. She wouldn't be interested in me."

"Oh, honey, you have so much to learn about women. You're tall, you're in great shape, you're good-looking. You have a good job, you're basically sweet and funny and smart. What's not to like?"

He flushed. "That's not me."

"It's exactly you. It was all there, all the time, just hiding behind a pocket protector." She narrowed her gaze. "I told you to throw them all out. Did you?"

He rolled his eyes. "Yes. I said I did."

"Good."

Her cell phone rang. She pulled it out of her purse and looked at the screen.

"Andrew or Zeke?" Matt asked.

"Joe." She turned off the phone. "Sorry."

Matt studied her. "How many guys are there?"

Not a question she wanted to answer. "This isn't a very interesting topic."

"It's interesting to me."

"I date but I don't get serious. It's no big deal."

"You meet a lot of different guys?"

"Sure. It's easy. They're everywhere." And men were not the least bit challenging to attract. Not that she was interested in keeping them around for any length of time.

Their server appeared. Jesse was relieved by the interruption. Talking about her personal life would only depress her and it might make him think she was...

What? Slutty? Isn't that what her sister called her? Stop thinking about Nicole, she ordered herself and opened her menu.

Matt waited while she placed her order first, then he listed his selection, even including a glass of wine.

"Very smooth," she said when they were alone. "The glass of wine is a nice touch. You know, we could go to the Chateau St. Michelle winery some-time. They have tastings. You could practice being snobby."

He laughed. "You want me to be a snob?"

"You never know when it will come in handy."

The server brought their drinks. Jesse stirred her iced tea. "You're making some great changes. How do you feel about that?"

"You're not going to get me to talk about my feelings," he told her. "It's a guy thing."

"Good answer."

"Are you playing me?"

"Maybe a little."

"I can handle it."

There was a quiet confidence in his voice she hadn't heard before. It matched his straight posture and the way he looked her directly in the eye.

Still looking at her, he asked, "What's your story? I know you're not really a lifestyle coach. So who are you and what do you do when you're not hounding me to go to the mall?"

At least they weren't talking about her personal life, Jesse thought as she wrinkled her nose. Not that the rest of her world was in much better shape. "There's nothing much to tell. I work in a bakery that my sister and I own. Well, my half is in trust until I'm twenty-five. I don't especially like working there, but that's more about me not getting along with Nicole than anything else."

"Why don't you get along?"

Jesse considered how much to tell. "I have a second sister. Claire. She plays piano and is kind of famous. She went off to tour the world right after I was born, so I don't really know her. When I was six, my mom took off to be with Claire and Nicole got stuck raising me. My dad wasn't much help. I was a handful, as they say. Nicole thinks I only ever screw up and I think she's the queen bitch of the West. Like with the bakery. I've begged her to buy me out so I can just leave, but she won't."

"What would you do with the money?"

"I have no idea."

"Maybe that's why she won't give it to you."

Jesse smiled. "If you're going to be reasonable, we can't have this conversation."

"Sorry."

"That's okay. Enough about me. I know you live with your mom. What about your dad? Are they divorced?"

"They were never married. My mom doesn't talk about him at all. It's always been just the two of us. She worked really hard when I was young. Money was tight. She did everything for me."

A possibly scary thought, although Jesse decided not to judge until she knew all the facts. "She sounds nice."

"She is mostly. She didn't care that I was into computers. She never bugged me to go outside or worried that I didn't have a lot of friends. She kept saying I'd grow into who I was meant to be and not to worry if things weren't how I wanted them now."

"Good for her," Jesse said.

"When I was fifteen, I got really frustrated by this computer game I was playing. I broke into their system, accessed the code and rewrote it. Then I took the new version to them. They licensed it from me. Our money situation got better then."

Jesse stared at him. "You licensed a computer game when you were fifteen?"

He nodded.

"For a lot of money?"

"It's a couple of million a year."

If she'd been drinking she would have choked. "So you're rich?"

"I guess. I don't think about it much."

"You're rich and you wore a pocket protector?"

"You've got to let that go. I said I threw them all out."

"You're rich." She couldn't get her mind around that fact.

"What's your point? Does it change anything?"

More than he knew, but warning him about women only after him for his money was something they could talk about later. She laughed. "It changes who's buying dinner."

CHAPTER THREE

Present day...

JESSE HAD ALREADY DECIDED to get all the reunions over as quickly as possible. It was like jumping in the deep end of a cold pool. Sure the shock nearly killed you, but it was over fast. So she did her best to shake off the conversation with Matt, ignoring the rapid pounding of her heart and the mass of memories that crowded her brain, then drove to a second unfamiliar address, guided by the trusty nav system.

This house wasn't gated, but it was nearly as large as the one she'd just left. Yet instead of being a testament to great architecture, it was a rambling two-story house that proudly announced a family lived there.

A tricycle and several toys littered the wide covered porch, while a minivan was parked in front of the garage. One of those decorative wreaths hung on the door, which made Jesse wonder if she had the right address. Nicole had never been the wreath type before. Maybe she'd changed.

Jesse tried to imagine it, but couldn't. Still, in the five years she'd been gone, not only had her sister married—a wedding Jesse hadn't been invited to—but she'd had a son and twin girls. The information came compliments of Nicole's fraternal twin, Claire, the sister Jesse had never really known.

She parked on the street and grabbed more pictures from her purse. Convincing Nicole who had fathered Jesse's child was nearly as important as convincing Matt, although for very different reasons.

She got out of her car and walked up the main path. As she approached the front door, her shoulders slumped. The old feelings she'd thought she'd gotten over returned. The voices that said she was nothing but a screwup. That she ruined everything she touched, didn't appreciate anything.

"Stop!" she said aloud, pausing in front of the steps. "I'm not that person anymore."

She wasn't. She'd grown up and changed. She was responsible, a single mother who'd made it on her own. When Jesse left, Nicole had claimed she would come crawling back in a matter of weeks. That hadn't happened.

After squaring her shoulders and raising her chin, she walked up the stairs, then pressed the bell and waited.

She heard yelling from inside, and the sound of running feet. The front door jerked open and a little boy stared up at her.

"Who are you?" he demanded loudly, his voice

competing with the sound of babies crying. Apparently both twins were awake and not happy.

"Eric, I've told you. Don't answer the door without checking with me first. And don't ask who the person is."

Eric had blond hair and blue eyes like his mom. He was the same size as Gabe and just about the same age. He sighed and addressed Jesse.

"I'm not supposed to answer the door on my own."

"I heard. So maybe you want to go get your mom."

"I'm here," Nicole said, walking around the corner, carrying a baby in her arms. "Can I help—"

She came to a stop. Her eyes widened and all the color left her face.

"Hi," Jesse said, feeling awkward and unsure of her welcome. "It's been a long time."

Nicole stared. "Jesse?"

"It's me."

"I can't believe it." In the distance, a baby continued to cry. Nicole glanced in that direction. "It's Molly. Holding them both when they need to be walked is impossible. Hawk's out of town. He didn't want to leave, but he and Brittany had planned the trip celebrating her graduation from college for a while and it didn't seem fair to cancel it because I have twins who aren't sleeping." She rocked the crying baby in her arms and looked desperate.

"I can help," Jesse said, stepping in the house without being invited. "Here. Let me take this one."

"Are you sure?" Nicole asked, obviously reluctant to hand over her baby.

"I raised one myself," she said.

"Right. Sure. Here."

Jesse took the wrapped baby and smiled down at her. "Hello, pretty girl. How are you? Keeping mom up? She'll remember and punish you later. You might want to think that through."

The baby's eyes focused on her face, then slowly began to close. Nicole hesitated a second, before retreating to the back of the house to collect Molly. Eric stared at her.

"Who are you?" he asked.

"I'm your aunt Jesse," she said as she closed the front door, stepped over several toys and followed him to a family room.

There was a sofa and television, along with toys and a couple of baskets of laundry. A stack of diapers sat in one chair. Shoes littered the hallway leading to the kitchen.

Jesse remembered Nicole's house being mostly tidy and quiet. It was a place Jesse had never felt at home. While this place made her feel at ease, she couldn't believe her perfect sister lived in chaos.

A small, hairy white dog raced through the room, followed by a slightly larger black-and-white dog. Pets? Nicole had pets?

"That's Sheila," Eric told her. "Rambo is her son. Like I'm my daddy's son." He seemed proud of the fact.

Nicole returned with a second infant and collapsed in a chair.

"Clear a space," she murmured, rocking her daughter with a desperation that spoke of many nights without sleep. "Come on, Molly. It can't be that bad, can it?"

Kim, the baby Jesse held, had quieted enough for her to ask, "Want me to put her down?"

Nicole shook her head. "She won't sleep. She'll wake right up."

"We can try," Jesse said, knowing getting the twins into their own cribs was the only solution that was going to let Nicole rest.

Nicole's gaze narrowed, then she shrugged. "Whatever. They're in the sitting area off our bedroom. They have a room upstairs, but it got to be too far to walk when I realized they weren't ever going to sleep."

Her voice was thick with emotion, as if she was inches from losing it all.

"I'll show you," Eric said. He'd been hovering by his mom. Now he led the way down a short hallway and into the master suite.

Jesse had the impression of space, large furniture and a view of a massive backyard. She followed Eric into what would usually be the master bedroom retreat area. A love seat and coffee table had been pushed to the side. Two cribs stood in the middle of the space.

"This one is Kim's," Eric told her, pointing to the one on the right.

She smiled at him. "Wow. You're very helpful. I'm

sure your mom is happy to have you around. You're a great big brother."

Eric beamed. "I'm the man of the house while Daddy's gone."

"Your mom is so lucky."

She eased the sleeping baby into the crib. Kim stayed asleep. Jesse wound the mobile above the crib and motioned for Eric to join her as she backed out of the room.

They returned to the family room. Nicole stared at her.

"She's sleeping?"

"Yes. Why don't I take Molly while you go grab a shower?"

Nicole hesitated, as if she was going to argue, then she handed over the infant and hurried down the hall.

Jesse gazed at the sleepy baby in her arms. "Do you have one of those chairs that rocks the baby?" she asked Eric.

He nodded and pointed to the far corner.

Jesse dug it out from behind a pile of towels and set it in front of the sofa. Molly fussed when she was put in, but quieted as the chair began to crank back and forth.

The piles of laundry needed attention first, Jesse thought. "Where are the washer and dryer?" she asked Eric.

He showed her the utility room off the kitchen. She loaded in towels, added soap and started the machine. She took baby clothes out of the dryer and quickly folded them, giving him socks to match up.

"Excellent job," she told him, as she cleaned off the kitchen table, wiped it down, then stacked the clean clothes in piles. "Are you thirsty?"

"Uh-huh. I can have juice."

There were boxes in the fridge. She got him settled with his drink, then loaded the dishwasher with as much as she could fit in before filling the sink and washing the big pots and pans by hand. She just started drying them when Nicole walked into the kitchen.

"Where's Molly?" she asked.

Jesse pointed to the slumbering baby in the rocking chair. "There's a load of towels going in the washer. The dishwasher is full, but I didn't know if it would pull too much hot water from your shower, so I waited."

Nicole sank into a chair at the table. "You didn't have to do this."

"I don't mind." She knew what it was like to be overwhelmed, to think she was never going to get enough rest to feel human again.

The doorbell rang. Nicole winced, but Eric went running. "It's Billy and his mom," he yelled. Molly started to cry.

"I'll take the baby," Jesse said.

"Thanks. Eric's spending the afternoon at his friend's house. I'll be right back."

While Jesse soothed Molly back to sleep, Nicole saw off her son, then returned to the kitchen, looking exhausted. They stood staring at each other for an awkward second.

"So, you're back in Seattle?" Nicole asked as she sank into a chair at the table.

"For now." Jesse remembered the pictures she'd brought and went to get them. When she returned, she handed them to her sister. "Gabe's been asking about his father. I've put off their meeting as long as I could, but I'm running out of excuses. So we're here, at least for a few weeks."

She hesitated because Nicole hadn't looked at the pictures. "I went to see Matt this morning. He wasn't expecting me." There was an understatement. "I'd told him I was pregnant when I left, but he didn't believe he was the father. Given the circumstances, I guess I can't blame him."

Now came the hard part, Jesse thought. She'd practiced what she wanted to say dozens of times, but suddenly couldn't think of any of her carefully prepared phrases.

"I didn't sleep with Drew," she said, jumping in and hoping her sister would listen. "I never slept with him, tried to sleep with him or thought of him as anything but your husband. He and I were friends. We would talk and that was it. I was in love with Matt."

Nicole stood and crossed to the dishwasher, where she pushed a couple of buttons to start the cycle. "I don't want to talk about this."

"We have to eventually."

"Why?" Nicole turned to face her, then sighed. "Okay. Maybe. But not today."

Jesse wanted to push. She'd felt awful about Nicole's hurt and anger for five years and she didn't want to wait any longer. But the mature choice would be to let her sister get used to the idea of her being back first.

"I'll leave the pictures," Jesse said quietly. "You can look at them later. There's a lot of Matt in Gabe. Especially in his eyes. It made it hard to forget."

Not hard. Impossible.

Nicole nodded. "I will." She crossed her arms across her chest. "I thought I'd hear from you when you turned twenty-five."

Meaning she thought Jesse would show up to get her half of the bakery. Their father had left the business to both of them, with Jesse's half held in trust until she was twenty-five. Once she'd graduated from high school, Jesse had bugged Nicole to buy her out soon and give her the money. Nicole had refused. It had been just one more thing for them to fight about.

"I don't want to be given anything," Jesse told her. "I want to earn my way in."

Nicole raised her eyebrows. "Meaning what? You want a job? I thought you hated working at the bakery."

A job? Jesse hadn't thought that far, but she could sure use the money. "A job would be great. But I have something else to offer. A brownie recipe. I've been working on it on and off for a couple of years. It's finally ready. It's better than anything out there."

Nicole didn't look convinced.

Jesse fought disappointment and the voice that

whispered her sister would never see her as anything but a screwup. The truth was, Jesse might know how much she'd changed, but Nicole had to be convinced. That was fine. Jesse wasn't going anywhere for a while.

"I'll bake a couple of batches," Jesse told her. "We can set up time for a tasting."

"All right. But if they're that good, why didn't you just start a business on your own?"

A genuine question or a slam? Jesse wondered. Five years ago, she'd taken the famous Keyes chocolate cake recipe, made the cakes out of a rented kitchen and sold them online. Nicole had been furious and pressed charges, throwing her baby sister in jail.

"They're that good," Jesse said calmly. "I could have gone out on my own, but I wanted to bring them to the bakery. I told you—I'm interested in earning my way back in."

Nicole stared at her, obviously not convinced. Jesse took that as a hint to leave.

"I'll call you," she said as she headed for the door. "So we can set up a time that works for you."

"How can I get in touch with you?" Nicole asked.

The question gave Jesse hope. Maybe her sister hadn't given up on her completely. "I left my cell number on the pictures."

"Oh. Okay."

Jesse reached the front door.

"Wait," Nicole called.

Jesse turned.

"Thanks for helping with the twins. I'm usually more together than that."

"Babies are tough," Jesse told her, pleased she'd been able to make a difference. "I'll talk to you soon."

"Okay. Bye."

Jesse walked to her car, smiling and feeling more hopeful than she had when she'd left Matt's. Nicole would take some convincing, but Jesse felt that she could earn her way back into her sister's good graces. She would have her family back and, right now, that mattered more than anything.

JESSE PARKED IN FRONT of the YMCA in Bothell. The Y in Spokane had been a big part of her life ever since she'd had Gabe. She'd taken baby CPR classes there, had gone to Mommy and Me classes where she'd met other young mothers. She'd worked out in the gym, knowing her son was safe in the day care center and the babysitting service they provided had saved her butt more times than she could count.

Now she walked in to pick up Gabe and smiled as she saw him playing with two other little boys. As always, he was laughing and in the center of everything.

One of the teenagers there came up to her. "Hi, Jesse. You're back early."

"My meetings went quicker than I'd thought. How was Gabe?"

"Great. He's really outgoing and he does so well

with the other kids. Especially the shy ones. He takes the time to draw them out. Bring him back anytime."

Jesse smiled and nodded. She wanted to take credit for Gabe's easy personality, but she knew it was just one of those moments of chance when the gene pool did something beyond right.

Her son looked up and saw her. His smile widened and he raced toward her. "Mommy, Mommy, I made new friends."

She bent down and grabbed him as he launched himself at her. "Did you? That's great."

"I had fun and I want to come back."

"We'll have to make sure that happens, won't we?"

He nodded vigorously.

Jesse signed the paperwork and left, Gabe chatting as he walked with her. He gave her a real-time account of his morning, every event more fun and exciting than the one before. More good luck, she thought as she helped him into his car seat. He was a cheerful, happy kid. She wasn't sure how she would have survived if he'd been any different.

She closed his door, then got in the driver's seat.

"Now what?" he asked. "Are we going back to the hotel?"

"We can," she said slowly, thinking about where they were and how far it would be to the hotel.

A thought pushed into her head. She tried to ignore it, but it just got bigger and louder.

Talk about crazy, she told herself. Hadn't she been

through enough for one day? Did she want to keep tor-
turing herself? Even though she knew it was a bad
idea, she heard herself say, "I think there's someone I
want you to meet."

Gabe's face brightened. "My daddy?"

"Um, not yet. But someone else. Your grandmother."

Gabe's eyes widened and he looked as if she'd just
offered him a puppy. "I have a grandmother?" he
asked, his voice low and filled with wonder.

"Uh-huh. Your daddy's mother." Gabe knew the
basics about grandparents, mostly that he didn't have
any. Well, except for Paula.

There was only one problem. Matt's mother had
always hated her.

It's been a long time, she reminded herself.
Maybe Paula had changed. If not, it would be a very
short visit.

Jesse drove into Woodinville, to the pretty house
Matt had bought for his mother years ago, after his
first computer game had been licensed for millions.

For the third time that morning, she pulled in front
of a house owned by someone who very well might
not welcome her back. But this time she didn't bother
with pictures. She had the real thing.

"Hurry!" Gabe instructed, as she unfastened him
from the car seat. "Hurry!"

He ran ahead of her, racing up the walk and then
reaching up on his toes so he could push the doorbell.
Jesse grabbed her purse, slammed the door and jogged

after him, but she was too late. The front door opened before she got there.

Paula stood there, looking a little older, but not all that different. Her hair was still dark like her son's. There were a few more lines around her face and she'd gained a little weight, but otherwise she was as Jesse remembered.

"Hi," Gabe said with a grin. "You're my grandma."

Paula stiffened as she gazed at the boy, then she looked past him to where Jesse stood halfway up the walk.

"Hi," Jesse said, knowing she would have handled the situation differently than her four-year-old, but it was too late now. "I probably should have called or something. We just got into Seattle yesterday."

Paula blinked several times. "Jesse?"

"I'm Gabe," he said. "You're my grandma."

Tears filled Paula's eyes. "You were pregnant?"

Jesse nodded, still not sure what was going to happen. She braced herself for screaming or nasty accusations. Instead, Paula smiled at Gabe as if he were a treasure she'd never expected to find.

"I've never had a grandson before. This is very exciting. Would you like to come in?"

Gabe nodded and stepped into the house. Jesse followed more slowly.

The place was as she remembered. She'd only been to it a few times, but each visit had been difficult enough for her to remember forever.

The colors were soothing, the furniture comfortable. The reason the awkward hours were etched into her brain had nothing to do with the house itself and everything to do with Paula.

"This way," Paula said. "You know, it's funny. I made cookies this morning. I don't usually make cookies, but suddenly I got in the mood." She smiled at Gabe again, looking stunned but pleased. "Do you like chocolate chip?"

He nodded in appreciation. "They're my favorite."

"Mine, too, although I really like peanut butter, too."

"Those are my favorite, too," Gabe told her, as charming as ever. "You're pretty. Isn't my grandma pretty, Mommy?"

Jesse nodded.

Paula looked as if she couldn't believe this was happening. "Can I hug you?" she asked him.

Gabe smiled and held out his arms. Paula dropped to her knees and held him close. Her eyes closed as her face took on an expression of such longing that Jesse had to look away. Wasn't this always the way? The two people who were more likely to welcome her had been cautious and unfriendly. The one person who had always hated her seemed thrilled she was back in town. Life was nothing if not perverse.

Fifteen minutes later, Gabe had eaten a cookie and finished a small glass of milk. He'd also brought Paula up to date on their trip from Spokane and how he was going to meet his daddy soon.

"Matt hasn't seen him yet?" Paula asked.

Jesse shook her head, then looked into the family room. "Gabe, would you like to watch TV for a little bit?"

It was a rare daytime treat. Her son jumped to his feet and followed her to the sofa. Paula found a channel for kids, then the two women retreated to the kitchen where they could keep an eye on Gabe without being overheard.

"I didn't know," Paula said as soon as they were seated. She leaned toward Jesse and touched her hand. "I swear, I didn't know you were pregnant. All I knew was what your sister said." She shifted uncomfortably. "I told Matt about that."

"I know. It's okay. There were complications." Jesse hated how, after all this time, the past still had the power to hurt everyone involved.

"It was a long time ago," Jesse told her. "Whatever you believe, you have to know I loved Matt. I would never have hurt him."

"I do believe you," Paula said, surprising her. "He was devastated after you left."

"Was he?" It was nice to know he'd missed her, however briefly. "I told him I was pregnant, but he didn't think he was the father. I told him there hadn't been anyone else, but he didn't believe me."

Once again Paula looked uncomfortable. "It's my fault. All of it. He was angry because of what I said. I'd held him too close for too long. I was one of those horrible, clinging mothers they're always discussing on talk shows. He was angry with you, but he never forgave me. We stopped being close after you left. We're still not close. I rarely see him."

"I'm sorry," Jesse said, and found she meant it. "You're his mother. Nothing will ever change that."

"Something he's managed to ignore," she said with a lightness that seemed forced. "So tell me. What have you been doing with yourself?"

"I've been living in Spokane. That's where I went when I took off. At least that's where the money ran out. I got a job in a bar. I was lucky. Bill, the guy who owns the place, took care of me. Found me a place to live, worked my schedule around Gabe." She smiled as she thought of her boss and friend. "He's the one who gave me the kick in the ass to come back here. Well, him and Gabe. Your grandson wants to meet his daddy. I couldn't keep saying no."

"Are you and Bill—" Paula's voice trailed off.

Jesse stared at her. "Are we…" she got the question "…involved? Oh, no. We're just friends. He says I'm too young for him." She smiled. "He's in his sixties, as are all his friends. They've been my family while I was gone. It was just so hard being away. It's only a few hundred miles, but I felt like I was in another world. I couldn't believe Nicole just let me go."

Jesse held the coffee mug Paula had given her but didn't drink. "It was always just Nicole and me. She was my bossy older sister. Claire, her twin, had gone away the year I was born, so I never knew her beyond the little Nicole told me or what I read in magazines."

"She plays piano?"

"Yes. She's pretty famous but I don't really know her beyond some e-mails and letters. She's been in touch with me over the years. She's the one who told me about Nicole getting married and all that." Jesse tried to keep the pain out of her voice. Despite everything that had happened between them, she loved Nicole and had hated being cut off from her. Nicole's life had gone on, as if she, Jesse, had never been a part of things.

"How long are you back here?" Paula asked.

"I don't know. A few weeks. I'm half owner of the Keyes Bakery, but I'm not asking Nicole for anything. I'm going to work there and give her my brownie recipe. I've been working on it for months. It's finally perfect and—"

Jesse pressed her lips together. "I'm sorry. I'm going on and on about my life when what you really want to hear about is Gabe. I just haven't had anyone to talk to in a long time."

"Me, either," Paula told her. "Where are you staying?"

"In a motel. I'm going to rent some place furnished in the University District. It will be cheap in the summer."

"That will make for a lot of driving," Paula said. "You could just stay here. With me."

Jesse didn't know what to say. Talk about an unexpected invitation. "Are you sure?"

"Come see the rooms, then decide."

Stunned, Jesse followed her upstairs. Two bedrooms sat at one end of the hallway, a shared bathroom between them. Both were set up for guests, with double beds and bright colors. The rooms were lovely, well lit and clean, so different from the seedy place she would have to rent, that she felt herself getting emotional.

"Paula, this is beyond generous," she murmured.

"They're both yours for as long as you want," Matt's mother said. "I've missed four years of my grandson's life because I was a scared, lonely woman terrified of losing the little she had. Well, I did lose it and I've been regretting that more than I can say. Stay here. Please. Let me have the chance to get to know you and Gabe. Let me make up for how horrible I was five years ago. You didn't deserve that, Jesse. This is the least I can do."

Actually, it was an irresistible offer, Jesse thought, looking at the rooms. One she wasn't about to refuse.

"Thank you," she said, feeling safe and welcome for the first time since arriving in Seattle. "You're being more than kind. Gabe and I would love to stay."

"Good. Why don't you head back to your hotel and pack while I go to the grocery and stock up. Oh, you'll have to tell me what you both like to eat. I've missed cooking for more than myself."

A beautiful place to stay and someone to do the cooking? It was a little corner of heaven, Jesse thought. And Paula was the most unlikely angel.

CHAPTER FOUR

MATT STOOD IN FRONT OF the large window as he spoke. He was still angry; he could feel the rage burning inside, although he did his best to keep his voice controlled. Not that his attorney was fooled.

"This isn't the time to make decisions," Heath told him. "Wait a few days, a couple of weeks. Nothing is going to change and you'll get a chance to calm down."

"You wouldn't be furious in my position?" he asked, glancing over his shoulder.

Heath sat on the edge of his desk. "I'd be beyond pissed," the other man admitted. "Not telling you she was pregnant and then taking off is unforgivable. We can sue her for that in civil court."

That wasn't going to happen, Matt thought grimly. Mostly because Jesse *had* told him she was pregnant—he just hadn't believed her. Or rather he hadn't believed the baby was his, which was about the same thing.

He didn't want to think about the past. That was a

different time and he was a different man now. More controlled and capable, not someone to be led by his emotions. He'd learned a damn hard lesson and he wouldn't make those same mistakes again. Just because he was the kid's father didn't change the fact that she'd slept with someone else.

"I want her destroyed," he said quietly. "Start with a thorough investigation. I want to know everything about the past five years. Where she's lived, what she's been doing, who she slept with, who she talked to. Everything. She used to sleep around, so that won't have changed. There may be other things."

Heath nodded. "We'll find whatever there is and use it against her."

It wasn't going to be enough, Matt thought. He wanted more. He wanted her broken and bleeding. He wanted her to lose everything and know that he'd taken it. He wanted revenge.

"There are a dozen ways to make her life uncomfortable," Heath continued. "Equal say in all decisions, getting an injunction so she can't leave Seattle. The big one is to sue for custody."

Take the boy from her. Matt considered the possibility. How she would react. "Do it," he said.

Heath cleared his throat. "You realize that if you win, you get the kid."

An abstract concept, he thought. "I'll deal with that when it happens." If he needed help, he would hire it. Nannies and boarding schools existed for a reason.

"Do it," he repeated. "Draw up the papers to sue for custody, but don't serve her until I tell you. I want to see how this is going to play out."

There were options to be explored. He was patient. He didn't have to rush in right away. He could wait and figure out the best way to play his hand. The best way to hurt her and the best way to win.

NICOLE HELD the front door open as Claire led both her children up the front walk. She greeted four-year-old Robby and two-year-old Mirabella before turning to her sister.

"You look perfectly rested," Nicole grumbled as they embraced.

"You were, too, before the twins were born, and you will be again in a few months." Claire smiled. "Actually, you're looking pretty good."

"I got some sleep yesterday afternoon while Eric was at a play date."

"The twins are getting into a routine?"

"Sort of."

Nicole waited until they were in the family room. Robby and Eric raced to the toy bin in the corner and began digging through the contents. Mirabella snuggled up next to her mom on the sofa. For once the twins were awake and not crying as they surveyed the world from identical baby seats.

Nicole sat in an oversized chair that faced the sofa and watched Claire as she spoke. "Jesse's back."

Claire smiled serenely, something she'd always done. It still made Nicole crazy. "Is she?"

"You're not surprised."

"She'd mentioned she was thinking of returning to Seattle for the summer."

Nicole stiffened. If not for the five children in the room, she would have been on her feet and swearing, which Claire knew and probably counted on.

"You've been in touch with her," Nicole said, working hard to keep the accusation out of her voice. This was so like Claire. All sweet and agreeable on the outside, but doing exactly what she wanted.

Claire sighed. "She's my sister, too. A sister I never got a chance to know. You two had the fight, not me, and when she went away, I felt like I'd lost her all over again. So yes, I've been in touch with her. We e-mail every month or so. I didn't think you'd want to know about it."

What Nicole wanted was to scream, and maybe throw something. She resented the logic of what Claire had said and that Claire had known Jesse was all right while Nicole had wondered and worried. She ignored the voice that said she could have gotten in touch with Jesse just as easily. After all, Nicole had always known where her sister was.

"So she came to see you?" Claire asked.

"Yesterday."

"Did you meet Gabe?"

"No. She brought pictures." Photos that Nicole

had looked at last night. "He looks a lot like her ex-boyfriend." Nicole had seen that at once. She glared at Claire. "Don't you say it."

"Say what?"

"That who Gabe's father is means something."

Claire glanced at her daughter, then lowered her voice. "She was never involved with Drew."

"How do you know?"

"She told me."

Jesse had tried to tell Nicole, too, only she hadn't wanted to hear it. Or maybe she just wasn't ready to play that old game of trying to figure out the truth.

"I'll never be sure," Nicole said at last.

"Sometimes you have to take a leap of faith. She's your sister. Doesn't that mean something?"

It meant Jesse had the power to hurt her more than most people. Something she'd done time and time again.

"I believe her," Claire said. "She's a part of my family and I have to give her the benefit of the doubt."

"I don't," Nicole said flatly. "She's had too many chances already."

"That was a long time ago."

"I don't believe she's changed. She's going to have to prove herself to me first."

"Is there anything she can do to convince you or are you setting her up to fail?"

Nicole considered the question, then gave an honest answer. "I don't know."

JESSE PULLED THE BROWNIES from the oven and stared at the pan. They looked perfect, as did the other three batches she'd already made that morning, but maybe she would try again.

"Obsess much?" she muttered to herself, knowing that she couldn't do any more than her best. Either Nicole would admit the brownies were fabulous, or she wouldn't and there was very little Jesse could do to change the outcome.

Being rational and calm were still attributes she was working on and this seemed like a great opportunity to practice. Wasn't it great how life was always teaching lessons?

She set the brownies on the cooling racks, then jumped when her cell phone rang. A quick check of the display showed her a 206 area code, which meant Seattle, and a number she didn't recognize.

"Hello?"

"Jesse? It's Matt. I'd like to meet my son."

Her heart jumped into overdrive while her throat tightened. Just like that, she thought, trying not to panic. No preliminaries or idle conversation. Just right to the point.

"He would like that as well," she said, hoping she sounded relaxed and at ease. She knew Matt's office was in Bellevue and remembered a large McDonald's close by, with a play area. Having fun stuff for Gabe to do would make the meeting more relaxed. At least that was the theory. "How do you feel about a burger and fries?"

"I'm not interested in lunch."

Apparently he wasn't interested in being friendly, either, she thought. She gave him the location and they settled on two in the afternoon. When they hung up, she glanced at the clock. The meeting was three hours away, which gave her far too long to panic and obsess.

TWO HOURS AND FIFTY-FIVE minutes later, Jesse pulled into the parking lot of the McDonald's and sent warm, fuzzy mental vibrations to whomever had decided that a big play area in the fast-food place was a good idea. Mothers around the country, maybe around the world, had benefited from the chance to let their kids out of the house in a safe play environment that supplied caffeine and French fries. What could be better?

Gabe practically threw himself out of his car seat. "Is he here? Is he here?"

"I don't know," Jesse said, nearly as excited as Gabe, but for very different reasons. Matt had been the only man she'd ever loved. Their most recent meeting had been awkward and difficult. She was hoping this one would go better.

To that end, she'd resisted the need to change clothes four hundred times. Not that she had anything fabulous to wear. Her world was one of jeans and T-shirts or sweatshirts, depending on the season. There wasn't any money left over from say, buying milk, to fill her closet with designer anything. She made do with what was on sale or in decent shape at the local thrift store. Besides, this meeting wasn't about her. It was about Gabe meeting his father for the first time.

They walked into the McDonald's. She saw Matt right away. He was the only guy in a suit. He rose and faced them.

God, he was good-looking, she thought taking in the chiseled features and dark eyes. He had an air of confidence and power that she imagined most women would find irresistible. Yet she knew a side of the man the rest of the world didn't see. She knew what made him laugh, what pissed him off, how he liked to be kissed and touched and how she could literally bring him to his knees if she…

Or she *had,* she reminded himself, fighting the need to touch him, to step into his embrace and have him hold her. He'd been the only person on the planet who could make her feel safe. Five years was a long time to miss that feeling, but it was something she was going to have to get over. This Matt was a stranger to her. She didn't know him anymore and she was going to have to remember that.

He barely looked at her, instead focusing his considerable attention on his son. Gabe walked up to him and smiled.

"Are you my daddy?"

"Yes," Matt told him.

But he spoke without emotion and didn't smile or

bend down to get on Gabe's level. Her son stepped back and frowned.

"Are you sure?"

"Yes." Matt turned to her. "We'll be doing a DNA test."

"Sure." She'd offered it before. Why would she mind now? But what about Gabe? Why was Matt acting like this? Didn't he plan to get to know his…

Then she remembered the disgruntled Electra and knew that Matt's actions had nothing to do with him being a jerk and everything to do with his lack of experience with children. He didn't know how to talk to a four-year-old boy.

She relaxed and put her hand on Gabe's shoulder. "It's okay," she told her son. "It's like the first day of school, when you don't know anyone. It feels funny inside, but you know you're going to be friends, right?"

Gabe shot her a look that spoke of disappointment. She remembered how Paula had welcomed him, literally with open arms.

She dropped into a crouch. "He's nervous," she whispered, although she wasn't sure if she cared if Matt heard or not. "You're his first little boy. So maybe we can give it time. He'll get used to you."

Gabe sighed. "Can I go on the slide?"

"Sure."

She watched him go and wondered if Matt cared that he'd disappointed his son. She knew Gabe had been hoping for *something* more than a semi-formal introduction.

She moved to a table where she could keep an eye on the play area. Matt hesitated, then followed. He'd seen his kid—did he consider the meeting over?

"He's doing really well," she said, deciding to just start talking. "He's been in preschool for a year now and it's been great. He's highly verbal and outgoing. He makes friends easily. The teachers like him."

Matt looked at her rather than Gabe. "He must get that from you."

"Maybe. He's good at math, which is probably your doing." She hesitated. "This has got to be strange for you. Seeing him like this. He's probably not even real."

"He's real enough."

So Matt wasn't going to make it easy. "What do you want?" she asked. "Have you figured that out?"

He stared at her. "An interesting question."

"We should probably set up some time for you two to get to know each other. You don't have a lot of experience with children, but that's okay. The two of you can work it out as you go."

"You sound very sure of yourself."

"He's an easy kid to be with." She smiled. "I want this to go well, Matt. You're his father. That means so much to him."

Jesse sounded earnest and sincere, Matt thought grimly. There was a time when he would have been young enough and stupid enough to believe her. Not anymore. She was playing him, which was fine. He was going to play her right back. He just had to decide how.

He followed her gaze and saw her watching the kid. Gabe had stopped to talk to a girl about his size. They were laughing, then the two of them went to the slide together. Jesse smiled, as if pleased by the exchange.

She didn't look all that different, he thought. Still blond, blue-eyed and pretty. She looked like she belonged on a surfboard, or modeling as a milkmaid. When she turned and caught him watching her, she smiled again. An easy, shared smiled. As if they had something in common. As if she'd never betrayed him.

"Gabe has a way with the ladies," she said. "I'm worried about how that will play out when he gets older, but one problem at a time, right?"

Matt nodded, not interested in Gabe, except as a means to an end.

"Why now?" he asked.

She didn't pretend to misunderstand him. "Gabe's been asking about you for a while now. I wasn't going to lie and tell him you were dead, so I told him the truth. That you didn't know about him."

"But I did know. You told me."

"You didn't believe me." She dropped her gaze to the floor. "I understand why. I mean, sure, it hurt, but given my past, I shouldn't have been surprised, right? Telling you I loved you wouldn't have changed anything, would it?"

She looked at him, all wide-eyed and hurt, as if remembering distressed her. Did she really think he would buy that?

"I hoped you'd think about it later and maybe wonder, but you didn't," she continued. "So we're back and we'll figure this out." She rose. "Could you watch him while I get him a snack?"

She was gone before he could say anything, leaving him responsible for a four-year-old kid.

Matt sat in his seat, not sure what he was supposed to do. What did he know about children? He turned his attention to Gabe, but the boy hadn't noticed his mother was gone. Instead he continued talking to the little girl. They were playing with a big truck and laughing.

A few minutes later, Jesse returned with milk, two coffees and a yogurt parfait. She handed one of the coffees to Matt. Gabe ran up and pointed at the parfait. "Is that for me?" he asked with a grin.

She ruffled his hair. "I'll share. Oh, look. Your shoe's untied."

Gabe looked at Matt, then bent down and slowly, carefully, tied his shoe. Jesse watched anxiously, as if this was a big deal. Matt realized he didn't know when kids were supposed to learn to tie their shoes. Was Gabe early, late or on time?

The kid finished and straightened. Jesse hugged him.

"Excellent job. Good for you."

Gabe looked at Matt, who gave him a slight smile. Gabe turned away.

"He's just learned," Jesse said by way of explanation. "It's tough for little kids. Their fine motor skills take a while to develop."

"Uncle Bill helped me," Gabe said as he took the milk.

Who the hell was Uncle Bill? Matt might not have any big interest in the kid, but he wasn't happy about Jesse's boyfriends hanging around him. Or was he more than a boyfriend? He dropped his gaze to her left hand.

"You married?" he asked.

Jesse choked on her coffee. "No." She cleared her throat, then laughed. "Married. That's a good one. I don't have time to get to the dry cleaners, let alone date. If only."

Was she telling the truth about dating? He would know soon enough. She'd always had guys around. She was that kind of woman. Men found her sexy and attractive. Even now, angry and looking for ways to punish her, he noticed how the light played on her skin and the easy way she smiled. If he let himself, he could remember how sexy he'd always found everything about her. Childbirth hadn't changed her body in any way that he could tell.

Jesse without a man? Impossible to imagine. So she was lying about that, too.

An older woman in a suit walked into the play area. Matt had never seen her before, but she looked official and out of place, so he waved her over.

"Mr. Fenner?" she asked. "I'm from the lab."

"DNA test," Matt said when Jesse raised her eyebrows.

She blinked at him. "Oh, right. Okay. Sure. What do you need?"

"A cheek swab. It doesn't hurt."

Jesse looked doubtful. "Can you do me first?" she asked. "I know you don't need it, but it would make Gabe feel better."

"I'll be doing it as well," Matt told her. "Is that good enough?"

She hesitated long enough to annoy him, then nodded. She called over her son.

"This nice lady needs to do a special test on you," she began, then held up her hands. "No needles. Look, Matt is going to show you what's involved so you can see you don't have to be scared."

Gabe looked doubtful, but stayed in place. The woman put on plastic gloves, then removed a swab from sterile packaging and asked him to open his mouth. Seconds later, she was finished.

"That looks easy," Jesse said cheerfully. "Did it hurt?"

"Not at all," Matt told her, feeling like an idiot. It was a swab. How could it hurt?

Gabe swallowed, then opened his mouth. When the test was done, he grinned. "I was brave."

"Yes, you were," Jesse told him. "This is to make sure Matt's really your daddy."

"But you said he was."

"I know, but this makes it official. Just to be sure."

Gabe obviously wasn't used to having his mother's word questioned. Give it time, Matt thought.

The woman from the lab left.

The boy slid close to Jesse. "When he's sure, will he like me?" he asked in a loud whisper.

Jesse shot Matt a look, then hugged Gabe. "He likes you now, honey. But the test will make everyone feel better."

Matt had the feeling of being judged, which didn't make sense. What had he done wrong?

Jesse picked up the kid and set him on her lap. "You're getting big," she said. "Some days I can actually see you growing."

Gabe laughed and turned to him. "When I reach the mark on the wall I get to have a real bike."

Jesse sighed. "Something I agreed to in a moment of weakness. A two-wheeler, but with training wheels."

Gabe sighed. "Yes, Mommy. But when Uncle Bill teaches me how to ride, I don't have to use them anymore."

Who was this Uncle Bill? This was the second time his name had come up. Matt made a note to make sure the investigator found out everything about him.

"Give me a break," she told her son, hugging him close. "Don't grow up so fast. I like you small."

"But I want to be big!"

Jesse laughed and her long hair swung forward. She turned to him then, happy and beautiful and so full of life.

He'd seen her like that a hundred times. He'd seen

her smile turn wicked as she reached for him. He'd seen her tired and sleepy and shaking with passion. He knew her body, or he had. He knew her scent and the feel of her skin. He'd once said he could find her blindfolded in a room full of women.

He'd loved her years ago; when he'd been young and stupid and thought everything would work out. But it hadn't. She'd betrayed him and now, still angry, he knew taking Gabe away from her wasn't enough revenge. There had to be more. But what?

"Do you like my mommy?" Gabe asked.

The unexpected question surprised Matt. "Of course," he said quickly, knowing he couldn't speak the truth. That he hated her with a passion that could burn through steel.

"Do you love her?" the boy asked.

"Shh," Jesse said quickly as color stained her cheeks. "That's one of those not-polite questions we've talked about."

"But why?"

"It just is."

She was embarrassed. Why? Out of guilt? Or did she still have feelings for him? As long as there was some kind of weakness, he wanted to exploit it. But how? There was no way to make up for what she'd done unless he did it to her. Get her to care about him, get her to expose her heart so he could crush her.

Was that the answer? Steal her heart *and* her child? That would leave her with nothing.

It was a ruthless and cruel plan, which made him like every part of it. He'd spent the past five years honing his skills with women. If he put his mind to it, Jesse wouldn't stand a chance. Then he would walk away without looking back.

CHAPTER FIVE

MATT STOOD. "I'M NOT a yogurt kind of guy," he said. "How about some fries?"

"Sure." Jesse watched him walk to the front of the restaurant and order.

He was so different, she thought, wishing they could all be more comfortable together. That would take time. She knew that. Most good things took time. Only this wasn't what she wanted—the distance, the strained conversations. She wanted them to be comfortable together…a family.

If only, she thought, not sure that would ever happen. So much time had passed. It hurt to remember how close she and Matt had been and how much had been lost.

He returned with a tray and three orders of fries.

"That's a lot of food," she murmured, knowing Gabe couldn't eat even half of the order and she shouldn't. Fries seemed to take a straight line to her thighs.

"Eat what you want and leave the rest," Matt told her.

She held in a laugh. Waste food? Not on her income.

Every crumb was accounted for. Not that he would understand that. Matt had been rich when she'd left and he seemed to have done well in the past five years.

Gabe returned to their table and eyed the fries. She smiled. "Yes, you may have some."

He grinned and grabbed one. Fries weren't a regular food in their house. All this eating out and fast food was going to go to his head.

Jesse reached for a fry herself, only to find that it didn't taste like much. She wasn't hungry at all. If anything, her stomach felt a little queasy. The old "I used to be in love with you and now I'm nervous" diet. Limited audience, but very effective. She grabbed her coffee.

"You were in Spokane the whole time?" Matt asked.

"Yes. I ran out of gas and money pretty much at the same time. Once I was working, I didn't feel the need to move on." She hadn't been hiding, just trying to get away. Not that anyone had come looking for her.

She felt bitterness rise up inside of her, but pushed it away. Both Nicole and Matt had been angry with her, thinking she'd betrayed them. That's why they hadn't hunted her down and dragged her back. At least that's what she told herself because it was better than the alternative. That neither of them had really cared about her at all.

"Have you seen your sister?" Matt asked.

Was he showing interest in her? Being polite? Was it possible he could get over being mad?

"Yes. I stopped by to see Nicole after I saw you."

"How did that go?"

"Not great. She's dealing with a lot right now. She has twins who are only a few months old, so that's hard. I'm going to start working in the bakery, just to help out. Plus I've created a brownie recipe I think she'll really like. I'm going to make some for her. Sort of a tasting."

Which couldn't be anything he was interested in. So maybe she should talk about something that would be more relevant. As much as it pained her to bring up the past.

"I wanted to tell you," she said, aware that Gabe was still sitting next to her, munching on fries. "I didn't know how. You'd been so angry and I was hurt. I felt guilty."

"About Drew?" Matt asked, anger flaring in his eyes.

She stiffened. "No. Nothing happened there. I told you that." She glanced at her son. "We'll talk about that later."

"Fine, but we *will* talk about it."

Because he didn't believe her, she thought sadly. Just like Nicole didn't believe her. She pushed away her fries and pressed a hand against her stomach. She felt queasy and uncomfortable. None of this was going the way she wanted. Her fantasy had been a perfect family reunion. Instead she'd gotten an awkward reality, which really sucked.

"I owe you child support," Matt said.

What? "No, you don't."

"Gabe is my son, my responsibility."

"None of this is about that." She wished she knew what he was thinking. She'd been able to read him before, but now he was a mystery. "I didn't come back for money. I came back so you and Gabe could get to know each other."

Matt didn't look as if he believed her, but he didn't say anything. Was that good or bad? Was it too late for him to connect with his son? She refused to believe that.

Gabe leaned against her and sighed.

"Getting tired, buddy?" she asked as she stroked his head. "You had a busy morning."

He looked at Matt. "I played outside with my grandma, then we read a story. I'm learning my letters. I know Q."

Matt's features tightened. "Your grandmother?"

Jesse swore silently. She'd meant to tell him about that.

"Uh-huh," Gabe said. "My grandma Paula."

Jesse put her arm around her son. "I went to see her, too. She's his only grandparent and I wanted them to meet. She was thrilled and invited us to stay."

"You can't," Matt told her. "Not there."

"Why not? There's plenty of room and she's great with Gabe. I want him to get to know all his family."

"You're not going to get any money out of her. However she pretends to care, she keeps the cash locked up."

Jesse's cheeks heated. "Is that what you think?" she asked as she stood. "That this is all about money? There are more important things."

"The only people who really believe that are the ones without any money. I'm guessing you're one of them."

"You're right. I don't have your millions and I don't need them. Gabe and I do just fine."

"That's crap and you know it. This is all about you getting in on what I have. Just admit it, Jesse. At least then we're starting from a place of honesty."

She couldn't believe what he was saying. Did he really believe that about her? Or was it not specifically her? Was it everyone?

"You're not interested in me being honest," she told him. "You believe what you want because it's easier. I can't stop you, so I won't try. What I do want to know is how you changed so much. You were never like this before."

He rose and stared at her. One corner of his mouth turned up in a mocking smile. "I am what you made me, Jesse. You should be proud."

JESSE STOPPED AT THE red light and did her best to wake up. She was still upset by her conversation with Matt the previous day. She hadn't slept much and had been up early to bake brownies.

Even breathing in their delicious smell didn't make her feel any better. She felt tired and beat-up. Telling herself to forget about Matt was good advice, but not something she seemed able to do. While she knew in her head that things were bound to have changed between them, her heart hadn't gotten the e-mail. Apparently some part of her had foolishly hoped there would still be a connection between them.

"Idiot," she muttered as the light turned green and she drove through the intersection.

Sure, she'd loved Matt once. He'd been everything to her, but he was gone now. So different that he might as well have been a complete stranger. Wanting more than a slightly cordial relationship with the father of her child was impossible. She would have to accept that and move on. And she would. Just as soon as she got through her meeting with Nicole and downed a triple-shot latte.

She pulled up in front of her sister's house and parked. The brownies were in a pink bakery box she'd bought. That morning she'd made two batches of each of the three flavors she wanted Nicole to taste. She'd cherry-picked a dozen of the best brownies of each flavor and put them in little paper cups. Presentation was everything, she reminded herself.

After collecting the box, she walked to the front door and rang the bell.

The door was answered by a tall, well-built, gorgeous guy who could have been an underwear model ten years ago.

"Hi," he said with a grin. "I'm Hawk. You must be Jesse. Come on in. I'm not allowed to stay for the tasting. Nicole says I don't have a subtle enough palate, but those brownies smell good so make sure she doesn't eat them all."

"Not to worry, I brought three dozen," Jesse said, immediately liking the man.

He led the way into the kitchen, which was much tidier than the last time she'd seen it. Nicole stood at the counter, pouring coffee. She turned as Jesse entered.

"Good morning," she said, not sounding especially excited to have company. "You brought the brownies?"

"Yes." Jesse set the box on the kitchen table.

Another woman entered the room. Someone as tall and blond as Nicole, with similar features.

Claire, Jesse thought, feeling strange at seeing her other sister—the one she'd never really known.

Claire and Nicole were fraternal twins, six years older than Jesse. At the age of three, Claire had sat down at a piano and started playing perfectly, despite the fact that she'd never had a lesson. By the time Jesse was born, she'd been whisked off to New York to study and play around the world. Jesse had grown up never really knowing Claire, only resenting her princess life-style as she moved from fabulous city to fabulous city, meeting the rich and famous and playing the piano.

Jesse and Nicole had been stuck back in Seattle, trying to grow up without much supervision. Nicole had always hated Claire for leaving, even though it hadn't been her choice, while Jesse had simply wanted to go with her on her travels.

Jesse still didn't know Claire very well, but she'd been the one to stay in touch when Jesse had moved away.

"You made it back," Claire said by way of greeting. "Is Seattle the same as you remembered?"

"Pretty much. There's a lot of new construction."

"That's the strong job market drawing people here." Claire took the mug of coffee Nicole offered. Jesse did the same.

There was a moment of awkward silence. Jesse felt uneasy. While these people were her family, they were strangers for one reason or another. And they all thought the worst of her.

Hawk moved next to Nicole and put his hands on her shoulders. He whispered something, then kissed her. His adoration was visible even across the room. Jesse felt a rush of pleasure that her sister had found someone so good for her and, close at its heels, envy, because she wanted the same thing for herself. She immediately thought of Matt, which was dumb. He might have been "the one" five years ago, but he wasn't anymore.

"I'll leave you ladies to your tasting," Hawk said. "Nicole, remember what I said."

She laughed. "We're not going to eat them all. You'll have plenty."

She and Hawk shared one of those intimate looks that passes between people who know each other and are secure in their love, then he left.

Nicole and Claire both sat at the table. Jesse joined them and opened the bakery box.

"I have three kinds of brownies," Jesse said. "Plain chocolate, chocolate with walnuts and peanut-butter chocolate."

"And these are your recipes?" Nicole asked.

Jesse resisted the urge to snap. "Yes. I developed them myself. I've kept records so there's a clear evolution of the process."

She hated that she had to explain herself, that Nicole just wouldn't trust her, but that was her sister's way. Nicole would never forgive Jesse for selling the famous Keyes cake online five years ago.

Nicole took one of each brownie. Claire did the same, then laughed. "I'm not really an expert. Is saying I like them going to be enough?"

"It is for me," Jesse said, then held her breath as Nicole took a bite.

Nicole chewed and swallowed without saying anything. She got up and filled a glass with water, took a sip, returned to the table and tasted again.

She ate slowly, and deliberately, tasting each brownie three times before finishing her water and turning to Claire.

"What do you think?" she asked.

"They're amazing. Really rich without being over-powering. I'm not usually big on the whole peanut-butter-chocolate combo, but even those are incredible."

Jesse didn't relax. Nicole wouldn't care what Claire thought.

Nicole pushed away the brownies. "They're good. I'd sell them in the bakery."

Jesse exhaled. "All three flavors?"

Nicole nodded.

Relief was sweet and instant. "Great. So now what?"

Claire rose. "I'm going to leave you two to talk business. I'll be in the back with the kids." She patted Jesse on the shoulder as she left.

Nicole leaned back in her chair. "What do you want? You said before you were interested in earning your way back in. Is that still true?"

"Yes." What did she want? A do-over. She wanted to somehow change the past. Except she wouldn't give up Gabe and she liked the person she'd become.

"I want to work for you for six months," Jesse began, making it up as she went. "After that period of time, we'll discuss me becoming your partner. During that six months, you'll get the brownie recipes. If things don't work out, I take them with me."

"And go sell them somewhere else? I don't think so. If you leave, the brownie recipes stay, but I'll pay you for them."

Jesse didn't like that, but she understood Nicole's concerns. She wouldn't want to sell something in the bakery for six months only to lose it and possibly customers.

Before Jesse could respond, Nicole said, "Or I

could just buy you out. You're over twenty-five now. I could get a loan and you'd get cash for half what the bakery is worth."

It would be a lot of money, Jesse thought. Enough for her to start her own business. But that wasn't what she wanted.

"I want to make this work," she told her sister. "That's why I'm here."

"I have trouble believing that," Nicole admitted. "But you're different. That's obvious."

"I don't care what I do at the bakery. You always need extra help. I'll provide that. I'm not saying I have to be in charge. You're still the boss."

Nicole shifted in her seat. "An interesting statement. Since having the twins, it's been really hard for me to get into the bakery much. We're stretched pretty thin. What I need is someone to help run the place. You have any management experience?"

"I've been running a bar."

Nicole's eyes widened. "You're kidding."

"No. I worked my way up from server. I would bartend and run the place a few nights a week. I've managed employees and drunk customers. A few businesspeople buying donuts and coffee will be easy. I also have my associates' degree in business."

"You went to college?"

"In the morning. I worked at night and did homework when I could."

"What about Gabe?"

"I raised him, too."

"You've been busy."

Jesse nodded. She felt a little pride and took pleasure in the fact that Nicole seemed impressed. Despite what Nicole believed, Jesse cared about what her sister thought of her. Which was why she was willing to shatter the moment of connection between them by saying, "We have to talk about Drew."

It was like a wall came down. "No, we don't," Nicole snapped.

"Fine. You can just listen. I didn't sleep with him. I never slept with him or had anything close to an inappropriate relationship with him." Jesse spoke quickly, afraid Nicole might bolt. "We used to talk, nothing more. He listened and I had a lot to say. One night…" She drew in a breath.

"That night I was upset. I'd found an engagement ring while I was helping Matt unpack. I knew he was going to propose. I loved him so much, but I was terrified, too. Terrified of blowing it. I'd never had a real relationship before. Could I have one with Matt? I wanted to, but I'd always managed to mess up everything good in my life. I didn't want to screw up with him."

Nicole started to stand. Jesse put her hand on her arm.

"You have to listen."

"I don't want to hear this."

"I need to tell you."

Nicole sank back in the chair and crossed her arms over her chest. "Go on."

"I was crying," Jesse said, thinking that not talking about this was so much easier. She hated the feelings that rushed up in her, the sense of being swept back into the past. "He sat on the bed and told me I couldn't change who I was. I would never settle for one guy. Girls like me didn't settle down."

She swallowed against the tightness in her throat. "I was stunned. Was he right? Was I going to hurt Matt? Worse, maybe I didn't deserve him."

She closed her eyes. Shame filled her. Shame that someone would think she was worth so little. "Drew kissed me. He kissed me and I let him because I'd always used guys to make myself feel better. Why should this be different? Then he pulled off my T-shirt and touched my bare skin and I lost it. I knew I didn't want anyone but Matt. That I had changed. I started to push him away."

There was more. There was how sick she'd felt inside. How she'd thought she was going to throw up. There was her terror that Nicole would hear them and come in, which was what had happened anyway. There was the rapid pounding of her heart and the knowledge that the very last piece of innocence buried deep inside had been shattered.

"That's when you came in," she whispered. "Drew jumped up and shouted that I'd been coming on to him. I knew you were going to believe him."

She opened her eyes. Nicole stared at her, but she couldn't read her expression. Did her sister believe her? Did she still hate her?

There was so much more she wanted to explain. She wanted to say that it had hurt so much to have Nicole turn her back on her. It had hurt to be shut out of her only family.

"I didn't sleep with him," Jesse repeated. "Nothing happened and not because we were interrupted."

"I want to believe you," Nicole told her. "For a lot of reasons."

Jesse's chest tightened. "But you don't."

"I'm not sure."

Why was she even surprised? "I can't give you proof." She wasn't sure what Drew had said about that night. "Sometimes you just have to have faith. I screwed up a lot when I was growing up, Nicole. I know that. But I never did anything to deliberately hurt you."

Nicole looked at her without speaking.

Jesse had tried and she would keep trying, but right now she was just plain tired.

"I'll be at the bakery on Monday morning," she said as she stood. "You know how to get in touch with me if you need anything before then."

Nicole nodded.

Jesse walked out without looking back.

She'd come home with high hopes and a lot of dreams. So far none of them had come true, but she wasn't giving up. She'd come a long way already. She was going to keep moving forward until every-thing worked out. The past five years had taught her to be strong and to dig deep for what was needed. She wasn't afraid of hard work or challenges. She was a survivor.

JESSE'S CELL PHONE RANG a little after three that afternoon. The number displayed was unfamiliar.

"Hello?"

"It's Matt."

Funny how, despite everything, her body still reacted to the sound of his voice.

"Hi."

"You're probably wondering why I'm calling," he said.

"I'm sure it's to yell at me about something."

There was a pause, then he surprised her by chuckling. "Okay, I earned that. Maybe I'm calling to say I'm sorry. That our meeting yesterday was too much, too soon. Maybe I have regrets."

Was she going to get that lucky? "When will you know for sure?" she asked.

"By tonight. I could tell you all about it over dinner."

"You could."

"Is that a yes?" he asked.

Was it? Did she want to see Matt again?

She was feeling raw from their last encounter—hurt and confused and a little sad about the changes she saw in him. But he was also Gabe's father, so she had to reestablish a relationship with him. If she were in the mood to be honest, she had some personal interest in getting to know him. He was still the only man she had ever loved.

"I could meet you for dinner," she said, grateful that she was staying with Paula and wouldn't have to worry about finding a sitter. Gabe adored his grandmother and the feeling was mutual.

"I know a quiet Italian place close to you," he said. "Grazies." He gave her the address and simple directions. "Seven?"

"That's fine. I'll be there."

JESSE PULLED INTO THE parking lot a couple of minutes early, which gave her a chance to check her makeup in the rearview mirror and try to get her breathing under control. She was beyond nervous and telling herself to get a grip wasn't helping.

Too much had happened too fast. Coming home, dealing with family, seeing Matt, knowing everyone in Seattle she cared about hated her. The irony with Matt was she hadn't done anything wrong. She'd fallen in love with him, nothing more. Yet he blamed her for so much.

"Deep breaths," she told herself as she climbed out of her car and walked toward the restaurant.

Matt was waiting by the front desk, looking tall and handsome in a long-sleeved shirt and slacks. He'd come a long way from that geeky computer nerd she'd first met in a Starbucks years ago. But were all the changes on the outside or had he transformed who he was inside as well?

They were led to a booth by a window overlooking the patio. Jesse slid in then took the offered menu. Despite how great everything sounded, she didn't know if she was going to be able to eat. Not sitting across from Matt.

He thanked their server and studied the wine list. "They have a nice selection of Italian wines," he told her. "Any preferences?"

"No. Whatever looks good to you is fine."

He nodded, still studying the wines.

She remembered the first time they'd gone to dinner at the Olive Garden. She'd thought he was adorable. She still remembered the flash of his smile and how she'd realized he was someone she might have to worry about.

"What are you thinking?" Matt asked.

"Nothing much."

"It was something. You had an interesting look on your face."

She didn't feel that telling him the truth was a good idea. "I saw Nicole today. We had a tasting for the brownies I've been working on and she liked them. We're going to start selling them in the bakery."

"That's good. Things are going well with her?"

Jesse thought about her sister's determination to think the worst of her. "We're making progress."

"You're still staying with my mother?"

"Yes." Did he want to hear about the woman who'd raised him? Did he miss her? "She's been wonderful.

Gabe thinks she's fabulous and she can't get enough of him. They play and watch movies and go for walks. I kind of feel guilty for having so much free time. It's been nice."

Matt's expression was impossible to read. She searched his dark eyes, but he wasn't giving anything away.

She hesitated, then said, "She's changed. Before she didn't want anything to do with me. I think she would have been happy if I'd been run over by a truck and left on the side of the road."

"Probably," Matt told her.

Ouch. Not that it wasn't true. "But she's different now. Open. She wants a relationship with me and Gabe." Jesse touched her water glass but didn't pick it up. "She misses you."

The server appeared. Jesse sighed at the timing. They placed their orders. When they were alone again, she said, "What happened between the two of you? You used to be so close. I know I got caught in the middle."

He stared at her for a long time. "I never forgave her for telling me about you and Drew."

His voice was low and flat. Despite her innocence, she flushed. The humiliation was hard to escape.

Paula had come to the house to do whatever she could to break up Jesse and Matt. Nicole had told her that Jesse no longer lived there and had gone into detail as to why. Paula hadn't wasted any time in rushing to tell her son about Jesse's supposed affair with her sister's husband.

Jesse still ached with the unfairness of what had happened. She'd gotten away with so much when she'd been a teenager, then she'd been damned by something that hadn't happened at all.

"I never forgave her for that," Matt said. "Not for telling me, but for being so happy about it."

"She's sorry," Jesse said, feeling that the Paula issue was more easily fixed than her own situation. "She misses you."

"You're taking her side?" He sounded surprised.

"Yes. I told you, she's changed. She's been great to me and Gabe. I wish she and I could have become friends five years ago. We both had you in common."

"You're giving her too much credit."

"I don't think so. We all make mistakes."

He looked at her. "Including you?"

"My list is long and impressive, but it doesn't include sleeping with Drew."

"Jesse," he began.

She shook her head. "No, Matt. I have to say this. I have to explain." For the second time that day, she told the story of that horrible night. When Drew had sat on the edge of her bed and she'd poured out her heart and he'd told her she wasn't a one-guy woman. She left out the part about finding the engagement ring, saying instead that she knew she was in love with him and terrified of messing up. An equal truth, she thought.

"I never slept with him," she concluded. "I never

wanted to. He was wrong about me. You were the one I was in love with. Just you."

She couldn't tell what he was thinking, if he believed her or not. She wished there were better words to convince him.

"I know you've spent the past five years thinking the worst of me," she said. "I know it's going to take a little time to consider that there might be another explanation for what happened. Can you at least be open to the possibility?"

"I can try."

"It's a place to start."

The server returned with their bottle of wine. After she'd opened it and Matt had tasted it, she poured them each a glass and left.

He picked up his wine. "To new beginnings."

She touched her glass to his and hoped new beginnings were possible.

They ate their salads and talked about how Seattle had changed. When the entrées arrived, she asked him about his business. "When did you go out on your own?"

"Four years ago. I had some ideas that didn't fit in with what I'd been doing at Microsoft. With the money I had from the games I'd licensed, I was able to start up without bank financing."

"And keep all the profits for yourself."

"How do you know there are profits?" he asked.

"I've seen your house."

"I've been fortunate."

More than that, she thought. "Now you're the boss. How does that feel?"

"I like it," he admitted. "Having a staff means I can focus on what I want to do. They take care of the details." He cut into his chicken. "You'd like my assistant. Diane. She's opinionated and does her best to run my life."

"I'm surprised you allow that."

"I don't, but she ignores me."

"Then she must be really good at her job."

"She is."

Jesse liked that Matt kept a mouthy assistant around, although she couldn't say why. Did it make him more approachable? More like the man she remembered?

"Are you ever going to believe me?" she asked. "Is this ever going to be okay?"

He looked at her for a long time before reaching across the table and touching her hand. "I want it to be," he said.

And for now, that was enough.

CHAPTER SIX

AFTER DINNER, MATT WALKED Jesse to her car. The meal had been an interesting combination of comfortable and awkward. They managed a few minutes of easy conversation, only to reach another bump. Jesse told herself that while she'd had years to work everything through, this was still new to Matt. She had to give him time.

She was oddly aware of him as they crossed the parking lot. It was summer, and the sun still hadn't completely set, despite the fact that it was near nine.

"Thanks for dinner," she said when they reached her Subaru. "We needed to talk."

He touched her cheek with the back of his fingers. "I understand why you're here," he told her. "I'm working the problem."

"Someone's been to management seminars," she teased.

He grinned. "More than I want to admit to."

"You must hate them."

"Every second."

"All that group bonding."

"Not my style," he admitted.

That hadn't changed, she thought. He'd always been more of a one-on-one guy. And speaking of one-on-one...

He seemed to be standing a little too close. He was still touching her cheek and she could feel definite heat where their skin brushed. His eyes were so dark, she thought, her brain getting fuzzy. She remembered when getting lost in them was the best way to spend a day. Was that still true?

"Dammit, Jesse," he murmured.

Was he upset about the past? Aware of the growing tension between them? Thinking about kissing her as much as she thought about kissing him?

She knew she had to keep things light. Try to establish a friendship so he would be in a good position to get to know his son. Anything else would be a mistake. Only this was Matt and he'd been the last man she'd kissed. She suddenly ached to feel his mouth on hers, his arms around her. She wanted to feel aroused and safe at the same time. She wanted—

He leaned in and kissed her, just as she'd hoped he would. A light kiss that allowed her time to adjust to the reality after years of living on fantasy.

His mouth was exactly as she remembered. Warm and firm, but just soft enough to make her want more. She leaned in slightly, putting her hand on his upper arm where she felt his strong muscles. He cupped her jaw, then tilted his head and licked her lower lip.

Electricity shot through her. Need burned hot and bright, melting every part of her. She went from interested to intense in a heartbeat.

He put his free hand on her spine, above her butt. He used just enough pressure to draw her closer, but not so much that she felt she was going to be forced. Which made her want to shift nearer on her own.

Parts of her began to ache. It had been forever, she thought dreamily, and here she was, back where she'd started. She couldn't help remembering how it had been between them—all passion and surrender. She wanted that again. Wanted all of it.

He deepened the kiss, then pulled back and kissed her jaw, the side of her neck before returning to her mouth. She felt herself getting swept away. The fact that they were in a restaurant parking lot didn't really matter. There was only the moment and the man.

He kissed her over and over, arousing her with each stroke of his tongue. But something was different and that difference was what brought her back to reality.

She became aware of the way he slowly circled her spine with his palm. It was deliciously exciting and made her want to purr, but it wasn't anything he'd ever done before. He dropped his hand from her jaw to her shoulder and lightly rubbed her bare arm. Again, thrilling but not Matt. Even his kisses were different. They were more perfect, more practiced. He was a man who knew how to arouse a woman in a matter of seconds.

She hadn't taught him that.

She drew back and told herself it didn't matter. That it had been a long time and of course he'd been with other people. But it hurt to have proof that his life had gone on.

"Jesse?"

She forced herself to smile. "Impressive. You know your way around a good seduction."

"I've always enjoyed kissing you."

It was true, Matt thought, knowing that getting Jesse into bed would be pleasurable for them both. So what if he had a good time? That didn't mean he wouldn't walk away when it was over.

"You're kissing differently," she said, then looked away as if she hadn't expected to admit that.

"I've had practice."

"I can tell."

There was something in her voice. Annoyance? Hurt? He'd done his best to be charming during dinner—all part of the plan—and now he reminded himself there was a goal. Still, his temper flared to life.

"Did you expect me to live like a monk after you left?" he asked.

She met his gaze. "No. I expected you to take everything I'd taught you and use it on someone else."

She *was* hurt and angry, he thought. Welcome to the club.

"Then you're not disappointed," he said. "I took everything I learned with you and put it to good use." When she shivered, he added, "Come on, Jess. It's not like you've been living a solitary life yourself. You've had guys around. That was always your style."

She stepped back. "I told you before. There hasn't been time. You have no idea what it's like to be a single parent."

"You're right about that." Because of her, he didn't know *anything* about being a parent. "What about Uncle Bill? Gabe likes him."

"He's a friend. Nothing more."

"Right."

She glared at him. "Where do you get off judging me? I've told you the truth."

"It's hard to believe. It's been five years. That's a long time to go without getting laid. And before you and I hooked up, you'd always had a guy around. No, wait. You had a guy around even when we were together."

"You know that's not true." Her mouth twisted. "But let's not let a little thing like the truth get in the way of your righteous anger. Once a slut, always a slut. Isn't that what you told me when you thought I'd slept with Drew? Except I hadn't done anything wrong. One day you're going to know that for certain, Matt. And when you do, you're going to have to accept the fact that I loved you, I was faithful to you and when I came and told you I was pregnant with your child, you threw me out. You weren't interested, and you couldn't begin to bring yourself to believe that there was even a *chance* the baby was yours."

He narrowed his gaze. "It's not like you tried to

convince me," he reminded her. "You knew what Nicole had told my mother and what she had told me. Why would I think your sister was lying? Why wouldn't I believe her?"

"Because you loved me," Jesse yelled. "Because you knew I loved you. You should have at least tried to listen."

"You weren't very convincing. You knew I was devastated and you left anyway."

"Oh, right. I went to Spokane, Matt. That's three hundred miles away. It's not like I was living off the grid. If you'd cared at all, you would have come looking for me. You would have found out for sure. But you couldn't be bothered." She opened her car and tossed her purse inside. "Here's the thing. If you want any kind of a relationship with your son, you're going to have to deal with me. Which means you'll have to make peace with the past and accept the fact that, for all my faults, I didn't lie to you. I just wish I knew if that was possible for you or if you like being pissed at me so much, you can never accept the truth."

She got in her car and slammed the door. He stepped back and watched her drive away.

The sun was warm on his back, not that he needed the heat. His temper blazed bright enough to chase away any chill.

She still thought he was that naive kid she'd fooled five years ago. But she was wrong. He was going to take her down, break her and leave her, just as she'd done to him. Then the past would be over and he would never look back.

JESSE ARRIVED AT THE Keyes Bakery a little before six in the morning. It was her first day working and she didn't want to be late. If things worked out and she actually filled in for Nicole, she would be getting there a whole lot earlier. Sid and Phil started at three and she would be expected in around four-thirty.

Years ago, she always complained about the early hours, but now she knew she wouldn't mind. She would be off by noon and able to spend the afternoon with Gabe.

She walked to the rear door and stepped inside. The sounds and smells were familiar—the scent of rising dough, the sweetness of the frosting and cinnamon thickened the air. She heard mixers and the hum of ovens, a radio playing and conversation. She headed for the latter.

She found Sid standing by a massive mixing bowl. He looked a little older, a little heavier. He wore all white and seeing his familiar scowl made her smile.

"Morning," she said loudly.

He turned toward her. The scowl lifted and he actually grinned.

"Jess! You're back. Nicole said you'd be working here again, but I didn't know you were starting today. Kid, how you doing?"

She rushed toward him and he held out his arms.

He hugged her tight, squeezing until her ribs hurt, but she didn't complain. It felt good to be welcomed.

"I'm great, Sid. How are you?"

"Same old, same old. Keeping busy. So what's this I hear about you making brownies?"

"I've been working on a recipe for a while now," she said as he released her. "They're really good."

"Uh-huh. I'll let you know what I think. It's one thing to cook in your kitchen, it's another to make big enough batches to sell. You think all that through, kid?"

"We'll find out."

She didn't mind him wanting her to prove herself. Sid had always been fair with her. If he liked the brownies, he would tell her. There wouldn't be any subtext or hidden agenda.

Sid led her around and introduced her to a mostly new crew. They all seemed nice enough.

"Where's Phil?" she asked.

"Florida, if you can believe it. He and his wife won a two-million-dollar lotto and took off for the sunshine. Lucky SOB."

He continued talking about Phil and his good fortune. Jesse took the opportunity to look around.

The equipment was exactly as she remembered. The same old machines in the same place. They all needed to be upgraded. She'd been doing a lot of research and she knew they could buy smaller, more energy-efficient ovens that worked better and faster than what they had now. The same with all the mixers. Not that she would mention any of that to Nicole. Her sister wouldn't be interested in her ideas—not for a while.

"I'm going to have to prove myself," Jesse murmured. "And I will."

Sid looked at her. "Talking to yourself? That's new."

She laughed. "Sometimes I was the only adult in the room. I'll try to remember not to mutter in public."

"That's right. You had a kid."

"A boy. Gabriel. Gabe. He's great."

"So you gonna bring him around to meet his uncle Sid?"

Jesse nodded then threw herself at the older man. "I missed you."

He smoothed her hair. "I missed you, too, Jess. I was real sorry that you and your sister fell out with each other. It was a shame."

Jesse didn't want to talk about that. "Can you show me my corner of the kitchen so I can get started with the brownies?"

"Sure. I've pulled off a couple of guys to help you. Nicole said you get the college help."

Jesse wrinkled her nose. Great. Her sister had assigned her the summer employees who had no real experience. Yet more evidence that Nicole wasn't exactly on board with the brownie idea. Not that it mattered. She was going to make this a success despite any obstacles thrown in her way.

"Any help is appreciated," Jesse said.

"Good attitude. Jasper's okay. Jasper. Can you

believe it? That's his real name. And D.C. He's got some attitude on him, but he does the work, so I ignore it and him." Sid pointed to a back corner of the kitchen where an ancient mixer stood by itself.

"You're kidding," Jesse muttered. It hadn't worked most of the time five years ago.

"Sorry. That's what the boss said. Oh, and she wanted me to tell you not to make too many brownies until we know if they're gonna sell." He shrugged. "You know Nicole."

"Oh, yeah. I know her."

Jesse found her help and introduced herself. They were both young and obviously just putting in their time to earn money for school. She collected the ingredients she would need, then set out the few special items she'd brought with her in her backpack.

"We're going to be making small batches at first," she told the guys. "I rented a kitchen to work out the problems of expanding the recipe and I don't want to go bigger than I've already done." She couldn't afford to make a mistake. She had a feeling that Nicole was more than ready to toss her out on her ass.

She sent D.C. to find the right size pans and had Jasper make sure the mixer was having a good and functioning day, then she smoothed out her recipe and went to work.

An hour later, she pulled the second batch of brownies from the oven and nearly moaned as she breathed in the rich, chocolate smell. She'd been telling herself that with brownies like this in her life, she didn't miss having a man. Of course, that had been before the hot, sexy, bone-melting kisses Matt had taunted her with. Now she had a bad feeling the brownies would come in second.

Matt. She didn't want to think about him, their evening together or the way it had ended. It made her sad and full of regret. Because on her dark nights she had always imagined what it would have been like if he'd believed her. If he'd at least waited to find out if the baby was his. They could have been married and had another child together. They could have been happy. They could have—

"Stop!" she whispered fiercely, hoping Jasper couldn't hear her. She didn't want to frighten the help on the first day. But she couldn't allow herself to get lost in what *hadn't* happened with Matt. She had plenty of reality to deal with.

She set the brownies on racks to cool. The first batch was at the right temperature to cut. She did it by hand, working slowly, carefully. D.C. helped put each cut brownie into an individual paper wrapper, then slid them onto a tray for the front case.

Jesse took one of the corner pieces and broke it in two, then handed part of the still-warm brownie to each of the guys.

"Damn," Jasper said, then grimaced. "Ah, sorry. Darn, that's good, Jessie."

She laughed. "Sid still has his no-swearing rule?"

"Yeah, and he gets real mad if he hears any."

D.C. licked his fingers. "Those are really good. They're the best thing in this place."

"Good to know," Nicole said as she walked around a rack and into their corner of the kitchen. "That's two votes in favor of what you're doing. Congratulations."

"Thanks."

But Nicole didn't look pleased. She studied the tray that would be taken up front. "Just one flavor?"

"Two. With and without walnuts. I thought I'd wait on the peanut butter ones for a week or so."

"All right. We didn't discuss a price."

"I have cost breakdowns," Jesse said. She took off her plastic gloves and dug a folder out of her backpack. "One of my business classes required us to do a business plan, including coming up with the pro-totype of the product. That's what gave me the idea for the brownies. I had to guess on fixed costs and just assigned a value based on my Internet research."

She handed Nicole the sheet with the information. "A dollar-fifty gives us a decent margin. If we add more flavors, we can charge more as the ingredients get more specialized and expensive."

Nicole studied the paper. "You were thorough."

Jesse started to say she got an A on the project but didn't. Nicole wasn't exactly enthusiastic about any of this. Better to give her time and let her see that the brownies were going to sell. It was the mature thing to do, even if she sometimes got tired of having to make the adult decision.

Jasper and D.C. motioned that they were leaving. Jesse nodded, a little surprised that even they picked up on Nicole's tension. Apparently it was obvious to people other than her.

"Do you want me to sign something?" Nicole asked. "A statement that if this doesn't work out I won't sell the brownies without your knowledge."

Jesse forced herself not to react. Steal. Nicole meant steal. It was a not-so-subtle dig at Jesse for the chocolate cake incident from five years ago.

"I'm willing to trust you," she said with a lightness she didn't feel. Obviously she'd been an idiot to think her sister would welcome her with open arms. Nicole was determined not to make this easy.

"We've already cleared a space in the main case," Nicole said. "You can take the brownie trays up whenever you're ready. Maggie is putting up a sign about them and we'll be handing out samples."

"Thanks."

Nicole started to leave. Jesse called her back.

"I missed you," she said. "It was hard being gone. Having Gabe on my own terrified me, but it also made me understand what you'd gone through, having your little sister to take care of. You were a kid yourself. You shouldn't have had the responsibility. I want you to know I appreciate all you did for me and all you had to put up with."

Nicole's mouth twisted. For a second Jesse thought—hoped—they were going to have an honest moment of communication. Then Nicole shrugged.

"We all do what we have to do. I'll let you get back to your brownies."

Then she was gone.

"YOU SURE ABOUT THIS?" Jesse asked.

Wyatt, Claire's husband, dumped more containers of fat snap-together building blocks on the family room floor. "We're making a castle," he said with a grin. "The castle is our favorite."

Robby, Claire and Wyatt's four-year-old, and Mirabella, their two-year-old daughter, sank down next to Gabe, who was staring intently at the blocks and the possibilities they represented.

"He's great with the kids," Claire said, as she led the way to the living room and the relative quiet and privacy there.

"I remember how he was with Amy," Jesse said, wishing Wyatt's daughter had been around. But Amy, now a pretty, accomplished teenager, was off at camp for the summer. "I can't wait to see her."

"You won't believe how much she's grown," Claire said with a laugh. "She's beautiful and that's making Wyatt crazy. Boys are sniffing around all the time. So far she's not interested in dating, but it's just a matter of time until that changes. We're holding out for a couple more years of relative peace."

"Good luck with that." Jesse settled on the sofa and faced her sister. "You're doing well. I read about you in the paper."

Claire dismissed the compliment with a flick of her wrist. "I'm performing less and less each year. I take tours when it interests me and when the scheduling works out, but with three kids, it's hard. I just don't have the drive anymore." She glanced at the gleaming baby grand piano in the corner. "I'll always have music in my life, but not in the same way. Oh, I'm teaching Eric and Robby together once a week. If you'd like Gabe to join them, I'd be happy to have him."

"Sure," Jesse said. "What mother doesn't want her child taught by the famous Claire Keyes?"

Claire laughed. "Don't expect much. We play more than we learn, but I want them to appreciate music and find it thrilling, not be a grind. If they're interested, they can work on scales and technique later."

"You're the expert. Just tell me when and I'll have him here." She paused. "Assuming it's all right with Nicole."

"Jesse, don't."

"Don't what? Be realistic? Admit it." Jesse kicked off her sandals and tucked her feet under her. "She doesn't want me to be successful, Claire. She's sorry I'm back."

"She's not sorry. She's dealing with a lot. Remember—we didn't give her any warning."

Which had been Jesse's request—that Claire not

tell Nicole she was coming back. "Maybe that was a mistake. Maybe I should have let you tell her. Not that I think it would have made any difference. She's still angry with me about something that didn't happen." Exactly like Matt. He was furious about the past he remembered, not the one that had happened.

"She'll get over it," Claire said soothingly. "Give it time."

"Do I have a choice?"

"Not really. She'll come around."

Jesse wasn't so sure. "It's unfair. I kept telling her before and she didn't believe me. Now it's five years later and she's still pissed."

"You didn't try very hard," Claire pointed out.

Jesse stared at her. "Excuse me?"

"You weren't very convincing back then. You kept saying nothing happened."

"Nothing did." Jesse couldn't believe it. She was being judged on the way she'd tried to defend herself?

"We thought you meant Nicole shouldn't be angry because you and Drew hadn't actually gotten far enough along to have sex."

"What?" Jesse couldn't believe it. "I meant nothing happened as in nothing happened. Not, gee, we were interrupted and I'm really bummed about it."

Why would they have thought otherwise? Why would—

She rubbed her temple. Nicole would have assumed the worst because she was used to her baby sister being a disaster. Because the worst was easier to believe.

"All this over words," she murmured. Lives changed forever, chances lost because of semantics?

"Words matter," Claire said. "Nicole was devastated. I'm not sure she would have listened to anything you had to say."

Claire was right, Jesse thought. But at least if she'd made her sister understand what she'd meant, they might be getting along better now.

"Nothing happened," Jesse repeated. "Drew and I were never involved, never had sex, never wanted to have sex." She paused. "Okay, he did, that last night, but I have no idea where that came from. I was in love with Matt and I was completely faithful to him. Drew was a friend, nothing more. Is that clear enough?"

Claire touched her hand. "I totally and completely believe you."

"Great. When you get a chance, pass it on to Nicole."

"Give her time. She'll come around."

Jesse nodded. It wasn't like she had much choice.

Claire smiled. "You've changed. You're a grown-up."

"A hard-won victory."

"An impressive victory."

"I have so much I want to do," Jesse told her. "So many things I want to achieve. Coming back here is just the beginning. Reconciling with Nicole is a part of that, but ultimately the decision is hers."

"I agree. So do what you can and then try to let it go."

"That doesn't seem possible." Let it go as in not care? "I appreciate that you stayed in touch with me."

"I didn't have the same emotional energy about you that Nicole did," Claire said.

Because they hadn't grown up together. They were still practically strangers who just happened to be sisters.

"I'll get through it," Jesse said, knowing one way or the other she would. "I'm strong. I think I was always strong, I just didn't know it then."

"You know now," Claire said. "Isn't that what matters?"

JESSE SAT IN HER CAR and pulled out her cell phone. She pushed the button to dial a familiar number, then smiled when she heard the slow, low, "Hello?"

"Hi, Bill."

"Hey, Jess. How you doing?"

"Okay. Good. Sort of."

He chuckled. "Still trying to decide."

"Oh, yeah. Nothing is like I thought."

"Better or worse?"

"Both."

"That happens."

She gave him a brief rundown of her time in Seattle. "I'm going to be staying six months and working at the bakery. I wanted to let you know so you could replace me."

"I'll never be able to replace you but I'll hire someone to take your place."

She laughed. "You're a charmer."

"That's what my mama said."

"She was right. And how sad it is that all your charm goes to waste."

"You appreciate it."

"You know what I mean," she said, the argument familiar. "Come on, Bill. It's been six years since Ellie died. You need to think about dating, finding someone. You should be happy."

"I tell you the same thing."

"The circumstances are different." The person *she* couldn't forget was still alive.

"Not that different, little girl. Now get off me."

"For now."

"I'm going to come visit you. I miss you and Gabe more than I want to admit."

"We'd love to see you." She gave him Paula's address and phone number.

"I'll be by in the next few weeks."

"Good."

"Now go find yourself someone," he instructed.

"I'm hanging up on you, Bill," she said.

He laughed and said goodbye.

She pressed the end button on her phone and thought about what he'd said. That she should find someone.

Maybe that was possible in the future, but not now.

Not until she'd resolved everything with Matt. She had to get some kind of closure, make sure she wasn't still in love with him. Only then could she put the past behind her and look into the future.

CHAPTER SEVEN

Five Years Ago...

JESSE STOOD IN FRONT of the house for a second, before approaching and knocking softly on the door. She should have told Matt she would meet him somewhere else, but he'd said his house and she'd agreed before she'd thought the plan through.

Seconds later the door flew open and a very angry Paula Fenner stood in front of her.

"What are you doing here?" she demanded, her voice sharp. "Don't you know what time it is?"

Jesse opened her mouth, then closed it, not sure what to say.

"He's out with someone else," Paula continued. "Another girl. He's not out with you. Don't you have any pride?"

Jesse couldn't figure out why Matt's mother hated her. They hardly had any contact. Jesse wasn't even dating Matt. She was helping him. Not that Paula saw any of that. For some reason the other woman believed

Jesse was a threat and attacked every time they were in the same room.

"I'm sorry to bother you," Jesse said and stepped back. "Good night."

Paula glared at her, not moving from the entryway until Jesse climbed into her car, then the front door slammed shut.

Jesse sighed. Paula and Nicole should get together and start a "we hate Jesse" club. They'd have to fight over who got to be president. They could hang pictures of her and throw darts at them.

The silly image made her smile, then reality intruded and her smile faded.

She wished that Paula wasn't so determined to have nothing to do with her, because Jesse sure had a lot to say to her. Paula was holding on too tight and that clinging was pushing her son away. Jesse could see it every time Matt talked about his mother. Paula was making him crazy and if she wasn't careful, she was going to lose her son completely.

"Not my problem," Jesse murmured as a car pulled up to hers.

Matt climbed out and approached the driver's side. "Thanks for meeting me," he said. "Want to come in?"

She eyed the door, then shook her head. "Your mom is still up and she wasn't exactly thrilled to see me."

Matt grimaced. "She's getting worse. Come on. I know an all-night diner. Want me to drive?"

"I'll follow you." It would be easier if she had her

own car and could just walk away at the end of the meeting.

As she started the engine, Jesse tried not to think about what Matt had spent the past few hours doing. And whom he'd been doing it with. After all, him dating was what she wanted. Her goal had been to bring out all his hidden potential and her lessons were paying off. He'd been on three dates this week alone.

He was exactly the kind of guy women wanted— funny, smart, caring, good-looking and wealthy. Not that any of his dates knew about his money. He'd wanted to keep that information quiet and Jesse had agreed. But even without the millions sitting in an investment company somewhere, he was still a catch.

The changes had been simple. A new wardrobe, an interest in current events, a working knowledge of how to ask a girl out and basic date etiquette had transformed him. There was only one teeny, tiny problem…

She'd fallen for him.

Jesse sighed. She wasn't about to admit it to anyone and barely believed it herself, but there it was. She liked Matt. She'd liked him geeky and she liked him even more now. He made her feel safe and that was a very unfamiliar state of being for her.

Still, her job was to help him become what he was always capable of being, not get involved with him. Like now—he'd asked for her to see him so they could go over the date together. Sort of a post-game review. They'd done it before. He'd told her how things had gone and she'd suggested improvements he could make. It was no big deal, except she'd found it harder and harder to listen to the great time he had with other women.

They met back up in the parking lot of the diner and walked inside. When they were seated at a quiet booth in the back, Jesse said, "So, tell me everything. How did it go?"

"Good." Matt rearranged the flatware on the Formica table. "Kasey is bright and pretty. She was a little too into her dogs, but that's not a big deal."

"What's too into?" she asked, trying not to smile. "Does she dress them in matching outfits?"

"No, but they sleep with her."

"I'm sure she locks them out of the room when a good-looking guy shows up to do the wild thing."

Matt grinned. "I'm not so sure. Fluffy and Bobo seem to be her closest friends."

Jesse snorted. "Bobo? Okay, yeah, the dogs could be a problem. How did it go otherwise?"

"Fine. She's into music, which I like. She wasn't turned off by the computer thing."

"A-plus," Jesse said, trying not to notice his dark eyes and the way his smile made her insides all quivery. "Any sparkage?"

Matt laughed. "No one says sparkage anymore, Jess."

"I do."

The waitress showed up and handed them menus. Matt ignored them and smiled at the older woman.

"Tell me about the pie," he said. "It seems like a good night for pie."

The waitress listed what was available. "The marionberry is the freshest," she said. "Or the double-chocolate. Those are my favorites."

"I'll take the marionberry," he told her. "Jess, you want a chocolate rush?"

"Sure."

"Great. And two decafs, please."

Jesse was pleased by the exchange. A month ago, Matt wouldn't have spoken more than his order. He hadn't understood the simple pleasure of connecting with someone for a few seconds. Now he seemed to move more easily in the world. She wanted to take credit, but she'd done nothing more than point out the obvious.

"You didn't answer the sparkage question," Jesse said, hoping they'd made out for hours. Maybe hearing about him falling for someone else would help her realize that he wasn't for her.

"I kissed her, if that's what you're asking."

"And?"

He shrugged. "It was okay."

She held in a whimper as she tried not to think about what kissing Matt would be like. He had a great mouth and an attention to detail that was intriguing. Except it was never going to happen between them. Not only was he obviously not interested, but she liked him and liking him made a relationship impossible.

Every time she got involved, things went wrong.

Somehow she managed to screw up everything. After a series of disasters, she'd given up on anything serious and settled for casual flings, although lately even they were losing their appeal. She liked Matt too much to risk destroying their friendship. Besides, now he had everything going for him so he would never be interested in her.

"There wasn't chemistry," he said. "I'm a guy and she was pretty, so sure, the kissing was nice, but there are degrees, you know? There's nice and then there's I-have-to-take-you-now. She was nice."

Jesse felt a rush of heat. When was the last time he'd had an I-have-to-take-you-now experience? She desperately wanted to ask and didn't want to know in equal measures.

"Maybe the next one will be better."

"Maybe." He looked up. "You remembered to turn off your cell. There haven't been any calls from Ted or Butch or Spike."

"I've never dated anyone named Butch."

"What about Spike?"

She laughed. "Once."

"I knew it."

She touched her purse. "No calls. I'm between guys."

In the past couple of weeks she'd ignored her ringing phone. She knew the reason. He was sitting across from her. She even knew what was different. She and Matt were friends. She'd never bothered with being friends before. Had never thought about more than the night. Now she found herself wondering… Talk about terrifying.

The waitress brought their coffee and pie, then left. Matt picked up his fork.

"I think I want something else," he said, hesitantly.

"What do you mean? Different pie?"

"The dating. It's okay, but every time it's the same conversation. Getting to know each other, trying to remember if I've told that story or not. I want a second date."

"You want a relationship," Jesse said, telling her heart it could get pouty later. "That makes sense. So ask someone out a second time. If it's good, ask her out again. That's how dating turns into a relationship."

"I haven't met anyone who interests me that way. No one I feel comfortable just hanging out with."

They were hanging out. She took a bite of pie to keep from saying that. Memo to self—Matt wasn't interested. He saw her as his teacher, nothing more. She should be happy. And she was…almost.

"Is that stupid?" he asked. "You don't do relationships."

"Which isn't something to be proud of. You know what you want. That's a good thing." If only he could want her.

Time for a subject change. "Have you been looking at condos?" she asked.

"Just those first ones."

"You've got to get your own place. It's time. You're never going to get laid if you don't get your own place."

He grinned. "Who says I haven't gotten laid?"

There was a confidence in the question, sexy maleness in his voice. A sharp jab cut through Jesse. Jealousy burned hot and bright.

"You're not going to get laid a lot," she said, going for normal and hoping she didn't fall short. "You need your own place."

He looked at her. "You okay?"

"I'm fine."

"I was kidding. I haven't slept with any of them."

Thank God. "It would be okay if you had. You're single, they're single. That's how it's supposed to be."

He studied her, as if searching for something. Humiliation heated her cheeks, forcing her to duck her head so her hair hung down, shielding her. She didn't want him to guess that she had feelings for him. He might pity her and that would be worse than anything.

"I'm a guy," he said. "I don't like shopping. Picking a condo is shopping on a grand scale. Come with me. That will make it easier."

Easier for him, maybe. Not that she would say no. She wanted to spend time with him, to pretend that hey, sure, it could work out.

"Just tell me when."

"YOU CAN SPEND MORE than this," Jesse murmured as they walked through the empty tri-level town house in Redmond. "Get something on the water. A place with a view."

"It's too big," Matt told her, ignoring her comment about price. "Three bedrooms. What do I need three bedrooms for?"

"One for you, one for an office, one for guests."

"I don't have guests."

Good point. Because any women spending the night would be in his bed. "Then use the third bedroom as a media room."

His eyes brightened. "Yeah?"

"Guys are so easy," she murmured. "Yes. Cram it full of electronics. Make the walls vibrate. But if you're going to do that, use the top-floor bedroom because it doesn't have a common wall with anyone and you won't annoy your neighbors."

"Good point."

They toured the kitchen, which was a good size and bright. "Nice appliances," Jesse said, pointing at the stainless-steal cooktop. "Double ovens. That's important."

Matt looked at her. "For all those multi-course dinners I'm going to cook?"

"It could happen."

They revisited the master.

"Nice shower," she said, pointing to the frameless enclosure. "Big enough for two."

"I heard that," the real-estate agent said as she came

into the room. "You're such a lovely young couple. Are you engaged?"

Jesse had been looking at condos with Matt for the entire afternoon. She'd climbed countless stairs, pointed out pluses and minuses and seen several perfectly acceptable places. But would he pick one?

She was hungry, tired and both happy and frustrated by spending time with him without actually being *with* him. In his mind, she was his faithful friend. Like a dog. She decided it was time for a little payback.

"Yes," Jesse said quickly, leaning against Matt. "But it's a secret."

The older woman smiled. "Congratulations. You seem very happy."

"Oh, we are." Jesse batted her eyes at Matt. If she'd been able to reach, she would have kissed him, but he was a little tall and she didn't think he would cooperate by bending. "Aren't we, my little snuggle monkey?"

His gaze narrowed. "Snuggle monkey?" he mouthed, then he leaned down. "You are so going to pay for that," he whispered.

"You deserve it. This condo is great. So were the others we saw. Pick one or I'll tell your mother we're engaged."

He ignored that, but didn't pull away when she continued to lean on him.

He felt perfect, she thought. Strong and capable. Someone she could count on. If only...

The real-estate agent glanced at her watch. "I have

another appointment, so I need to run. If you want to look around a little more, just lock the door behind you when you leave. There are more condos, if you want to see them."

Matt shook his head. "I've seen enough. Let me pick one this afternoon, then we can get together and fill out the paperwork."

"Wonderful. You have my cell number. I'll be available anytime after four."

She waved and left.

Jesse stepped back. "You're serious? You're going to buy one?"

"Probably this one. You're right. It has everything I need, so why not?"

"But you haven't wanted to make a decision."

"I haven't wanted to make a change," he corrected. "You were right about that, too. It's time for me to be on my own. I've taken the easy way out, staying with my mom. She isn't going to like me leaving, but she'll get over it."

"Wow. Great. I think this one is the best of them, but it's your decision. Imagine the fun you'll have picking out new furniture." She moved into the bedroom. It was big enough for one of those massive sleigh beds. With the fireplace in the corner and rich bedding, the room could be masculine *and* romantic.

"The dining room is beautiful, with that coved ceiling. And you can go crazy with your media room."

She turned and saw him watching her. There was

something about the look on his face, something she'd never seen before.

"Matt?"

"I don't think I realized it until just now," he said slowly.

"Realized what?"

"That somewhere along the line I became more than a project to you. When did that change?"

She froze, unable to move, barely breathing. Here it was—the one thing she'd wanted to avoid. That moment of total humiliation. Because he wasn't some poor geek who needed her help anymore. He was masculine and capable and someone she was wildly attracted to. Emotionally, he could crush her like a bug.

"I don't know what you're talking about," she said as she started backing out of the room. "Look. It's late and I should probably be going."

Except they'd come in the same car. Damn. Now what?

"Jesse."

The way he spoke her name made her shiver. "What?"

"You didn't answer my question."

"I can't."

"Why?"

"Because I'm scared."

There it was. The truth. All of it, leaving her exposed. What if he laughed? What if, even worse, he said he appreciated her feelings but he thought it would be best if they were just friends. What if—

He crossed the space separating them, cupped her face in his large hands and kissed her. Just like that. Mouth on mouth. Lips pressing, touching.

It was a soft kiss, a gentle kiss, as if he was giving her a chance to get used to being close to him. She raised her arms, then lowered them to her sides. For the first time since she was maybe thirteen, she wasn't sure what to do back. How to respond. What would be right? What would be too much?

He tilted his head slightly, but didn't deepen the kiss. Seconds ticked by. She was aware of the pounding of her heart and the heat she felt inside. Heat and wanting and fear. Finally she couldn't stand it anymore and she pulled back.

"I can't," she whispered. "I can't do this."

"Why not?"

She turned her back on him and folded her arms across her chest. "Because I'm not what you think. I'm not anyone you want to be with."

He moved behind her and wrapped his arms around her, pulling her against him. She let herself lean on him, just for now. In a second she would be strong again.

"You're exactly who I want to be with," he told her. "You're smart and funny and kind. You're also sexy as hell."

"You're just grateful because I helped you see your potential."

"I'm a whole lot more than grateful."

He moved her hair off her shoulder, then leaned in

and kissed her neck. Immediately tingles rippled through her. He opened his mouth and licked the spot he'd kissed, then blew on her damp skin. He nipped her earlobe, making her jump. She half turned. He put his hands on her shoulders, bringing her all the way around until she faced him.

"You're so beautiful," he murmured between kisses along her jaw. "That's what I remember from the first time we met. The sun in your hair, how your smile hit me in the gut. It was the best and worst moment of my life. Best because I met you and worst because of what you'd seen."

"Matt, I never thought badly of you," she said, barely able to speak. She was on fire, burning everywhere he touched and many places he didn't.

"I know. It was amazing to me. You saw beyond what I was on the outside. And every time I went out with someone else, all I could think about was that I would rather be with you."

He kissed her then, hard and hot. She parted because she didn't have a choice, didn't want a choice. She welcomed him inside of her mouth, brushing her tongue with his, feeling her breasts swell.

Her nipples ached, as did that place between her legs. She gave herself up to the feeling of being close to him and wrapped her arms around him.

They pressed together everywhere. He was already hard, which thrilled her.

When he nudged her backward, she went willingly.

They moved until she bumped into something. Then he picked her up and set her on the bathroom counter.

She parted her thighs and he moved between them. His hardness nestled against her. Then they were kissing again, his hands moving up and down her back.

She touched his shoulders, his chest. He was all muscle and far too much a gentleman. She grabbed his hands and put them on her breasts. His breath caught as he cupped her curves.

It would be so easy, she thought sadly. She knew the drill. She could slip off her jeans and panties. He could be in her in seconds. Here, in the empty house, they could be together. They could fuck. And then what?

Tears burned in her eyes. Regret choked her. She pushed him away, jumped to her feet and ran.

He caught her by the front door, grabbed her arm and held her in place.

"Why are you running away?" he demanded.

She did her best not to cry. "I can't talk about it. I'm sorry. Let me go."

"Jess, no. Talk to me. Tell me what's going on."

She forced herself to look at him. Maybe it was time to tell the truth. She could get it over with now. It would be like cutting off an arm. One quick slice and it would fall away. Then she could get used to being without him.

She pulled free and thought longingly of the door. Then she squared her shoulders. Time to sharpen the blade.

"You're right," she said quietly. "You're a lot more than a project. I didn't mean for that to happen. I just wanted to make a difference, you know? To do something right. I saw you and you had so much going for you. Then we started hanging out and I realized you were even better than I thought."

"You adore me and I like being adored. So where's the bad?"

Despite everything, she laughed. "It's not you, Matt. It's me. I'm not who you think."

"You've said that before and it's not true. I know you."

"No, you don't. You know who I've let you see, but that's not who I am. I've always been wild. My sister calls me a professional screwup and she's right. I started drinking when I was twelve. I got into drugs when I was thirteen. I got bored with both when I was fourteen, mostly because I discovered boys."

She walked to the window because looking out at the trees was a whole lot easier than staring at him and watching the disappointment fill his eyes.

"I learned very quickly that putting out was an easy way to be popular. I also enjoyed the sex itself. Mostly to be close to someone, to feel like I mattered, even if it was just for a few minutes. I was the school slut all through high school. Nicole found out and put me on the Pill so I didn't get pregnant. I was lucky, because I never got any diseases. But there were guys, Matt. A lot of guys. There are some I don't even remember."

She swallowed. "Those guys who call? I sleep with them. All of them."

She fought tears. "And then I met you and you were great and it was easy and suddenly there I was. Wanting more. Wanting to be different so you would want me. Like me. But so what? You can do a whole lot better than me. I'm completely drifting. I don't have any direction, I live with my sister, I can't seem to commit to my future. You don't need that. You need someone as focused and great as you are."

There. She'd said it. All of it, or close.

"Are you done with the other guys?"

She bowed her head. "Yes. I don't want to be that person anymore. I want—a lot of other things."

He walked toward her. She braced herself for the attack, but he only turned her toward him, then put his arms around her. She kept hers folded protectively across her chest, but he just held her closer.

"Don't you know none of that matters?"

She stared up at him. "You can't mean that."

"Do I look as if I'm lying?"

He looked like a man who was very sure of himself. He looked like someone she could trust.

He touched her face again. "Jess, your past changes nothing. You're the one I want to be with because of who you are right now."

He was making it too easy.

"I want to believe you," she whispered.

"Then try. Give it time. I won't let you down." His

mouth twisted. "And I won't push you sexually. Even though I want to."

She smiled. "If anyone should be holding back, it's me."

"You don't scare me."

How was that possible? "I mess up a lot. I destroy relationships that matter."

"No, you don't."

"Matt, you have to listen."

"Jesse, do you want to go out with me? Do you want to be with me?"

"Yes."

"Then be with me. The rest of it will work itself out. I can handle whatever you throw at me. Do you believe that?"

"I want to." More than he knew.

"Then trust me. Just a little. I'm not going to let you down. I swear. No matter what. Just give me the chance to prove myself."

She nodded because she didn't have a choice. Walking away was impossible to imagine. Maybe he was right. Maybe she could trust him. Wouldn't that be a miracle?

CHAPTER EIGHT

Present Day…

MATT REMEMBERED GROWING up in small apartments. His mom's salary as a dental hygienist had only stretched so far. But while they'd struggled financially, he'd never much felt the lack. His mom had made simple moments seem special. She'd always found the money for what mattered…like the computers he'd taken apart, repaired and put back together when he was ten or eleven. Selling those had paid for the next he'd bought, along with the parts, but he'd never considered what she'd had to give up to buy the first broken computers.

He'd paid her back a thousand times over when he'd licensed his game modification. They'd moved out of their crappy apartment into the house in Woodinville. Money had never been a problem again. He'd been all of sixteen when he'd insisted on setting up a trust fund for her so she never had to work, if she didn't want to. The house had been bought with cash. He'd wanted to do that for her, because she was his only family. Because it was the right thing to do.

Now, as he stood in front of that house, he wondered if he had it to do all over again, would he be so generous? He wasn't sure. They'd barely spoken in the past five years. He had Diane send her a gift at Christmas and flowers on her birthday. He called on Mother's Day. Nothing more. Because he'd never forgiven her for telling him about Jesse and Drew.

No, not for telling him. He'd never forgiven her for being *happy* about the news.

But he had to deal with her now. He'd wanted to see Gabe again and the kid was staying in her house.

When Jesse had phoned and suggested he spend a little time with his son, he'd agreed. Not because he had any burning desire to get to know him, but because it furthered his plan. What he resented was the casual way she called the shots. Not for long, he told himself. Soon he would be in charge.

Reminding himself of that helped with the anger that continued to grow inside of him. He'd blown it at dinner, he knew that. And kissing Jesse had been a mistake. He'd found himself reacting, wanting her. After all this time, how was that possible?

He knew that instant passion had always been a part of his relationship with her. Apparently time hadn't changed that.

He moved up the walkway and rang the bell,

ignoring the memories of living there. The door opened immediately, as if his mother had been waiting for him.

She stood in the entryway, staring at him with an expression that was equal parts hope and pain. She smiled, but there were tears in her eyes.

"Oh, Matthew," she whispered. "I've missed you so much."

The words surprised him, as did her air of vulnerability.

"Come in, come in," she said, motioning for him to enter the house. "How are you? You look great. Gabe's very excited about your visit. He's been talking about it since he got up this morning. He's such a happy child. He wakes up excited about the new day."

There was the sound of footsteps, then Gabe skidded around the corner, before coming to a stop and staring at Matt.

Matt stared back, not sure what to say or do. This was the part he hadn't thought through. Actually dealing with a child.

"Ah, good morning," he said.

Gabe blinked.

Matt felt like an idiot, something he didn't appreciate and for which he blamed Jesse. Paula touched the boy's head.

"Your dad is going to spend the morning with us. That will be fun." She smiled at Matt. "We made sugar cookies yesterday. I thought we could frost them this morning. Gabe's excited about that, aren't you?"

The boy had his eyes, Matt thought. "I like sugar cookies," he said, not knowing what else to say. "Do you?"

The kid nodded. Hadn't Jesse said he was verbal? Shouldn't he be talking?

Paula ushered them into the kitchen. The room looked different. Matt guessed she'd remodeled sometime in the past five years. He wondered what else was different in her life.

"Here we go," she said, pointing to the cookies she'd spread out on the kitchen table. There were pastry bags filled with colored icing. Paula eyed his suit jacket. "You might want to leave that in the other room and roll up your sleeves. This is going to get messy."

Fifteen minutes later, he knew she wasn't kidding. What Gabe lacked in skill, he made up for in enthusiasm as he gushed icing all over the cookies, the table and himself. He grinned and laughed as the gooey frosting oozed everywhere.

Paula leaned over his shoulder. "Is that a dog? I think that's a dog."

Gabe beamed. "Uh-huh. With spots."

Matt stared at the mess of green and orange icing. How was that a dog? It wasn't close to anything. How had his mom figured it out?

Matt used the white icing bag to put stripes on a few of the cookies. He felt uncomfortable and out of place. Gabe kept looking at him, as if expecting something.

Paula handed the kid several round cookies. "We talked about putting numbers on these," she said. "Gabe, why don't you start. You do the first number and your dad will do the second."

"Okay." Gabe grabbed a bag of purple icing and drew a fairly steady straight line. "That's a one."

"Good for you," Paula said, then looked at Matt. "Isn't that good?"

Matt nodded. "It's great," he said, feeling stupid. Jesse had gone wild with the praise when the kid had tied his shoes. Evidently, that was the way to a child's heart.

"Now you do two," Gabe said.

"Sure." Matt squeezed out a two on a cookie.

Paula clapped her hands. "That's terrific. What's next, Gabe?"

"Three," he said and bent over the cookie. He concentrated so hard, his face turned red. Slowly, a shaky three emerged.

They worked their way up to ten. When they'd finished, Paula looked at him. "Gabe knows his letters, as well, and he's learning to read."

"Okay." Matt didn't know if that was impressive or not. At what age did kids start reading?

Paula helped Gabe to the sink and rinsed off the icing. Matt did the same in the guest bathroom, all the time wondering what the hell he was doing here. Sure, he had to spend time with his son because that was part of the plan, but nothing about it felt right or comfortable. Maybe he just wasn't a kid person. That happened, right? He'd grown up without a father and he'd turned out fine. He'd—

As he dried his hands on a small towel, he unwillingly remembered a middle-school announcement about "Bring your dad to school" day. All the other kids had been talking about their dads, but he hadn't had anything to say. He sat there, his stomach hurting, feeling more out of place than usual. He'd never told his mother. What was the point? She wouldn't have been able to change anything.

But this kid thing was tough. Heath had been right to point out that if he won his lawsuit against Jesse, he was going to end up with a child. His son. There was no way he could handle that on his own.

When he walked back into the kitchen, Gabe was gone. Paula turned on him.

"Did you know Jesse was pregnant?" she demanded. "Did she tell you?"

"Where's Gabe?"

"Up in his room, figuring out which toys he wants to show you. Not that you'll even pretend to be interested. Did she tell you?"

He didn't know which attack to deal with first. "She mentioned she was, but I never thought the kid was mine. She'd been sleeping with—" Other guys. With Drew. Except she said she hadn't and Gabe was obviously his. "I never thought the baby was mine," he repeated.

Paula glared at him. "How could you let her just walk away without finding out the truth? You were raised to take responsibility. What kind of man doesn't bother to find out if his girlfriend is carrying his child?"

Matt stared at his mother. "Where is this all coming from? Last I knew, you hated Jesse."

"I made a mistake about that," she told him, her eyes bright with anger. "Which isn't the point. Do you know what we both lost? What can never be recovered? Years, Matthew. Years of seeing your son, my grandson, growing up. Of being there when he was born. All the firsts are lost. All those precious moments and memories. It's gone because you couldn't be bothered to find out the truth."

"Hey, wait a minute. You're the one who told me she was sleeping with someone else. And you were pretty happy about that fact."

"I was wrong," Paula said, looking him in the eye. "I was wrong about a lot of things and I've certainly paid for my mistakes. But I never knew Jesse was pregnant. If I had, I would have gone after her. I would have insisted she stay until we could confirm paternity. We're talking about your child, Matthew. Your son. Doesn't that mean anything to you?"

Before he could answer, Gabe ran back in the room carrying a large fire truck that was nearly as big as he was.

"Look!" he said, obviously proud and excited.

Matt looked at his mother, who glared at him. No help there.

"That's a really, ah, big truck."

Gabe nodded. "It's my favorite. I can ride on it. Want to see?"

"Sure."

Gabe set down the truck, straddled it, then pushed himself around with his feet. He headed into the family room.

"Go with him," Paula said in a low, angry tone. "Do something."

"I don't know what to do. I don't know him."

"Whose fault is that?" she snapped.

"You could help."

"I could, but I'm not going to. You created this problem, you fix it," she said and turned away.

He followed Gabe into the family room where his son looked expectantly at him. Matt stood there, not sure what to do, furious at his mother and Jesse.

"Want to, ah, play a game?" Matt asked.

Gabe sighed heavily, then shook his head.

"Watch a movie?"

The boy rose and returned to the kitchen, where he ran straight to Paula, grabbed her around the legs and started to cry.

"I didn't do anything," Matt said when she glared at him.

"I know. And that's the problem." She stroked Gabe's hair. "Matthew, you have a lot to learn about children."

Feeling angry and confused, not to mention dismissed, he stalked out of the house and slammed the front door behind him.

It wasn't supposed to be like this, he thought grimly, although he couldn't say how it was supposed to be.

JESSE STOOD ON THE sidewalk of the strip mall, sucked in a breath, then entered the small Chinese restaurant. Matt was already there, at a booth against the side wall. He rose as she walked over.

"Thanks for coming," he said.

She nodded and tried to smile, but there were too many emotions rushing through her for her to pick just one and go with it.

She wanted to tell him she was only here because Paula had said his meeting with Gabe had been a disaster, but the truth was more uncomfortable. She was here because she'd missed him.

Seeing him the other night, being with him, talking and then kissing him, had opened too many doors to the past. She'd been caught up in what they'd once had together. Worse, she'd been unable to shake the passion he'd stirred in her. Passion that had disturbed her sleep with vivid sexual dreams and left her restless and aroused.

When she was seated, he leaned toward her. "Did she tell you how badly my meeting with Gabe went?"

Jesse sighed. "Shouldn't we start with more neutral conversation? I could ask about your day. You could ask about mine."

"If you'd like. How was your day?"

"Busy. The brownies are selling well, which is exciting for me, but I think it's pissing off Nicole."

"You're still having trouble with her?"

"Trouble isn't the right word. She's distant and, I don't know, angry maybe. It's like we're strangers."

"Give her time."

"But I want it fixed now."

He surprised her by smiling. "You were never big on patience."

"I had more of it than you did."

"Low blow."

Now it was her turn to smile. "It was the only thing I beat you at."

"Not true."

"Oh, please. You were smarter. And successful."

"You had a great sense of humor."

"True."

His eyes crinkled. "You're prettier than me."

She wasn't sure she would agree, but she appreciated the compliment. "If you say so."

"I do. You still wear your hair long. It looks great."

She tried not to fidget. He'd always liked her long hair and because of that, she'd been unable to cut it. Which made her a fool, but there it was.

"Thanks," she said. "How was *your* day?"

"Good. We're getting ready to launch a new game so we're pretty busy. There's going to be a big party. I know I'm getting old because I found myself thinking it was going to be loud and way too long."

"You're not old. You're barely thirty."

"A couple of guys on the team are in college. Compared to them, I'm practically an old man."

The server appeared. Matt ordered several dishes for them to share, along with beer. When they were alone, Jesse said, "Tell me what happened with Gabe."

Matt grimaced. "What did my mother say?"

"That you don't have a lot of experience with children and that you'll do better next time."

"I doubt she was that kind."

He was right. Paula had ranted, but Jesse wasn't going to kick him when he was obviously down. "It's what she meant."

Matt stared at her. "I don't know him, Jess. I'm not going to be an ass about it. What happened is done. We're here now. I've got a kid and I don't know anything about him. How do I change that?"

She desperately wanted to believe that he'd accepted their situation and was dealing with it, but she wasn't sure. He'd been so angry before. Still, he was Gabe's father and she wanted the two of them to figure out a relationship.

"Gabe is very easygoing," she began. "He likes everybody. He's got a great sense of humor, which is fun to watch develop. He likes doing things outside. In Spokane, we go for long walks in the summer. There's a trail along the river that he enjoys. We play in the snow in winter."

"Has he been skiing?"

"A sport you enjoy?" she asked.

Matt nodded.

And he wouldn't even think twice about how much it would cost. "No, but I'm sure he could learn. He's pretty athletic. He's about average size for his age and he's always been healthy." Given the fact that she'd barely been able to afford basic health insurance for him, she'd been really lucky.

"My mom said he knew his letters."

"A requirement for most kindergarten classes these days, so he's ahead of that," Jesse said. "He can count to twenty and he's just starting to recognize words." She stared at him. "Matt, he wants you in his life. That's not a question. He'll be interested in whatever you're interested in. You could show him how to play a game on a computer or talk about your work. He'd listen. As for getting involved in his life, just be interactive. He likes board games and playing with his toys. Or just go for a walk and talk about what you see."

"You make it sound easy."

She wanted to say it *was* easy, but she had the advantage of familiarity. "It'll take practice and time together. Next time you come over, we'll all play a couple of games. Then there will be less pressure. You can just be yourself and get to know each other."

"Okay. Thanks."

Their beers arrived, along with a plate of dumplings. As she scooped two onto her plate, she said, "So

I'm guessing none of the women you've dated have had children."

"No." He frowned. "Maybe. I don't know."

"How could you not know?"

"I didn't ask. I go out. I don't get involved."

"How can you not get involved with someone you're seeing?"

"I don't do relationships. After three or four dates, I move on. I'm not interested in anything long-term."

A twinge of guilt flickered inside her chest. "Why not?"

"I don't see the point. I like variety. In my position, I can have anyone I want. Settling down isn't very interesting."

That was new, she thought. The Matt she'd known wanted someone he could care about. "Doesn't it get boring, going from woman to woman?"

He picked up his beer. "Never."

"And none of them try to make you stay longer?"

He grinned. "They try."

"So you don't ever invest yourself emotionally. It's just about having fun and getting laid."

"Pretty much."

She'd done that before she met Matt and knew how empty it could be. "Don't you want more?"

"No."

She hated hearing that. Hated thinking she might have done this to him. "You used to be a nice guy. What happened?"

"Nice is a lot less fun. Come on, Jess. You didn't think I'd stay that ignorant kid forever, did you?"

"You were never ignorant." Inexperienced, maybe. Lacking in confidence. "I hoped you'd stay honorable."

"Have I violated some moral code? The women I see are very clear on my terms. I'm not exclusive and I don't do relationships. If they don't like that, they don't have to accept the invitation."

It sounded fair, but Matt's dating philosophy left her with a sick feeling in her stomach. She'd come back to Seattle for a lot of reasons, the biggest being to help Gabe connect with his father. She'd also secretly hoped to find something still alive between herself and Matt.

While the passion lived on, she wasn't sure about the man across from her. Was that really him? Knowing what she did about his past and how he'd loved her, she wanted to say no. But it had been a long time. People changed.

"I need to use the restroom," she said and slid out of the booth.

She walked into the bathroom and pulled out her cell phone. Paula picked up on the first ring.

"Can you do me a favor?" Jesse asked quietly. "Can you call back in five minutes and tell me Gabe has a fever?"

Paula knew where she was and whom she was with. Jesse expected a lot of questions. Instead the other woman just sighed, then said she would.

Jesse returned to the table. Matt talked more about the new game his company was launching. As she listened, Jesse wondered how she could be so attracted to him and so sad at the same time. Who was he, really? Was he this new and not-improved version of himself or did the other Matt still exist? How was she supposed to find out?

She didn't have any answers when her phone rang.

"RED OR WHITE?" Paula asked, holding up a bottle of each.

"I'm not in a place where I'm going to be picky," Jesse said.

She'd just put Gabe to bed. Being with him had helped shake some of her mood after her aborted dinner with Matt, but not all of it.

"Red then." Paula opened the bottle and poured them each a glass. "The tannins are supposed to be good for us."

"I need something that is."

They went into the family room. Paula settled on the sofa while Jesse curled up in a wing chair.

"I'm so confused," Jesse admitted. "I know he's angry. Part of me wants to understand and part of me wants to point out that I did try to tell him the truth. I can't figure out what he's thinking or what he's after."

"He was totally out of his element with Gabe," Paula told her. "I probably should have helped, but I was too angry. I can't believe he let you go, knowing you were pregnant."

"He never thought the baby was his."

"Still. He should have been sure."

Jesse agreed, but that didn't change the past. "I know this is all a surprise to him and that his son is a stranger. Matt is trying, but there's still so much anger. Does he really want a relationship with Gabe? Can he get past wanting to punish me?" And, Jesse added silently, had his kisses meant anything?

"A lot of this is my fault," Paula said. "I never expected to have kids. I grew up poor and always had terrible taste in men. If they weren't hitting me, they were running off with my money. I knew I wanted more. I wanted to be respectable, so I worked three jobs to save the money to learn how to be a dental hygienist."

"That can't have been easy," Jesse said, trying not to react to Paula's confessions. She'd had no idea the other woman had struggled so much when she'd been younger.

"It wasn't, but I made it. On my thirty-fifth birthday I met my last deadbeat. He ran off with my savings and left me pregnant. I knew I hit bottom and I was done trying. It was too much. I went out for a drive and when a truck crossed the double yellow line and headed right for me, I didn't bother trying to swerve. I was going to take the easy way out."

Jesse held in a gasp. "I had no idea."

"It's not something I'm proud of. I figured I'd be dead and all my troubles would be over." She took a sip of her wine. "Except I didn't die. I don't remember anything about the crash. I woke up on the side of the road. The car was totaled and there wasn't a scratch on me. I decided God had sent me a message and I was going to listen. I'd been given a second chance and I was going to make the most of it."

Jesse understood, because she'd been given that same second chance. "Your baby."

Paula nodded. "I vowed to be the best mother I could, no matter what. I did everything I could think of for Matthew. Maybe too much. I know I kept him too close to me. I liked that I was the most important person in his life and I didn't want that to change. I was lonely and he was all I had."

"You didn't do anything wrong," Jesse told her.

"You're lovely to say that, but we both know I made plenty of mistakes. I kept him dependent. I didn't push him to try new things. I held on too tight."

Jesse sighed. "We do the best we can with what we have. Didn't Maya Angelou say that? And when we know better, we do better."

"I wish I'd known better sooner. I might not have lost him. That's the irony. I thought I was losing him to you, but in the end, I pushed him away myself."

"I never wanted to take him from you. Not the way you thought. I just wanted him to be the best he could be."

"I should have seen that. Instead, I reacted. Matthew's right. I was happy when I went to see you and Nicole said those things. I knew he would never forgive you. I'm so ashamed of that."

Jesse knew she could be angry at Paula and justify the emotion. But to what end? "We both made mistakes. Maybe I shouldn't have left. Except I needed to stand on my own. I guess I had to grow up, too. But I wasn't deliberately trying to cut you out of Gabe's life. I honestly never thought you'd be interested."

"I know," Paula told her. "With all that happened, what else would you think?"

Jesse felt bad. "I want us to be friends now. I really appreciate you letting Gabe and me stay here. And I know it's important for Gabe to know his family."

"I'm happy to have you. As for Matthew, maybe he just needs time."

Jesse wasn't sure. "I can't figure out who he is. The good guy or the bastard."

"Maybe he's both."

Maybe. But where did that leave her?

CHAPTER NINE

HEATH WALKED INTO MATT'S office and tossed a folder onto his desk. "The DNA test results are back."

Matt didn't bother picking up the papers. "He's mine."

Heath nodded and sank into a chair. "You already guessed that."

"Now we're both sure."

"This means you can move forward with the paperwork anytime you're ready. It's ready to file."

"Good to know."

He could set the wheels in motion with just a phone call. Threaten what Jesse cared about most. Take her son from her.

But Gabe wasn't just her son. Matt was his father.

It had been a week since the disastrous visit to his mother's and he'd been unable to forget the sound of Gabe crying. He'd disappointed the boy and he didn't have a clue as to what had gone wrong. He just knew he never wanted to feel that bad again. He never wanted to make his son cry.

"You know much about kids?" he asked his lawyer.

Heath raised his eyebrows. "Hell, no. Why would I want to?"

"You'll have them someday."

"I guess. I'm not the family type. Just like you."

Matt nodded slowly. These days he avoided entanglements, but years ago, he'd seen himself married, with a family. He'd wanted that in his life.

It had been the usual vague fantasies, him teaching some faceless child to ride a bike. Which he could do now, with Gabe. Assuming Uncle Bill didn't get there first.

"What about the investigation?" he asked.

Heath shrugged. "I have a preliminary report." He nodded at the folder. "It's early yet, but so far, there's nothing incriminating. Jesse lives quietly in a small rented house in a typical neighborhood. There's no evidence of a boyfriend. She doesn't party, doesn't go out at all. She worked, went to college, took care of her kid."

That wasn't possible, Matt thought. "What about Bill?"

"He's her boss at the bar. Old guy. The investigator is still digging, but so far he hasn't found anything on the two of them. Looks like Bill was just her boss and a friend."

Heath's expression turned sympathetic. "We haven't found anything we can use against her in court. There's the fact that she had the kid without telling you. The judge won't like that."

Except they didn't have that, Matt thought angrily. She had told him and he hadn't believed her. Wouldn't have believed her. She had to know that. When he'd found out about Drew, it was as if he'd found out she'd been mocking him the whole time.

"How far back can we go?" he asked. "What about who she was before she got pregnant?"

"You know something?"

"I might." Enough to leave her bleeding on the side of the road.

"Let me know if you want me to use it."

Matt nodded, knowing there was plenty to be found. Jesse had told him herself. But while he could remember exactly how she'd looked as she'd confessed her past to him all those years ago, he couldn't imagine sharing her secret. Not when she'd been so broken and ashamed in the telling.

He'd promised her the past didn't matter. Back then, it hadn't. Now? Now he wasn't so sure, except for one thing. He was never going to be the nice guy again.

"Tell your PI to keep digging," he said. "There has to be something."

"Will do." Heath rose. "And then what?"

Interesting question. "Hell if I know," Matt admitted. "I guess I win."

JESSE SAT IMPATIENTLY beside Nicole, trying not to fidget as her sister studied the layout for the ad Jesse had designed for the Seattle paper.

"Two dollars off six, five dollars off a dozen?" Nicole said, raising her eyebrows. "That's a big giveaway."

"We want to generate interest. So far brownie sales have been excellent, but more is always better."

"Excellent is a bit of a stretch," Nicole said, returning the sheet to Jesse.

"They're completely above target." Jesse opened her folder and pulled out the projections she'd been working on. "Here's what I had hoped we would sell in the first two weeks. We've nearly doubled that. As you can see, we made money on them the first day. With a little advertising, they can become a great seller. Buying a cake requires a commitment, but brownies can be an impulse purchase. Plus, I want to talk about them in gourmet terms so they become something people serve as dessert. I have some ideas for seasonal displays."

She handed those over to her sister, along with the sales projection.

Nicole's gaze dropped to the bottom of the sheet. "Internet sales?"

"They're an obvious next step."

"You want to do that again?"

Jesse took a deep breath. She knew she was being baited. She told herself to remain calm. That everything was fine. She was mature and able to deal with her sister. The fact that Nicole kept bringing up Jesse selling the famous Keyes cakes on the Internet five years ago was simply an annoying quirk.

"This is totally different," Jesse said with a smile. "Internet sales are easy. Brownies travel well, the customer pays the cost of shipping and handling, which means our profits aren't compromised. The prepared packages will be picked up by the carrier of our choice. It's not a high-risk operation."

"We don't have room to do shipping here," Nicole said. "We're already jammed in as it is. And before you suggest it, another location would be too expensive for a trial effort that's probably going to fail."

Jesse felt her temper slipping. She grabbed on with both hands and held it in.

"I know you're happy with the sales," Nicole continued, sounding more like a mom than a business partner. "But this is the rush of something new. They're going to level off. Let's see what the real numbers are before we make any commitments."

"We've barely begun to figure out even a piece of the market," Jesse told her, hating the sense of being talked down to. "There's buzz. We're already getting calls from people who've moved out of the Seattle area and have heard about the brownies from their friends who still live here."

"I know you want these to be the next big thing, but they're not," Nicole told her. "That sounds harsh, I know. I don't mean it that way. I'm just saying—"

"You're just saying you want me to fail," Jesse snapped. "This isn't even about the brownies. It's about the past. It's about Drew. Despite the fact that I have *told* you nothing happened, you don't believe me. Or maybe you could but you don't want to. It's easier to blame me and be angry."

"Why should I believe you?" Nicole asked flatly.

That hurt. Jesse sucked in a breath. "Don't. Call your ex-husband and ask him." Not that Drew had told the truth before, but hopefully enough time would have passed for him to be willing to come clean. It wasn't like she had a choice.

"You should have tried harder," Nicole yelled as she came to her feet. "You should have fought him off. Why didn't you? Why didn't I hear you scream?"

Jesse couldn't have been more surprised if Nicole had physically slapped her. She stood, not bothering to head off the anger exploding inside of her.

"Is that the condition of your forgiveness? Rape? Sorry to disappoint you. I wasn't violated. Not that way."

"That's not what I mean," Nicole snapped.

"Of course it is. I wasn't after Drew. I didn't try to get his attention. But that's not good enough. If he didn't attack me, I'm the bad guy. He blamed me and you believed him. You assumed the worst about me. You're my sister. You're supposed to know me better than anyone."

"I did know you," Nicole yelled. "I knew what you'd been in high school. Why would you have been any different with Drew?"

Once a slut, always a slut, Jesse thought sadly. That's what it came down to.

She told herself it didn't matter, except it did. It mattered and it hurt and she didn't know how to make anything better between them. All she had was the present and today she was focused on her brownies. She took another deep breath.

"I can't change the past," she told her sister. "I've told you what happened and you either believe me or you don't. I don't know what else to say or do. So I'm done trying. As far as the brownies go, you're wrong. We haven't even begun to tap their potential. I want to run the ads. I'm an equal partner in the bakery and this isn't an extraordinary expense."

Nicole's mouth tightened. "What happened to earning your way in?"

"I'm working my butt off here and you know it. While I'm willing to put in the time, I'm not willing to let your feelings about the past keep us from being successful."

"Fine," Nicole snapped. "Run the ads. Bake your brownies, but don't get your hopes up. They're not all that."

Jesse collected her papers and walked out of her sister's office. She made her way to the back where she could duck into the women's restroom and try not to cry.

Why did it have to be like this? Why couldn't Nicole give her at least half a break? Why did she have to assume the brownies were going to fail? Talk about a lack of faith and forgiveness.

She slowed her breathing. Gradually the burning behind her eyes faded. She sniffed, then made sure she hadn't leaked mascara on her face. Once she decided she could probably pass for relatively normal, she left the restroom and the building.

But when she got in her car, she found she wasn't ready to go back to Paula's. She felt restless and uncomfortable in her own skin. Without considering her actions, she picked up her cell phone, scrolled through her recent call list and then pushed the send button.

"Matthew Fenner's office," a woman's voice said. "May I help you?"

"Uh, this is Jesse. Is Matt around?"

"Just one moment, please. I'll check."

Meaning the woman would go ask him. She shouldn't have called, she thought. Why go looking for more pain?

But before she could hang up, she heard him say, "Jesse? Everything all right?"

"Sure. I don't know why I called." Then she remembered her vow to not lie. "That's not true. I called because I just had another fight with Nicole. The brownies are going great, but does she want to listen to any of my ideas? Of course not. She only wants to see me as a screwup. She wants me to fail. It's getting to me. That's all. I need to talk, but I know you're busy—"

There was a pause, then he stunned her by saying, "Or you could come by the office and rant in person."

"Really? Now?"

"Sure. Where are you?"

"At the bakery."

"Come on over. I'll order lunch in. You can call your sister all the names you want and I'll agree."

Despite everything, she smiled. "I'd like that."

Thirty minutes later, she parked by the large building that housed his company and made her way to the elevator. She went to the top floor where a well-dressed receptionist directed her toward a long corridor. Jesse tried not to feel underdressed in her jeans and T-shirt. She'd come straight from the bakery and working in the back meant comfortable clothes she didn't mind getting dirty.

Rather than notice how great everything she saw looked, she glanced into the offices and noticed that the closer she got to the end, the bigger they got. At the end of the hallway, she turned left and saw a fifty-something woman sitting at a desk.

"You must be Jesse," the woman said. "I'm Diane. Matt is waiting."

"Hi," Jesse said, wondering if this was the woman who told Matt what to do.

Diane walked into Matt's office. "Jesse is here," she said.

"Thanks, Diane. Have them hold lunch until I call for it."

"Sure."

Diane smiled at Jesse, then moved out of the room. She closed the door as she went.

Jesse stood in the middle of the big space and tried not to look as stupid as she felt. She shouldn't have called, shouldn't have come. She didn't belong here. The Matt she'd known years ago had changed and the successful, wealthy stranger walking toward her didn't look all that approachable.

"Sounds like Nicole's giving you a hard time," he said by way of greeting.

"I should go," Jesse murmured.

"Don't. You're here now. Have a seat."

He led her to a sofa with a view out the big windows. She sat down, then wished she'd brushed her butt first. Who knew what possible ingredients she might have on her jeans.

"Talk," he said as he settled at the other end of the couch and faced her.

That made her laugh. "You're a guy, Matt. You don't do talk. You fix the problem, conquer your enemies, then go celebrate with a big, loud brawl."

"I'm more evolved than that and I was never one to brawl. Now talk."

She didn't want to dump on him, but she didn't have that many friends in Seattle. Not anymore. She'd lost touch with most of them when she'd moved away. While Paula was wonderful, she was already doing so much by helping out with Gabe. Complaining seemed a poor way to repay her.

"I just—" Jesse began, then sighed. "I don't know why she bothered to agree to let me try to earn my way back into the bakery. She's hoping I'll fail. Or at least the brownies will. She's not doing anything to help with the launch and she's standing in the way of everything I want to do."

"You're part owner, aren't you? Can't you force her to do what you want?"

Jesse shrugged. "I played the 'I'm a part of this, too' card earlier. She didn't like it. It's just so frustrating. I'm not asking for special treatment here. I'm just asking that the brownies be given a chance. That she doesn't always assume the worst. It's been five years, but she's not over any of it. I've changed, but she can't see that."

She looked at him, at his dark eyes, at the familiar mouth that now kissed so different. "I guess you two have that in common."

"I know you've changed," he said.

"You're not acting like it. I didn't cheat on you, Matt. How many times do I have to say that? How many times do I have to keep explaining?" She stood up. "You know what? I'm tired of it. I'm tired of it from her and from you and you can both go to hell."

He rose. "Feel better?"

"A little. I'm just really pissed off."

"Seriously? Because I didn't get that from what you were saying."

Against her will, despite everything that was happening, she smiled. Then she laughed. "Dammit, Matt, I'm not kidding."

"Neither am I." He motioned to the sofa. "Are we ready to sit again?"

She felt a little foolish as she settled back down. "Sorry. I'm kind of on edge."

He angled toward her. "Jesse, you've known for a while you were coming back. You've had a chance to make plans, think it all through. You know what you want and how you're going to get it. We don't have that advantage. You show up here, unannounced, and expect me and Nicole to be okay with that. We're still trying to catch up."

As much as she didn't want to admit it, she saw his point. "I don't like it when you use reason against me."

"Sorry. It's all I've got." He stared at her. "I'm mad as hell about Gabe. Sure, you told me you were pregnant, but you knew I didn't believe you. You never tried to get in touch with me again. You never bothered to let me know when he was born. What the hell was up with that?"

Now she was the bad guy? She stood again. "What about all those things you said to me? You told me you didn't care if the baby was yours?"

He rose. "I was wrong, but so were you. You knew Gabe was mine. You should have tried harder."

She didn't want to hear that. "You wouldn't have listened."

"We'll never know what I would have done."

She stared at him for a long time. Shame filled her. "Matt," she whispered, fighting tears. "I'm sorry." She'd come here to cry on his shoulder. This wasn't the conversation she'd expected. "You hurt me so much."

"I know. I'm sorry. You have no idea how much I regret what I said."

Jesse wanted to believe him. Matt could see it in her face. But she wasn't sure if she could trust him. If she'd known these past five years, she would know she couldn't, but despite everything, Jesse had always believed in people, which was to his advantage.

She stared at him now, her big blue eyes dark with tears. God, she was beautiful. That hadn't changed. If anything, she'd improved with time. The lines of her face were a little sharper and more defined. She was all grown up and about the sexiest female he'd ever seen.

He accepted the fact that he wanted her. It couldn't be avoided. Sleeping with her would be a pleasure for both of them and where was the bad in that?

Now, as he moved toward her, sensing her vulnerability, he almost meant everything he said. Because caring about Jesse had been easy, too. Not that he was going to let himself forget what she'd done.

"You're confusing me," she admitted.

He rubbed his thumb against her bottom lip. "Part of my charm."

"You always were charming."

"I was some computer nerd who still lived with his mother."

She smiled. "I never saw you that way."

She really hadn't, he thought, remembering how easily she'd helped him. She'd changed everything and along the way he'd fallen for her. It had stunned him when she'd admitted having feelings for him. He could still recall the sense of impossible victory. He'd gotten the girl—the only girl who mattered.

He wasn't that foolish anymore, he told himself. No one mattered now. He didn't let them.

Just to make sure he didn't forget, he leaned in and kissed her. He touched his mouth to hers, claiming her, teasing, testing to see how far she would let him go.

At first she did nothing. She accepted the kiss, without kissing him back. He didn't move, determined to make her feel something, feel *him,* when she softened slightly, eased forward and put her hand on his shoulder.

He wrapped both arms around her and drew her against him, holding her close, holding her tight, determined to keep her for as long as he wanted. He thrust his tongue into her mouth, as much to claim her as to please her, but she didn't seem to mind. If anything, she met him stroke for stroke, touching, teasing, rubbing. Her hands moved up and down his back, her hips and belly pressed against him, daring him not to be aroused, not to be interested.

He was hard and ready and it was all he could do to keep from taking her right there in his office. The desk, a voice in his head yelled. The desk would work.

Heat burned through him, making it impossible to remember why he'd started the game, reminding him that now he should only be concerned with finishing it. Her mouth was hot against his, yielding, offering. He tasted her kiss and wanted to taste other parts of her, all of her. He wanted to touch her everywhere, rediscover the body he had known better than his own. He wanted to breathe in the scent of her, hear her gasp as pleasure claimed her. He wanted to push the thought of any other man out of her mind until there was only him.

He wanted more than sex, more than making love. He wanted to take her and mark her and hear her scream as she totally and completely lost control in his arms. Then he wanted to hear that final, breathless sigh of perfect contentment.

Need grew powerful. Wanting filled him. It wasn't pretend anymore. It was real and alive and it pulsed within him. He wanted Jesse the same damn way he'd always wanted her. Heart and soul. Forever. In that moment he knew he would walk away from his vow of revenge if only he could—

They pulled apart. Matt wanted to say he'd been the one to end the kiss, but he couldn't be sure. Maybe it had been her. Maybe she'd figured out the danger of an out-of-control fire. They stood staring at each other, both breathing hard. He could see the wanting in her eyes and knew she saw the same in his.

She started to speak, then shook her head and turned away. In a matter of seconds, she was gone. When he was alone, he continued to stand in the center of his office, his breathing too fast, his body burning for her as it had five years ago.

The game had just gotten interesting, he told himself. There was a whole new dimension at play. A dangerous one. Because she still had power over him. He was going to have to be very careful and make sure she never found out and used it against him.

What he didn't admit, even to himself, was that maybe it wasn't a game anymore. Maybe it was something else entirely.

CHAPTER TEN

Five years ago...

THE LOBBY OF THE HOTEL looked like something out of an old movie. There was dark wood everywhere, antiques and an air of elegance that made Jesse wish she'd worn something other than jeans and a sweater. She felt like she should be in a dress and heels. She also felt young, out of place and scared.

Don't be crazy, she told herself. She was fine. So she and Matt had gone away for the weekend. So they were going to have sex. That was hardly new for her. She couldn't count the number of times she'd done it.

Except everything about Matt was different. Everything was new and exciting and just a little terrifying, but in a good way. At least she hoped it was good.

Matt finished registering them. "Want someone to bring up our bags?" he asked.

She glanced at the small wheeled suitcase she'd brought and his leather duffel she'd made him buy a couple of weeks before.

"I think we can manage," she murmured, knowing a bellman would only make her more uncomfortable.

As it was, she felt like everyone was staring at her, judging her. It was as if they all knew about her shameful past and were thinking, "Here she goes again. Sleeping with someone else."

But it wasn't like that, she thought, wanting to defend herself. Matt was different. *She* was different. Being in love with him had changed her. Not that she expected anyone to believe her.

Jesse shook her head, determined not to think about her sister or anyone else. Matt had brought her to Portland for the weekend so they could spend some time together and have fun. She wanted to have fun…if only she could catch her breath.

The elevator was old and beautiful, with a brass railing and carved ceiling. They rode up ten floors, then walked down a long, carpeted hallway. Even the doors to the rooms were ornate and looked heavy. Matt used the key and let them into their room.

He stepped back and motioned for her to go first. She stepped into the space and frowned. There was no bed. Just a sofa, a couple of chairs and a view of the river.

She turned in a slow circle, taking in the beautiful furniture, the air of elegance. Then she noticed the open doorway and walked toward it.

Here was the bed, she thought as she stared at the carved canopy, the matching armoire and the lovely linens. The bathroom had a tub built for two, or maybe five, a double shower and real marble floors. The walk-in closet had automatic lights that went on as soon as the door opened.

"Makes me wish I'd brought more clothes," Jesse murmured, trying not to let him see how out of place she felt. This was too nice, too special. She was used to doing it in the back of a car, or a basement. On the sly, fast, as if the act was something to hide. As if she wasn't worth anything else.

Her throat was tight. Matt had obviously gone to a lot of trouble to find this place, make reservations. But it was all too much.

He came up behind her and put his hands on her shoulders. "You okay?"

She nodded.

"Don't panic," he said lightly, squeezing her, then letting her go. "There's a second bedroom. I wasn't assuming."

She turned to stare at him. "What?"

"There's a second bedroom. Want to see it?"

Another bedroom? Because he hadn't thought this was a sure thing? "We're away together. In a hotel. Why would you get a second bedroom?"

He frowned. "We never talked about anything other than going away. I didn't want to assume that you were ready for us to be lovers."

But he knew about her past. She'd told him. Not everything, but enough. And still, he treated her like… like… She couldn't even think of what it was like.

He smiled. "Jess, I'm not going to push you. I want us to spend time together. I want to enjoy the weekend. But if you need a little space of your own, that's fine."

He was perfect, she thought, unable to believe this was happening. Kind and gentle, smart, funny. He treated her like a princess. Like something precious. He took care of her without trying to change her. He believed in the best of her.

"I'm scared," she admitted. "I've never been scared before."

"You don't have anything to be scared about."

She looked into his dark eyes and knew he was wrong. She was scared because there was so much on the line.

The truth came to her then, in a blinding flash. She hadn't just fallen for him—she loved him. And that's what terrified her the most. The other guys hadn't mattered. If she blew it, there were another five to take that one's place. But not with Matt. There was only him and if she lost him, she would never recover.

She loved him. All of him. The way he was so intense about everything. How he had millions and didn't flaunt it. How he took care of not just her, but even his annoying mother. He was a good man, in every sense of the word. And when he kissed her, she burned down to her soul.

What if she hadn't been in that Starbucks on the first day they met? What if they'd never found each other?

What if he'd fallen for one of the other women he'd been dating? What if someone else had gotten him first?

It was little more than a quirk of fate that they'd found each other, she thought. For once in her life, she'd been lucky.

She crossed to him, raised herself on tiptoe and kissed him. He kissed her back, his mouth warm and firm, yet gentle, as if he didn't want to hurt her. As if he worried about her. Then his arms were around her and he was pulling her close.

She went willingly into his embrace, wanting to feel his body against hers. She parted and he slipped his tongue into her mouth.

He tasted of the wine they'd had at the tasting and something darkly sexy. She wrapped her arms around his neck, holding on to him so that everything stayed where it would. No matter what, Matt would keep her safe. She knew that. She'd known it from the first moment they'd met.

He ran his hands up and down her back. When he went lower and cupped her rear, she arched against him. Her belly brushed his hardness and he groaned.

He pulled back and cupped her face. "I want you, Jesse."

His dark eyes were bright with fire. His words made her shiver. "I want you, too," she whispered.

He took her hand and led her back into the bedroom. After he drew back the covers on the bed, he picked up her right hand and kissed her palm.

"This isn't my first time," he told her. "I thought you might be wondering."

She hadn't been, but it was good to know. On the heels of that thought came a wondering about how many others there had been. Who were those women? Why had they let Matt get away? Did he still see them? Think about them? Want them?

She wanted to ask, wanted to scream, wanted to jump out of her skin. The feelings of jealousy were new and uncomfortable. She tried telling herself she was here now and that's what mattered, but it wasn't enough.

What if they didn't click together sexually? What if he thought she was boring in bed? What if—

"Jess?"

She drew in a breath. "I'm making myself insane, worrying."

"About?"

"That you'll be disappointed."

He smiled. "That's not going to be a problem."

"You can't know that for sure."

"Stop thinking," he told her, just before he kissed her again.

She gave up to the feel of his mouth on hers. When her brain offered other ways for her to panic, she pushed the thoughts away. Better to enjoy what she could and let the crisis occur on its own.

She tilted her head and parted for him. He swept into her mouth, arousing her with each brush of his tongue.

Over and over, he kissed her, drawing out the

process until she began to relax. They weren't going to rush. That was good. Because despite her past, everything felt oddly new and unfamiliar.

He ran his fingers through her long hair, then pulled it aside so he could kiss her neck. He moved down to the hollow of her throat, the warm, erotic touch making her shiver slightly.

Wanting moved through her, sluggish at first, then growing. Her breasts began to ache. She felt heat burn between her legs.

He moved his hands over her back, then to her waist. She felt the weight of them through the layers of her clothing. He cupped the curve of her hips, but didn't move either higher or lower, as if he were comfortable taking things just this far.

He kissed her again. With each touch of his tongue on hers, her need cranked up a few degrees. When he nipped her earlobe, she quivered. Sensation flowed from where he touched her breasts. She could feel her nipples, tight and aching inside her bra.

She wanted to pull off her clothes and be naked. She wanted him urging her legs apart so he could fill her. She imagined his erection, big and straight and thick enough to make her scream.

Her skin yearned to feel his touch and still he only kissed her. Over and over, making her squirm.

At last he drew back far enough to pull off her sweater. At the same time she kicked off her shoes. He put his hands on her waist. She caught her breath in anticipation. Her breasts throbbed with each heart-beat. She was getting desperate.

He bent down and pressed his mouth to her bare shoulder. He licked the skin and she gasped. Slowly, more slowly than should be allowed, he moved his hands higher. Closer to her breasts. Closer and closer. At the same time, he kissed her collarbone, then her neck.

His hands moved higher. She silently urged him on. Just a little more. Just a little—

He cupped her curves in his large hands. Just held them for a second, before beginning to move, exploring her. She let her head drop back as she focused solely on his touch, the way his fingers moved over all of her. Then he brushed his thumbs across her nipples and she nearly screamed.

She stood frozen, wanting only to feel what he was doing to her. The irony was, he was barely touching her through her bra. In theory, they hadn't even gotten to the good stuff. How was she supposed to survive that?

He stepped back slightly and unfastened his shirt, then tugged it off. She stared at his bare chest, at the defined muscles, the dark hair. Then he pulled her against him.

She went willingly, wanting to feel skin on skin. He wrapped his arms around her, cocooning her in his strength. She clung to him, wishing she could crawl inside of him and never leave.

It was a perfect moment and they hadn't even done anything. Maybe it was because she knew for Matt, this was about being with her. She wasn't just some easy way to get laid. She was unique to him, and she'd never been that before.

His hands moved on her back. She felt a slight tugging on her bra, then it was loose. He pulled at a strap. She eased away enough to let it fall.

She was bare to the waist. He gazed at her, as if he found her beautiful, then he bent down and took her left nipple in his mouth. He sucked and licked, sending ribbons of sensation all through her body. She had to hold on to him to keep herself upright. Pressure built inside and when he used his hand to tease her other breast, she thought she might come right then.

It was as if he knew exactly what to do, exactly how to please her. He moved back and forth between her breasts, caressing her until she couldn't help moaning.

"Matt, please," she breathed. She was so ready, so on the edge. She wasn't used to this kind of foreplay, the drawn-out dance performed by a man determined to shatter every part of her.

He straightened and smiled at her. "I like how your breath catches and the little sounds you make."

She was making sounds? That was kind of embarrassing. How to explain she was used to sex being more…direct and quick. Or maybe she didn't want to. This way was a whole lot more fun.

He reached between them and unfastened her jeans. He pushed them down, along with her bikini panties and she stepped out of them. Then she was naked and he was easing her onto the edge of the bed.

She sat, her legs hanging down.

"Lay back," Matt told her.

She hesitated, knowing the position would leave her vulnerable, yet wanting to do what he said. Slowly, she lowered herself onto the sheets. He knelt on the floor.

"You're so beautiful," he murmured between kisses along her calf to her knee. "Your skin, your hair, your smile. The way you say my name."

He kissed and licked and nibbled his way up her thighs, getting closer and closer to the hungriest part of her. She stirred restlessly, parting her legs more, wanting what she knew was coming next. Wanting it all. She felt a whisper of breath, then his tongue found her most sensitive spot and she groaned.

He licked her gently, exploring her. At the same time, he moved his hands up her body until he touched her breasts.

The sensations were incredible. His tongue between her legs, loving the very center of her, his skilled fingers on her nipples, moving in perfect rhythm. She closed her eyes and gave herself up to the sensation, the liquid desire pulsing through her.

He moved slowly, around and around. Her muscles tensed. Wave after wave of deliciousness washed over her, pushing her higher and closer. As if sensing that, he went a little faster, a little harder. The movement of his fingers was more insistent. Need increased, pressure grew. She grabbed at the sheets and pushed toward him.

Faster and harder and more. She got closer and closer, losing herself. Her orgasm hovered just out of reach, teasing her with promise, making her ache and strain.

"Matt," she groaned.

He shifted slightly and sucked on the very core of her.

It was too much, she thought in the half second before she shattered.

Her orgasm claimed her with an unexpected intensity. She shook and cried out, unable to control her body. She might have begged, she wasn't sure. She just knew he couldn't stop—not until she was done.

She came and came, shuddering as he continued to touch her. Partway through, he thrust a finger inside of her. That sent her off on a new wave. She gave herself over to him, grinding herself against him, taking all of it on and on until finally she was still.

Jesse lay on the bed, her legs dangling, feeling more naked than she ever had in her life. She'd always enjoyed sex, but never like that. She felt as if she'd exposed her very soul. It was all she could do not to start crying. Or run away. She knew for sure she had to cover herself somehow.

She sat up and looked for an escape. Then Matt was there, pulling her to her feet, holding her. His strong arms held her close. He whispered that it was all right. As if he knew. As if he understood.

She began to cry then, big, fat tears she couldn't

explain. She cried as if her heart were breaking, probably terrifying him, but she couldn't stop. She cried like she'd come, with an out-of-control effort that left her drained and shaken.

"I'm sorry," she gasped, feeling his skin get wet beneath her cheek. "I'm sorry."

"It's okay." He stroked her hair, then kissed her forehead. "Just relax. I'm here."

He was there and he didn't sound the least bit freaked out. She managed to get her tears under control. "Why aren't you running as hard and as fast as you can?"

He smiled. "Why would I?"

"Because I'm a mess. I'm supposed to be glowing, not losing control. I don't know what's wrong."

He cupped her face, then wiped her tears. "I love you, Jess. Every part of you. You feel what you feel."

He loved her? Seriously?

Her heart stopped. She felt it freeze in her chest. How could he love her? She wasn't close to being anyone he should care about.

"Matt, you can't."

His answer was to kiss her. A gentle kiss filled with promise. She kissed him back, wanting to show him how much this meant to her. There had never been anyone like him before, anyone who cared. Sure, guys had told her they loved her, but only because they thought they had to so she would have sex with them.

He ran his hands up and down her body, touching her as if he couldn't get enough of her. She touched him back, then tugged at his belt.

He stepped back. While he pulled off the rest of his clothes, she got into bed and stretched out on the sheets. When he was naked, he moved next to her and stroked her. She saw the condom in his other hand.

Because that's just how he was, she thought, fighting tears again. He would protect her and take care of her, no matter what.

She pushed him onto his back and smiled down at him. "Brace yourself, big guy."

He laughed. "I can take it."

"I hope so."

She kissed him on the mouth, then trailed down his neck to his chest. Her hair was loose and stroked him as she moved.

She paused long enough to lick his nipples, then blow on them. From the corner of her eye, she saw his hands close into fists, as if he were fighting for control.

Good. She wanted to amaze him as much as he'd amazed her.

She continued kissing her way down his muscled stomach, then shifted so she knelt between his thighs. When she was in place, she took the condom from him and opened it, but didn't put it on him. Not yet. Then she leaned down and took him in her mouth.

She moved up and down a couple of times, retreated and licked the tip. He exhaled with a hiss. She closed her lips around him and sucked, then used her tongue to caress him.

Blood pulsed, making him even harder. His thighs tensed.

"Jesse," he groaned and reached for her.

She knew what he meant. Not like this. Not the first time. He wanted to be inside of her and she wanted that, too.

She slipped on the condom, then straddled him, taking all of him in one movement.

He filled her so completely, she nearly cried out. It was almost too much, she thought, then eased up and down again, more slowly. Her body stretched, adjusting to his arousal. She bent forward and braced herself on the bed. He reached up and cupped her hips.

"Jesse," he said, his voice strained and low.

She smiled. This was what she wanted—the chance to please him. She let him set the pace with his hold on her. She slid up and down, wanting to push him to the edge.

"Come with me," he told her.

"No. I want to watch."

She pushed down again and felt him stiffen. She moved faster, forcing him over the edge. He held on to her, as if trying to keep control, then he groaned again and was lost.

She rode him until the hands at her hips held her still. His eyes closed, his features tightened. She waited until he looked at her, then she bent down and kissed him.

"I love you, Matt."

He wrapped his arms around her and rolled so that he was on top, then kissed her. "I love you more."

"Impossible."

"Want to bet?" he asked.

"Sure."

"I'll prove it."

She laughed. "I can't wait to see you try."

CHAPTER ELEVEN

Present Day...

JESSE SAT DRINKING her morning coffee, trying to wake up. For once she didn't have to be at the bakery in the predawn hours, so sleeping in until seven was a treat. Or it would have been if she'd been able to sleep. Unfortunately, she'd had a restless night, unable to relax. When she'd finally dozed off, she'd dreamed about Matt. He'd haunted her with his kiss and his touch until she'd awakened uncomfortably aroused.

It was because of what had happened in his office, she thought with a sigh. Because of how he'd made her feel. She'd wanted to give him everything, had wanted to surrender to what he offered. The incredible passion she remembered so well still lived between them and it wasn't a place she could go. Not until she was sure of him. Or maybe not until she was sure of herself.

She cradled her mug of coffee in both hands and breathed in the scent as Paula hurried into the kitchen.

"Do you know where to look?" the other woman asked as she handed over the paper.

The ad for the new brownies along with the coupon was supposed to be in today's paper. "I don't have any idea," Jesse said, feeling both nervous and terrified. "For all I know, Nicole decided not to go forward with any of it."

"She wouldn't do that."

Jesse wasn't so sure. Her sister was pretty angry at her these days.

She divided the paper into sections, gave Paula half then began turning pages, looking for the quarter-page ad they were supposed to buy. She'd barely started looking when Paula began to laugh.

"It doesn't matter what she did," Paula said. "If you're right about her, she's going to be so pissed."

"Why?"

Paula tightened the belt on her robe, then sank onto one of the kitchen chairs. She cleared her throat and began to read.

"I confess I'm not a baked-goods kind of person. Scones leave me cold. Coffee cake makes me yawn. But I'm a huge fan of chocolate, so when a friend raved about the new brownies at the famous Keyes Bakery, I figured I'd give them a try. After all, a reporter has to be willing to do the really hard work. So I went in and bought one of each of the brownies. They're available with and without nuts."

Paula looked up and grinned. "Brace yourself, Jesse."

Jesse nodded, unable to do anything but listen and pray that the review was good.

"Seattle, we have a new nirvana. Forget the mocha-cinnos, the double-shot lattes and any other form of decadent delights in your life. Drop whatever it is you're doing and head directly to the Keyes Bakery. Order as many of their brownies as you can afford, then indulge yourself with a delicious, rich, incredible chocolate treat that will give you a rush unlike any you've ever experienced."

Paula continued reading, but Jesse wasn't listen-ing. She didn't have to. The brownies were a hit. She'd done it. She started to laugh. It was going to be a very good day.

JESSE SHOWED UP FOR her shift at ten in the morning. The entire building was in a state of confusion. The parking lot was overflowing, there were a dozen people standing in line and a very unhappy-looking Nicole met her before she'd gone five steps into the bakery.

"Did you know about this?" her sister demanded. "Did you know about the review?"

"Not until I read about it in the paper."

Nicole didn't look convinced. "We don't have enough. We're going to sell out within the hour. Then what am I supposed to tell people?"

Jesse stared at her. "I didn't know," she said. "If I had, don't you think I would have told you? Don't you think I would have wanted us to be prepared for the rush? At the very least, you have to think I'd want to rub it in."

That seemed to convince her sister. "It's a mess," Nicole murmured. "They're buying a half-dozen at a time. We're making them as fast as we can, but we have limited production capability. It wasn't supposed to be like this."

Jesse ignored the implication that her brownies couldn't possibly take off. They had a bigger problem right now.

"Are there phone orders?" she asked.

Nicole's expression tightened. "A few."

Which Jesse would guess meant a lot. "This is only going to get bigger. What if we rented a kitchen short-term? We don't need much space. A couple of commercial ovens would do it. There's virtually no start-up costs with that."

"That's a fairly permanent solution for a short-term problem," Nicole said.

Jesse didn't think it was short-term, but she decided not to push on that. "We could sell the extras over the Internet."

Her sister groaned. "Are you ever going to let that go?"

"No. It's a great idea. It's easy money. I have the Web site ready. All I need is to hook up with a server and we'll be online."

"Another of your community college business classes?"

"Yes," Jesse said, trying not to be annoyed by her sister's continuing doubt. "I've researched the right shipping material and boxes. It would take two days to get us up and running. We could even use it as spillover for bakery customers."

"I don't think so," Nicole said.

"You can't even muster one ounce of enthusiasm about any of this, can you?" Jesse asked, feeling bitter and defeated. "You're not happy because it's my recipe."

"I'm cautious because I have a responsibility to this business and my employees. I can't throw around resources just because you think it's a good idea. We're talking about a lot of money. I have payroll to meet. People depend on me. I can't afford to make a mistake."

Jesse pointed to the parking lot. "That isn't a mistake."

"It's not today, but what about in a week? A month? Do we hire new people then turn around and fire them if this doesn't work? I won't play with people's lives on a whim. I have more to worry about than your brownies, Jesse. I'm sorry if that bothers you.

"If you want to learn about the business," Nicole continued, "I would welcome that. I'm happy to give you a chance. But there's a lot more to the bakery than the flavor of the week. I have to remember that even if you don't."

Jesse didn't know what to say. Fortunately she saw Sid walking toward them. She couldn't read his expression, but it was one she'd never seen before.

"What's wrong?" Nicole asked.

"Nothing. Line two. You need to take this call."

Nicole crossed to the old wall phone, punched a button then picked up the receiver.

"This is Nicole," she said, sounding wary. She listened for about thirty seconds, then asked the caller to hold on. She handed the phone to Jesse. "It's for you." She thrust out the receiver and walked away.

Jesse stood staring after her. What on earth? "Hello?"

The female caller sighed. "Who am I talking to now?"

"Jesse Keyes."

"Really? That's great. Finally. You were not easy to track down. The number I found for you in Spokane was forwarded to another line, but you never picked up. I didn't know what else to do."

Jesse frowned. "I forwarded it to my cell."

"You might want to keep that turned on, you know. It would make it easier to reach you."

"Who *are* you?"

The other woman laughed. "Right. Sorry. Margo Walkin. I'm a producer here at *Good Morning America*. I'm in New York, but I used to live in Seattle. It's my birthday and my mom sent me some of your brownies as part of my present. Oh. My. God. They were incredible. Then she said they're getting all this buzz out there, so I thought I could do a segment on them. Or you. I know there's a story. So I want to set up a phone interview so we can talk and then I'll get a team out there for some filming. What do you think?"

Jesse looked at the crowd of cars in the parking

lot and thought about the article in the newspaper, then she laughed. "I think it's going to be a really, really good day!"

NICOLE SAT ON THE COUCH, then threw herself sideways and buried her face in a cushion. "I'm a horrible person," she muttered.

"You're not."

Claire's voice was warm and loving. The perfect supportive sister. Nicole knew she didn't deserve it.

"I'm hideous," she mumbled into the fabric. "I should have to wear a sign and a bell so people can be warned that I'm coming and can run away. Like I'm some kind of emotional leper."

"You're not an emotional leper," Claire told her. "Although you are dramatic. You're usually more rational than this."

"I can't seem to be rational about Jesse. I think that's the problem."

"Apparently. Now sit up. You'll hurt your back if you stay like that."

Nicole straightened. One of the things she most loved about Claire was that her sister always saw the best in people. Claire would listen and try to make Nicole feel better. Unlike Jesse, who would point out Nicole was acting like a bitch, then say she deserved what she got.

"I miss her," Nicole admitted. "I missed her while she was gone and now that she's back, I miss her more. I hate what's happening. I hate how I'm acting. I hear the words and I can't believe they're coming out of my mouth."

"Why are you saying them? Are you still angry at her about Drew?"

"I don't know. Maybe. Yes."

"Do you believe that she didn't sleep with him?"

Nicole didn't want to go there. "Yes, I believe her, but I'm still so hurt and upset. I can't seem to let it go. It's been five years. Shouldn't I be over this?"

"Probably, but you're not."

Nicole eyed her. "I always think of you as the helpful sister."

"I'm trying. Look, it's been five years, but nothing's changed for you."

"It's the Oprah moment all over again."

Nicole hadn't meant to say that and as soon as the words were out, she wished she could call them back.

"What's the Oprah moment?" Claire asked, sitting next to her on the sofa and rubbing her back. "Is that like the lightbulb thing?"

"Nothing that positive," Nicole muttered, feeling smaller and meaner by the second. "I was on *Oprah* about ten years ago. Someone sent her one of our chocolate cakes and she liked it so much, she brought me out to the show so I could talk about it."

Claire's eyes brightened as she grinned. "You never told me. That's incredible."

"It was supposed to be, only I didn't get to talk

about the cake. Between inviting me and my going to Chicago, someone on her show found out about you. So instead of showing off the famous Keyes chocolate cake to America, I answered questions about what it had been like having a twin sister who was a child prodigy. I hired extra workers, got in the ingredients, all for nothing. We got an extra dozen or so orders and that was it."

Nicole shrugged. "It was back when you and I weren't speaking, so I wasn't thrilled."

"I'm sorry," Claire told her.

The bitch of it was, she meant it, Nicole thought. "You're too soft-hearted."

"You're too mean, but I love you anyway."

"I don't want to be mean," Nicole said, knowing that might be something she couldn't change. "I'm so proud of what Jesse's done. She had that kid all on her own and she's done a good job with him. She's all grown-up and capable. That's a good thing. I should be happy."

"But you're not," Claire said and hugged her. "It's okay."

"It's not okay. She's my sister. I love her so much and I can't seem to let go of the past. I can't seem to trust her to get it right. I'm angry and resentful. Why can't I talk about the good stuff? She went to college. Did she tell you that? She got her AA by herself while raising Gabe and working full-time. Without any help. Who does that? Amazing people. People who are way better than me."

Nicole sucked in a breath so she wouldn't cry. "I

miss her and I love her and I think I hate her. What's wrong with me?"

"You're human."

"I'm a total bitch. I need to let the past go. I want to."

"Do you?"

Nicole continued to fight tears. "I hate it when you're insightful, but go ahead. Say it. You should and I probably need to hear it."

"If Jesse isn't the villain then you have to deal with why your first marriage failed. You have to accept responsibility."

"Why would I care about that? It's been five years. I love Hawk. Drew's long gone and I would never want him back."

"This isn't about him. It's about you. It's about admitting you screwed up."

"I accept responsibility for what I do wrong," Nicole said, feeling a little stung. "Jesse's the one who always—"

Except Jesse wasn't like that anymore. Jesse seemed to have her act together.

"I'm happy she's back," Nicole said. "I just don't know how to deal with all the crap that's coming to the surface."

"You'll figure it out."

"I'd better. I don't want to lose her again."

"Does my daddy like me?" Gabe asked.

Jesse wished she wasn't driving so that she could

pull her son into her arms and hug him until he never had to think anything bad again in his whole life.

"He does like you," she said instead. "He likes you a lot. But he doesn't have any experience around kids, so he doesn't know what to say. That makes him afraid of saying or doing the wrong thing. Grown-ups really hate that, so instead of making a mistake, he won't do anything."

Was this too much information for a four-year-old? Sometimes she just wasn't sure.

"But it's okay to make a mistake as long as you say you're sorry," Gabe said.

She laughed. "It is and I'll remind him of that."

"Good. Because I want him to be my daddy."

"I want that, too," she said and climbed out of the car.

She helped him out of his car seat, then collected the board games she'd brought for the evening at Matt's house.

Getting together had been her suggestion. She'd been nervous about calling after their encounter in his office, but as getting Gabe and his father connected was a major part of her reason for moving back to Seattle, it seemed silly to avoid him just because of how easily he caused her thighs to go up in flames. That was her problem, not his, and she would deal with it like a grown-up.

They walked up to the large double doors in front of Matt's house. Gabe looked around. "Is this a hotel, Mommy?"

"No. It's just a big house."

Gabe looked confused. "Is there another family here?"

"No, honey. Just your daddy."

"Just him?"

Jesse remembered the redhead who had been there when she'd first shown up. "Most of the time."

She wasn't going to think about Matt's other women or their kiss or anything else that could cause a problem. Tonight was about her son and his father and making sure they learned how to communicate.

The door opened before she could ring the bell. Matt stood there, all tall and sexy in jeans and a T-shirt. Casual. It was a good look for him. Of course, so was naked, although she'd promised herself not to think about that.

"Hi," she said, suddenly feeling nervous.

"Hi, yourself." He glanced down. "Hi, Gabe."

Her son seemed to brace himself. "Hello," he said quietly.

"Want to come in?" Matt asked.

Gabe looked at her, then nodded and walked into the house. Jesse followed him.

The entryway was as big as her rental back in Spokane, she thought as she stared at the wall in front of them. It was two stories high, with water rushing down.

Gabe stared wide-eyed. "It's raining *inside,*" he breathed. "Mommy, look. It's raining."

She thought about explaining that it was a water feature, albeit an expensive one. But maybe it was better to let her son think it was actual rain.

"I see," she said. "Pretty cool, huh?"

Matt walked over to a side wall and flipped a switch. Instantly the water on the wall fell into the pool below, then there was silence.

Gabe's expression turned to awe. "You can do that?"

Matt grinned. "So can you. Come on. I'll show you."

The switch was a little high. Jesse started to move toward them, but Matt simply reached down, grabbed Gabe around the waist and lifted him so he could reach. The boy turned on the switch and the water began to fall again.

Gabe laughed. "Mommy, can we have one of these?"

"Not for a while," she said, thinking there was a whole lot of other stuff they needed first. Of course, she didn't have Matt's millions.

He put Gabe down. "I'm ready to play some games," Matt told him. "What about you?"

Gabe nodded.

"Through here," Matt said, leading them down a short hall, past a kitchen large enough to serve two hundred and into an open family room. At least Jesse assumed it was a family room. The ceiling stretched up a couple of stories. There were wall-to-wall windows with a perfect view of Lake Washington. The fireplace could double as a guest room if it wasn't in use and there were four sofas scattered throughout the space.

Who lived like this? Okay, obviously Matt did, which was so weird. What had happened to the guy who'd complained that a three-bedroom town house was too big?

He went toward a sofa, but Gabe dropped onto the soft rug by the fireplace. Jesse smiled at Matt. "We play on the floor."

He looked doubtful, but joined them.

She set down the games she'd brought. "Chutes and Ladders and Candyland. Two perennial favorites." She glanced at Gabe and grinned. "Let's start with the easier one first. He's new to this."

Gabe laughed and reached for Chutes and Ladders.

Jesse set up the game. "Do I need to explain the rules?" she asked, thinking that teasing him would help with the sexual awareness she felt arcing between them. If they were laughing and focused on Gabe or the game, it was a whole lot more safe. At least for her.

"I can figure it out as we go," he told her, his dark eyes bright with amusement.

Gabe picked up the dice. "Here," he said. "You can go first."

"Very nice," Jesse whispered.

"He's new," Gabe whispered back.

"I can hear both of you," Matt grumbled and threw the dice.

Five minutes later, Gabe laughed as both she and Matt slid down chutes while he just kept going up and up on ladders.

"He's going to win," she told Matt.

"I can see that. It's because he has more practice."

"Maybe. Or he's just really good at the game."

Matt threw the dice and groaned as he landed on yet another chute.

He was being a good sport about it, she thought, pleased with how the evening was going. There was a lot less tension and while Matt wasn't exactly talking directly to Gabe all that much, they seemed more comfortable together.

When Gabe ran off to look out the big window, she turned to Matt.

"How are you doing?" she asked.

"Fine."

He looked comfortable enough, stretched out on his side on the rug, his head propped on his hand.

"Is he less scary or are you faking it better?" she asked.

"I've been doing some reading online. On his age group. What they like, where they are developmentally."

Did that mean he was starting to see Gabe as a person and his son? Was it too soon for that? Before she could figure out a way to ask, Gabe returned to her side and threw himself on her.

"I love you, Mommy," he said as he landed on her stomach.

She rolled, taking him with her, landing with him on his back. All the easier to tickle him. "I love you, too," she said as she wiggled her fingers against his side.

He shrieked with laughter and rolled closer. She

laughed, too, then pulled him against her. They hugged and she breathed in the little-boy scent of him.

Her heart kept growing and growing, she thought. It had to be getting bigger, otherwise it couldn't possibly hold all the love she felt for her son.

She turned and saw Matt had sat up. He was a little apart from them, looking slightly tense and out of place. There was something in his eyes, an emotion she couldn't read. Guilt? Concern? Then he blinked and it was gone.

Without warning, Gabe lunged for Matt's foot. He grabbed it and tickled. Matt pulled back so fast, he nearly tumbled over. Gabe's mouth fell open.

"Mommy, he's ticklish!"

Apparently, the news was nearly as exciting as the inside rain had been. A grown man who was ticklish? Was it possible?

Gabe lunged for him. Matt held out his arm, even as he continued to move back. "Wait a second. This isn't a good idea, Gabe. Tickling someone can be dangerous business."

Gabe wasn't listening and Jesse couldn't decide if she should intervene or not. She kind of liked the idea of Matt less than in charge and maybe on the run. When her son grabbed at Matt's toes, Matt scrambled to his feet.

"Who wants brownies?" he asked. "I stopped by the bakery and picked up some."

Jesse stood and pulled Gabe into her arms. They all went into the kitchen.

"I got both kinds," Matt was saying as he opened a familiar Keyes Bakery box. "Gabe, would you like milk with yours?"

"Yes, please."

"Jesse?"

He was acting so casual, she thought, feeling a little wicked. As if nothing had happened. As if he hadn't scrambled away like a little girl. She made a clucking sound.

He looked at her. "Are you all right?"

She clucked again. "Chick, chick, chicken."

His gaze narrowed. "I'm not a chicken. I have strong reflexes. I didn't want to risk hurting Gabe by accidentally kicking him."

"Uh-huh. You're ticklish and you didn't want him touching your feet."

"It's about reflexes."

She clucked again.

Without warning, he grabbed her arm, hauled her against him and stared into her face. His mouth was inches from hers. Heat burned everywhere they touched and wanting exploded.

"Say that again," he instructed, his voice low and very much in control.

"Are you daring me?" she asked, a little breathless.

"Absolutely."

"Can I have my brownie now?" Gabe asked, tugging on her shirt.

Reality crashed into her. She pulled back from Matt, who seemed to let her go just as quickly.

"Sure, honey," she said, picking him up and putting him on one of the tall seats by the high counter. "Without walnuts, right?"

"Uh-huh."

"You want milk with that, right?"

They worked in the kitchen, getting Gabe settled. Jesse asked Matt where the napkins were. He moved Gabe's chair closer to the counter. They acted as if nothing had happened, although she was desperately aware of every move he made.

Her body ached with need. She wanted—

Her cell phone rang.

She grabbed her purse and pulled it out. The number was local, but unfamiliar.

"Hello?"

"Jesse? It's Claire. You have to get down here right away." Claire sounded frantic.

"What's wrong? What happened?"

"It's the bakery. Oh, God, I can't believe it."

There were noises in the background. Loud noises and screams.

"What do you mean? What happened?"

"There's a fire. It's all on fire."

CHAPTER TWELVE

JESSE STOOD WITH HER sisters in front of the still-smoldering ruins of what had once been the Keyes Bakery. Most of the flames had been put out but the smell of smoke lingered in the air.

Over the past few hours, the building had been reduced to a pile of rubble. Nothing had been saved. When Jesse had arrived, flames had climbed toward the sky, like some frightening form of entertainment. The heat had kept them back. Now there was nothing but embers and ashes.

"I can't believe it's gone," Nicole whispered, sounding as stunned as Jesse felt. "Just like that."

Claire stood between them, her arms linked with theirs. "No one was hurt. That's the most important thing. The rest is just stuff and can be replaced."

Jesse didn't bother fighting the tears that flowed down her face. "*Good Morning America* isn't going to be coming out now," she said. "There's not much of a story."

Small business destroyed by fire. Who cared about that?

"It's not the end of the world," Nicole said. "We can fix this. We have insurance. We'll rebuild. It will just take some time."

Jesse didn't say anything. What was the point? She'd come back to Seattle to prove something. She'd given herself six months to make her point—that she could be a viable part of the business, that she could make a difference. But with the bakery shut down, that was impossible.

"What are you going to do until then?" Claire asked.

"I don't know," Nicole admitted. "Oversee the building."

It was the death of her dream, Jesse thought sadly. She would have to go back to Spokane and pick up her quiet life working in a bar. She would never get the chance to show that she had good ideas and could make a difference. She was—

"We can rent a kitchen," she said without thinking. "We'd have to cut down on some of the items, but not all of them. We can get the word out about the location. And we can use this time to go live on the Internet. The CDs with all the programming and information is at Paula's house. I could find a server in the morning. It wouldn't take long. Then we would still have most of the business during the reconstruction."

Nicole shook her head. "It would never work. Jesse, I know you keep pushing this, but it's not possible. This isn't the right time. You can't ship baked goods across the country. They won't pack well and even if you've solved that problem, they'll be stale when they arrive."

"Not if we use overnight shipping."

"No one's going to pay for that."

"How do you know?"

Nicole pulled free of Claire and turned on Jesse. "Maybe in your pretend world at community college they will. But not out here. No one is going to spend all that money to get brownies or a cake to Cleveland."

"You don't know that," Jesse said, frustrated by Nicole's constant refusal to admit her plan could work. "I did a lot of research and it wasn't in the pretend world. I checked out how other companies with delicate products did it. Yes, having to pay overnight will cut into sales, but it won't eliminate all of them. The start-up costs are so minimal, it's crazy not to try."

"I have spent years in this business," Nicole snapped. "I know my customers."

"You know the people who come into your store. You don't know the rest of the country and I don't know why you won't consider the possibility. There is more to life than just what you see."

"I'm aware of that," Nicole said through obviously clenched teeth. "But what you want is impossible."

"Because you say it is. You won't even try."

"Okay, that's enough," Claire said as she released both of them. She stepped in front, then turned to face them. "No more fighting. Not tonight. We've been through enough as it is." She looked at Nicole. "It's going to take a while to get everything figured out. The cause of the fire, designs for a new place, construction. We're talking months, maybe a couple of years. I don't know. In the meantime, you have employees. Are you going to let them go?"

Nicole shook her head. "I don't know. It's all too much right now."

"I agree," Claire said. "But Jesse's right. A rented kitchen is a fast way to get going and there isn't much in the way of start-up costs. The same with the Internet sales. If she has a Web site ready to go, we only have to deal with hosting. That won't cost much. So what if the sales aren't spectacular? There will be some and at the very least, you can keep a few employees on."

Nicole sighed. "You're right."

"I know. As to the rest of the business, what about selling to restaurants locally? Have you ever looked at that market? Between the cake and the brownies, you should be able to generate some interest."

Jesse glanced at Claire. "Restaurants? I never thought of that."

"Me, either," Nicole admitted.

"I am so much more than a pretty face," Claire told them. "You need to remember that."

That made Jesse smile.

Nicole laughed. "Fair enough. We'll start by finding a kitchen to rent and get the Internet site up and running. I need to call everyone and let them know what's happened. What time is it?"

Jesse glanced at her watch. "Nearly three."

"Sid will be getting here soon." Nicole sighed. "This is going to be hard for all of us."

Jesse didn't say anything. While she was pleased that Nicole had finally come around, she resented that her sister would consider the idea of a rented kitchen when Claire mentioned it, but not when she, Jesse, did.

There was a loud crack as another beam fell. Jesse blinked against the smoke and wondered what the fire department would say was the cause. Old wiring maybe. A faulty piece of equipment. The place had been around forever.

"Nicole? Jesse?"

Jesse turned and saw Sid walking toward them. He was dressed all in white, with a clean apron in his hands.

"What the hell?" he asked.

Jesse and Nicole moved toward him.

"No one was inside," Nicole said. "We're still not sure how it started. I was going to call, but I don't have anyone's number with me."

Sid stared at the smoldering flames. "I can't believe it. The whole thing is gone."

"We're going to rent a kitchen," Jesse told him. "It will take a couple of days to get up and running."

"What?" Sid shook his head. "Right. Yeah, rent a kitchen. That makes sense. Jesus. How does something like this happen?"

They didn't have any answer. Instead they talked quietly until more employees arrived, then went through everything with them. Jesse huddled in the darkness, cold and exhausted, but not ready to leave. Around four, Matt showed up, carrying containers of coffee.

Jesse hurried toward him, pleased he'd come. "What are you doing here?" she asked, wishing she could throw herself at him. Right now she could use a good holding. "It's the middle of the night."

"I guessed you were still here," he said as he handed out coffee. "I woke up and couldn't get back to sleep. So I came to see if I could help."

She took the coffee he offered. "Thanks."

He looked around at the smoldering ruin. "They couldn't save any of it? That must have been some fire."

"It was incredible." Jesse didn't want to think about all they'd been through. She was exhausted and not feeling up to coping, even though there was so much to do. She sipped the coffee and felt the warmth spread through her.

"Nicole's insured, isn't she?" he asked.

"Yes."

"Then you'll be able to rebuild, but it's going to take a while."

"I know. We're coming up with a plan now." She suddenly had to struggle to keep her eyes open. "Sorry. I'm not feeling too perky."

"A delayed reaction to stress and shock," he said and took her by the arm. "Come on back to my place.

You can shower and get some sleep. I'll bring you back here later to pick up your car."

"I should just go back to Paula's."

"It's four in the morning. You'll wake everyone."

Oh, right. Good point. "Let me tell Nicole and Claire."

She spoke with her sisters, then allowed Matt to lead her to his car. It was a sleek Mercedes two-seater that probably cost more than she'd made in the past five years.

"You'll need a different car," she mumbled as she put her coffee in the cup holder, then fumbled with the seat belt. "Kids need to be in the back. It's the front-seat air bag."

Matt smiled at her. "Interesting subject change. I'll keep that in mind. You going to be okay for the trip back?"

"Uh-huh. I just need a shower and a chance to rest."

Normally she would have skipped the shower, but she smelled like smoke. She didn't need the visceral reminder that her dreams had gone up in flames.

"Maybe not," she murmured. "If we do the rental kitchen and the Internet sales, I still have a chance."

"At proving yourself?" he asked as he pulled into the quiet street and headed for his place.

"Uh-huh." She leaned back in the seat and closed her eyes. "I gave myself six months to get it right. Did the fire have to be now? Couldn't it have been a year from now?"

"It's not personal, Jess. It's just one of those things."

"It feels personal. The fire hates me." She was starting to drift. "Nicole still hates me, but Claire's making her try out some of my ideas."

"Your sister doesn't hate you."

"Ha! A lot you know. You still hate me, too."

"No, I don't."

"You're mad. I can tell you're mad. But you're doing better with Gabe and he matters a lot more than me."

"Because you love him?"

"He's my son. I would die for him."

The car stopped. Jesse opened her eyes to see if they were already at Matt's place, but they were just stopped at a light. She glanced at him and found him staring at her.

"What?" she asked.

"You're not what I expected."

"You didn't expect me at all. I'm a surprise."

"In more ways than you know."

JESSE MUST HAVE FALLEN asleep because the next thing she knew, Matt was helping her out of the car. She managed to get through the house and upstairs. He helped her into a huge bedroom she would guess was the master. There was a massive bed and beautiful, custom furniture. At least she guessed it was custom based on how perfectly it fit into the space.

He tugged her hand and led her into what was supposed to be a bathroom, but needed a different word to describe it. There was a fireplace and a flat-screen TV over a jetted tub that could probably fit five. The shower was frameless with plenty of heads and jets and who knew what else.

"You awake enough to manage?" he asked as he set several very fluffy towels onto the marble counter. "I don't want you drowning in my shower."

"Me, either." She eyed the controls. "How do I turn it on?"

He went to a control panel on the wall. "Twenty minutes enough?" he asked.

Shock made her feel more awake. "You have a remote control *shower?*"

"There's a control panel inside as well. This sets the temperature, the water pressure, how many of the jets are to be used. I'm giving you the works. You'll like it."

He disappeared into a stadium-size closet and returned with a terry-cloth robe. "Leave your clothes here. I'll toss them in the wash while you're sleeping."

"Such service," she said lightly, trying not to think about being naked in Matt's house or who else had worn this robe. Did he have it laundered after each use or were there Electra cooties still on it? She decided it would be better not to ask.

He pushed a button and the water in the shower came on. "Just leave your clothes next to the towels," he told her and left.

She stared after him. There was a time he wouldn't have left. When him joining her in the shower wouldn't have been a question. Of course, that had been a long time ago, when they'd both still been in love and all that mattered had been being together.

She missed that. She missed a lot of things.

Jesse stripped quickly, left her clothes where he'd said and stepped into the shower. The water was hot and steamy and seemed to come from every direction. Sore muscles were soothed, smoke washed away. It was a little piece of heaven.

Fifteen minutes later she was clean and smelled like his shampoo and soap. She managed to turn off the water before stepping out and grabbing one of the towels. Her clothes were gone, which meant Matt had been in the bathroom while she'd been in the shower. Had he looked? Or maybe he hadn't even been tempted. She hated that she even wondered.

It had been a long time for her…five years to be exact, but that wasn't the reason she kept thinking about them being together. It was more because Matt had been the only one to touch her soul. She'd loved him and that had made all the difference.

She finished drying off and picked up the robe. It smelled of fabric softener rather than someone else, which was good. She didn't want to think about the other women in his life.

She put on the robe and used the blow-dryer to get most of the wetness out of her hair, then walked into the bedroom from the bathroom. Matt did the same from the hallway, carrying a mug of coffee. He handed it to her.

"I put your clothes in the wash," he told her.

"I saw that. Thanks." She sipped the coffee, feeling awkward and exhausted. The night was a blur of fire and smoke and shattered dreams. Except maybe she still had a shot at her dreams. Maybe it was all going to work out.

There was so much to do, so much to think about. She set down the coffee and rubbed her temples. "I think my head is going to explode."

"You don't want that," Matt said. He guided her to the bed. "Come on. Try to sleep. At least for a couple of hours."

He pulled back the covers. The sheets were beige and striped and looked expensive. Had he bought them himself? Did he have a designer or did one of his women take care of that sort of thing. Maybe the nice secretary she'd met at his office helped out. And how many women had there been in the past five years? A few? Many? Herds?

How could he have done that? Slept with them? Hadn't he missed her at all? Hadn't he loved her like he said, or had they just been the age-old words men had uttered since the beginning of time to get what they wanted?

"Don't cry," Matt said, touching her cheek and wiping away tears she hadn't felt fall. "You have a plan with the bakery. That's what matters."

She nodded, because speaking seemed impossible. Besides, what was the point? He actually thought she was only upset about the bakery. How just like a guy.

"I'm just tired," she managed to murmur. "It's a lot to take in."

He nodded and stepped back.

She stood by the bed feeling broken and alone, knowing she'd better get used to this because it wasn't going to change. Until that moment, she hadn't realized that talking about the bakery and making it there, reconciling with Nicole, had all been crap. Sure, it was important, but it hadn't been the real reason she'd come back. She'd come back for Matt. She'd come back to see if there was still something between them because she couldn't seem to move on. No other man had interested her and plenty had tried. She'd come back to see if he still loved her.

Looks like she had her answer.

It shouldn't hurt so much, she thought, even as pain sliced through her. She shouldn't be surprised. He'd never come looking for her, so of course he'd moved on. Still, a part of her had wondered if maybe, deep down inside, he'd felt it, too.

She'd been a fool.

There was no way she was going to sleep now, but her clothes were in the wash, so she was stuck for the next hour or so. Better to be alone in his bed than trying to make conversation with him.

"Do you have a T-shirt or something I can borrow?" she asked, hoping the twisting in her stomach went away soon.

He went into the jumbo closet and opened a built-in drawer, then returned with a soft, well-worn Seahawks T-shirt. He started to hand it to her, then swore, tossed it on the bed, grabbed her by the collar of the robe, dragged her close and kissed her.

It wasn't a gentle kiss. It was determined and hungry, taking as much as it offered. He used his lips to claim her, his tongue to arouse her and, dammit all to hell, it worked.

She found herself straining toward him, kissing him as intensely as he kissed her. She put her hands on his shoulders, then his upper arms and felt the strength of him. The fire she remembered returned, consuming them both. He broke the kiss and stared at her.

"You're just standing there, so calm and reasonable," he said, his eyes dark with passion. "You're naked, Jess, and that's not something I can ignore."

"I'm wearing a robe."

"*My* robe. How do you think that makes me feel?"

His? Not one of the girls'?

The pain in her stomach faded as if it had never been. "I can solve the problem of the robe," she murmured and shrugged out of it.

The heavy fabric fell instantly, pooling at her feet. His breath hissed, then he was touching her everywhere, his hands skimming her body. She gave herself over to him, kissing him, touching him, feeling the hard planes of his body, so wonderfully familiar.

He pulled back enough to jerk open his shirt. Buttons popped and scattered. He threw the ruined shirt on the floor, quickly removed his shoes, socks, jeans and briefs, then grabbed her around the waist and tumbled them both onto the bed.

They landed on the soft sheets, legs tangling, bodies touching. His erection pressed against her bare belly, his mouth on hers, his hands reached for her breasts. Heat was everywhere. She was already wet and swollen, just from being close to him. She felt herself drowning in sensation. The combination of past and present was too much, and exactly what she wanted.

He shifted so he could brace himself on the mattress, then gazed down at her. "You're so beautiful," he said as he stroked her hair. "You haven't changed."

There were a few changes, she thought, but they were mostly on the inside and she didn't want to talk about them.

"Matt," she said, loving the sound of his name.

He rubbed himself against her thigh, then groaned. "You've always had that power over me. What is it?"

"I don't know. Chemistry."

"Something."

He bent down and took her nipple in his mouth. The combination of tongue and lips caused her to arch her back. Her body clenched in anticipation. Wanting built, along with pressure.

He moved to her other breast, pushing her further along the road. She squirmed as her body began to remember how good all this could be. He licked her tight nipple, then sucked, causing her to gasp.

Each time he drew her deeply into his mouth, there was an answer pulse low in her belly. A flare of desire. She began to shift her hips, trying to hurry him along. Preliminaries were nice, but it was like being at a cocktail party when she was starving for dinner.

She could feel how swollen she was. Long dormant parts were insistent that it was time. She wanted to come, but it wasn't so much about the orgasm as it was about coming specifically with Matt. She wanted to know if it was still the same between them.

"Be in me," she breathed.

If he was surprised, he didn't show it. His dark gaze found hers for a second, then he nodded. He opened the nightstand drawer, pulled out a condom, then put it on.

She parted her legs and braced herself. Did that part shrink from lack of use? Had having a baby made anything different? Was there—

He pushed against her. Despite being wet and ready, she was tight, she thought as he eased inside. Tighter than she remembered.

Inch by inch he filled her, stretching her. Nerves began to quiver, then dance as he rubbed them, going deeper and deeper. It was as if he could go deep enough to touch her soul.

She pushed down as he pushed in, taking all of him, feeling full for the first time since…since…since the last time.

He withdrew and thrust in again. Her body tensed,

prepared for release. While Jesse knew it was going to be good, she was almost disconnected from the process. Because this moment wasn't about sex for her. It never had been. It was about finding the connection with the only man she'd ever loved.

Everything was different, she thought sadly. Everything was technically better. His pace, the intensity. He shifted so he was able to reach between them and rub that one swollen spot. It pushed her over the edge in a matter of seconds. Even as her orgasm claimed her, she knew it was as much about technique as anything else.

Then she was lost in the wave and nothing else mattered. There was only the release and all that went with it. She came and came as he filled her and withdrew. The pleasure was endless, causing her to hang on to him, gasp for breath.

When he came himself, she allowed herself to believe it was just like before. That they were together and he loved her and nothing else mattered. It was a beautiful dream that ended when her body was finally still.

He withdrew, then stretched out beside her. They faced each other as they had dozens of times before. She wanted to believe she saw something in his eyes, something that meant he'd felt the pull from the past, too. But she knew that was just wishful thinking on her part. Nothing more.

"That was unexpected," he told her. One side of his mouth turned up. "Not that I'm complaining."

"Me, either."

He touched her cheek, a tender gesture that made her throat get all tight. "Jesse…"

She waited, not breathing, praying that he would say something, anything, to make her believe that there was still a spark between them. That he regretted letting her go all those years ago. That he'd been wrong to judge her and wanted to make it up to her.

He withdrew his hand.

"I'm sorry about the fire," he told her.

Right. The fire. For a few minutes, she managed to forget the destruction. She rolled onto her back and pulled up the covers.

"We have a plan. We'll see how well it works."

"You'll figure it out," he told her.

She nodded. At least thinking about the five million things she had to do so the business could be up and running again meant she didn't have to think about Matt. Business was a whole lot easier to deal with.

"I can't believe Gabe and I were here last night," she said. "It feels like weeks ago."

"Thanks for bringing him over. I want to get to know him more."

She looked at him and smiled. "You were doing much better."

"He's a good kid."

The right words, but did he mean them? Did he see Gabe as his child yet? Had being apart for those first few years destroyed the relationship they should have had? Was that her fault?

She'd always comforted herself with the fact that she'd been very clear about the baby being Matt's. He'd been the one to refuse to believe her. But now she wondered if she'd tried hard enough. He'd complained that she hadn't bothered to tell him after Gabe was born. Maybe he had a point. Maybe she should have called or something. Not that he would have listened, but she could have tried harder.

"Do you want to try some one-on-one time with him?" she asked. "You could take him to the aquarium."

Matt sat up. "Am I ready for that?"

"Probably not, but you're only going to get ready by doing it. The aquarium gives you something to talk about. He's small, he won't last long before getting tired. You'll spend more time driving there and back than actually looking at the fish." She frowned. "I guess you'll have to borrow my car, or your mom's." She smiled. "Hers is newer and probably less embarrassing for you."

He shook his head. "I'll buy something. What's the safest car out there? A Volvo? I'll do some research online."

Now she sat up. "Matt, you don't have to buy a car to take Gabe out. That's crazy."

"Why? He's my son. I'll be seeing more of him. I need a safe car. I'll get one this week."

Of course he would. Because for him, buying a

new car was as much an expense as her picking up a pack of gum.

She slid back down in the bed and sighed. Everything was different. On the surface it all looked familiar, but that was an illusion. They'd all changed and pretending otherwise didn't alter reality.

She'd had a baby with Matt, had just made love with him and still she didn't know him. Didn't know what he was thinking, what he wanted, what he needed, what made him laugh, what he resented. He was a stranger with a familiar face, nothing more. No matter what her heart kept telling her, she had to remember that.

"Jesse?"

"Hmm?" She turned toward him.

He rolled toward her and kissed her. A slow kiss that reminded her of how it used to be. A kiss that made her wonder and maybe even hope.

"Get some sleep," he said. "I'll wake you in a couple of hours."

And then he was gone, leaving her alone in his bed.

CHAPTER THIRTEEN

"Check the ovens," Jesse called Monday morning as she carried in a stack of boxes and set them in the rear of the kitchen they'd rented. It was smaller than they were used to, but only a short-term solution. A restaurant had closed and the owner was renting to them until a new tenant was found, but for now, it was enough.

Sid opened the top oven door and checked the temperature. "We're on," he said. "Four hundred."

"Great." Ovens that worked were the most important thing.

"Where do you want these?" Jasper asked, carrying in two laptop boxes.

"Out front," Jesse said. "We'll take orders and do shipping in the front of the restaurant." Why not? They didn't need the tables and chairs for anything else. It would give them the space to spread out and keep the kitchen clear for baking. "Are the phones working?"

Jasper picked up the receiver. "We have a dial tone," he yelled.

"The phone company said they'd be forwarding

calls by nine." Jesse glanced at her watch. It was eight-thirty. "Call the old number and see if the referral is working yet."

Jasper began to dial.

Jesse moved around the rented kitchen, energized by the work and the possibilities. Once the rest of their supplies were inventoried, they could start baking. Brownies would go out that day. Tomorrow, someone on the other side of the country would taste one of her brownies and his or her life would change forever. At least that was the plan.

"Controlled chaos," Nicole said as she leaned against the counter and looked around.

Jesse nodded, not sure what to say. So far her sister hadn't talked very much. She seemed to be staying out of the setup. Was that because she was giving Jesse a chance to prove herself or was this more about being pissed off? Jesse wasn't sure she wanted to know.

"We had our delivery this morning," Jesse told her. "I did a preliminary check and everything seems to be here. You saw the shipping supplies. We have our first pickup this afternoon."

Nicole frowned. "What are you talking about? What pickup?"

"For our orders."

"How can we have orders?"

Jesse didn't understand the question. "I told you the Web site went up yesterday."

"I know that, but we already have orders? Is that possible?"

Jesse laughed. "It's beyond possible. Come on. I'll show you."

She led the way to the front of the restaurant to where D.C. had opened the boxes and was setting up the two laptops they'd already bought. Jesse walked over to her computer, sat down and typed in the Web address.

"The site went up yesterday. Normally it would take a while for people to find us, but with the publicity about the fire, we've had more activity than expected."

The site loaded quickly, a clean, appealing page featuring enticing pictures of the brownies and the famous Keyes chocolate cake. She scrolled down to a small icon in the bottom corner, clicked on it, then typed in the user name and password. The page changed to columns of numbers.

"Here's the latest info on hits," she said as she pointed. "We're getting—" She stopped and blinked. "That can't be right."

"What?" Nicole peered over her shoulder. "What's wrong?"

"This says we're getting over a thousand hits an hour. That's not possible."

"Sure it is," Sid told her. "Didn't you watch the news last night?"

"I was too busy debugging the site. Were we on it?"

"Yeah. A great story about how Keyes Bakery had been in business for years and burned down unexpectedly. And how we're using technology to stay in business. You looked good, Nicole."

Jesse stared at her sister who straightened, looking uncomfortable. "You were interviewed by the local news and didn't tell me?"

"They were covering the fire. I was in shock. I barely remember what I said."

"You told them about going online and how you wanted to keep your employees working until you could rebuild," Sid told her. "That there were many business models these days and you were going to take advantage of what the computer age offered."

Jesse felt as if she'd been hit in the stomach. What was going on? Her sister could get all excited about what they were doing away from her while being difficult and uncooperative in person?

"It was a good story," Sid repeated. "Maybe it got picked up by some other local stations. You know they're always looking to fill time, especially on the weekends. That could explain the hits."

Something had to, Jesse thought. She clicked on the order page and gasped. "We have one hundred and twenty orders."

Nicole stared at the screen. "That's not possible."

"Apparently it is." She scrolled through the list. "Mostly brownies, which is good. They're faster to make. There are a few cakes, though. We'll have to sort through the orders and figure out what we're baking first. Our overnight delivery pickup is at five-thirty.

We've got to get as many of these orders out today as possible." She looked at Nicole. "We're going to need more help."

"I'll call Hawk. Maybe some of his players or their friends want a temporary job."

Temporary meaning they would be replaced by full-time workers, or temporary meaning this wasn't going to last?

Jesse decided not to ask. She had enough going on without fighting with her sister right now. They had the illusion of getting along and she didn't want to disturb that.

"I'll get the inventory finished so we can get baking. We have orders to fill."

The sisters went in different directions. As Jesse counted large bottles of vanilla and bins of walnuts, she found her mind straying toward Matt and what had happened a few days ago…after the fire. Except she didn't want to think about him, either. It was too confusing.

She glanced at the computer. The order count was increasing by the hour. Adrenaline kicked in. At last a crisis she could get behind.

MATT HOVERED AWKWARDLY as Gabe climbed out of his car seat. His new BMW 5 Series had state-of-the-art safety, including curtain air bags. Still, he'd driven to the aquarium slowly and carefully, never once going over the speed limit. If this had been anywhere other than Seattle—the land of polite drivers—he would have been pushed off the road by passing cars.

"I'll get the door," he told the boy and slammed it shut. "I was, ah, doing some research online. There's an area where you can touch a lot of stuff. Plants and animals." He frowned. "I guess not animals. Marine life." Starfish. He remembered that they would be able to touch starfish. Which were what? A kind of fish?

Gabe looked up at him as they came to a stop at a light. "Are we crossing the street?" he asked.

"Yes."

"You gotta hold my hand."

"Oh. Sure."

Matt took the small hand in his own. He felt over-sized and inept. What had he been thinking, wanting to spend time alone with Gabe? He didn't know what he was doing. He hadn't even known which car seat to buy, let alone how to put the car seat into his car. His mom had helped with that.

The light changed and they crossed the street. When they arrived at the aquarium, Matt paid for their admission, collected a map and led the way inside.

"They have different talks all day long," he said. "I thought maybe you'd like the octopus one."

Gabe's eyes brightened. "Yeah. That's good."

Matt pointed to the map. "What else interests you?"

Gabe glanced at the open paper, then back at Matt. The light faded from his eyes. "I can't read, Dad."

Matt swore silently. "Sorry," he muttered, feeling like an ass. "Let's walk around and see what's fun."

Gabe sighed heavily as he followed at his side.

It shouldn't be like this, Matt thought, more frustrated by the second. The was his *kid*. They should be able to spend a couple of hours together without bumping into each other on the curves.

Not knowing what else to do, Matt followed the signs to the Underwater Dome. They walked in through a tunnel that opened up into an area in the middle of a massive aquarium. They were surrounded by water and fish. Gabe pointed and ran over to the glass.

"Look! Look!"

He raced from side to side, unable to take it all in. Matt watched him and relaxed a little. Maybe everything was going to be okay.

They spent a long time in the Underwater Dome. At one point, Matt saw a couple of boys eyeing Gabe. They were older, bigger and each had a squirt gun in their hands. He strolled over, came up behind them and put a hand on their shoulders.

"Don't even think about it," he told them.

They looked up, swallowed, then took off.

"Want some ice cream?" he asked his son.

Gabe nodded.

They got ice cream and soda, then went to the octopus talk. Gabe listened attentively for about fifteen minutes as he licked his cone and got ice cream all over himself, then he started squirming. Matt led him out and was about to ask where they should go next when Gabe stumbled, clutched his stomach and promptly vomited all over the cement floor.

A woman in an aquarium uniform stopped next to him. "Poor kid. Too much ice cream, huh? The bathroom is over there. I'll call for a cleanup."

Gabe stood there, looking miserable. Matt didn't know what to do. He hadn't thrown up since a long night of drinking in college, but he remembered it wasn't fun.

"Come on," he said and ushered the boy into the bathroom. "You done?" he asked. "You need to throw up again?"

Gabe shook his head. Matt grabbed paper towels, dampened them and began wiping Gabe's face. He didn't know what to say. The ice cream had been kind of large. Matt hadn't finished his, but Gabe had gotten the whole thing down…except the part that had melted on him. And the soda. That had been a mistake.

Who bought a four-year-old a large ice cream and soda? An idiot, that's who. He was beyond stupid. There was no way in hell he should be allowed out with his son on his own. This time he'd gotten him sick. Next time it could be worse.

Frustrated and angry, he scrubbed the kid's arms, then his hands. Gabe's shirt and shorts were clean, but his shoes weren't, so Matt wiped them as well.

He continued to berate himself, knowing that his plan to suck Jesse in, destroy her and take the kid had a massive flaw. While he wanted his former lover taken down, he had nothing against Gabe. Putting the child in mortal danger by hanging out with him was wrong. He had to—

A small sob caught his attention. He looked at Gabe and realized big, fat tears rolled down his cheeks.

Matt dropped the paper towel and grabbed him by his upper arms. "What's wrong? Are you sick? Do you need to go to the hospital? Tell me. What is it?"

Gabe cried harder. Matt crouched down in front of him, feeling helpless.

"You gotta tell me, buddy," he said. "I can fix it, whatever it is. Your stomach? Does it hurt?"

Gabe shook his head.

Okay, not that. "Your head? Your back?" What else could hurt on a four-year-old?

"You're m-mad at me," Gabe sobbed.

"What?" Mad at him? "No. Why would you think that?"

"You're h-hurting me." He pointed to a red spot on his arm where Matt had scrubbed a little too hard. "You l-look mad and you w-won't talk to me." There were more tears and a couple of heartbreaking sobs.

Matt felt like shit. Total and complete shit. He'd been so busy beating himself up, he hadn't paid any attention to Gabe. Yet another way he was a danger to his son.

"I'm not mad," he said, wishing Jesse was here and could take over. But she wasn't. He was on his own. He knelt on the cement bathroom floor and wiped

Gabe's cheeks with his fingers. "I'm not mad at you." He deliberately made his voice calm and friendly. "I'm kinda mad at myself."

That got Gabe's attention. The boy wiped his nose with the back of his hand. "Why?"

"You got sick because I bought you a big ice cream. I wanted to get you something you'd like, but I didn't think that you're still growing. I didn't know it would make you throw up. The soda didn't help, either. I felt bad and then I got mad at myself."

"You're not mad at me?"

"No. I'm having a good time with you."

Gabe smiled through his tears. "Me, too," he whispered, then threw himself at Matt.

His body was small and thin. Matt could feel his bones. The weight leaning against him was unfamiliar, but right. Not knowing what else to do, he hugged the boy. Skinny arms wrapped around his neck. He could feel Gabe's heartbeat.

This was his son, he thought, understanding dawning for the first time. His child. He was responsible for him being alive.

He tightened his hug, then quickly relaxed, not wanting to accidentally hurt him again. Gabe hung on.

"How you feeling?" he asked.

"Okay," Gabe said. "Tired."

They'd been at the aquarium all of an hour, but maybe at four, that was enough.

"Want to go home?" he asked.

Gabe nodded.

Matt waited, but the kid didn't let go. That was going to make it hard to walk. Then he said, "Want me to carry you?"

Gabe nodded again.

Matt carried him back to the car. Gabe hung on like he was never going to let go. Matt held him close, vowing that no matter what, he would protect this child. Take care of him. Unfamiliar emotions battled for space in his heart, but the one that got his attention the most was burning anger for all that he'd lost.

GABE SLEPT MOST OF the way home. He woke just as Matt pulled up in front of Paula's house. Matt helped him out of the car seat then watched as Gabe ran to the front door where Paula waited and began talking about his trip. Jesse appeared, hugged him, then walked toward Matt.

She looked tired. His mother had told him that the temporary business was booming with plenty of Internet orders. Jesse was taking the early shift, arriving at work around four and staying at least twelve hours.

"He sounds like he had fun," she said as she approached.

"He got sick. I gave him too much ice cream and he threw up."

She winced. "At that age, it's a pretty developed reflex. Did he get better right away?"

Matt nodded.

"Then he should be fine," she told him. "Were you freaked? I should have warned you that could happen."

She was beautiful, he thought. The long blond hair that had haunted him for months after she'd left. Her blue eyes. The shape of her mouth. Every inch of her appealed to him. Everything about her made him want her. Making love with her should have been nothing more than a way to further his plan, yet he'd been sucked in to the moment.

"You shouldn't have to warn me," he said, letting the frustration and anger boil up inside of him. "I should know."

She looked confused. "How could you? You haven't spent any time with Gabe."

"You're right. I haven't. Whose fault is that? Who made sure I didn't get to know my son?"

She took a step back and crossed her arms over her chest. "You did," she told him. "You refused to believe the baby was yours, so don't put this on me." Only she didn't sound totally convinced of what she was saying.

He had a reputation for being a ruthless bastard and he'd earned it by never letting a moment of weakness go unexploited.

"It's more than that," he said, narrowing his gaze. "You knew there was no way I would believe you after what I'd found out."

"No," she snapped. "Not found out. After what

you'd been told. I never slept with Drew, remember? There was nothing to find out."

"All right. You knew I wouldn't believe you after what I'd been told. You knew I'd think you'd gone back to your old ways—if you'd even given them up. But did you try to convince me again? Did you bother to get in touch with me after you had Gabe?"

"You didn't come looking for me. You didn't bother to find out."

"I wasn't the one who was pregnant," he yelled. "You had a responsibility to give me the chance to be a father. You took that from me. You stole four years of my son's life and there's no way for me to get that back. You didn't have the right, Jesse."

She seemed to shrink into herself. "I wanted you to know him," she said, obviously fighting tears.

"No, you didn't. You liked being a single parent. You liked being right and thinking I was nothing more than the bastard who let you down. You got to play the victim card and that was always your favorite."

She raised her hand like she was going to slap him. He grabbed her wrist. "Don't."

"Stop attacking me."

"I'm telling the truth," he said coldly. "You're the one who is suddenly so big on the truth. You kept him from me on purpose. You were punishing me for not believing you."

"Maybe I was," she screamed and pulled her hand free. "Maybe I was. You hurt me, Matt. You said you loved me. You said you'd always be there for me but at the first sign of trouble, you couldn't get rid of me fast enough. You never meant anything you said."

"That's bullshit and you know it. You're the one who couldn't handle our relationship. You're the one who ran."

She flinched. "Maybe, but you didn't come after me and I know why. You were already having regrets about us. You wanted out and I gave you a convenient excuse."

She couldn't have been more wrong, he thought, remembering how it had felt to hear his mother tell him Jesse had been cheating on him for their entire relationship. He wouldn't have believed Paula—he knew she wanted Jesse gone. But learning that Nicole had thrown her sister out of her house for sleeping with Drew had made the impossible real to him.

He'd been beyond devastated. Her betrayal had made him question everything they'd had together, made him question himself. In the dark, ugly pain of losing her, he'd vowed to never care about anyone ever again.

"If you think I wanted out, you didn't know me at all," he told her.

"Just like you didn't know me," she whispered. "What was it you said? Once a slut always a slut?"

He'd regretted the words as soon as he'd said them. Now was the moment to tell her he was sorry. But he was so angry about Gabe, so enraged at what she'd done, that instead he said, "My opinion hasn't changed."

"How dare you?"

He noticed she didn't try to slap him again.

"It's pretty easy, Jess," he told her, deliberately trying to provoke her. "Gabe talks about his 'uncles' all the time."

"I've told you who they are."

"Yeah. You've told me." His tone made it obvious he didn't believe her. "Why did you come back? Was this just more of your game? You wanted to make sure you showed me exactly what I'd been missing? You wanted me to suffer more? You picked a hell of a good way to do it. What I've lost with my child can never be recovered. You deliberately stole that. You decided I wasn't going to be his father in anything but name and you made that happen."

She went pale. "That's not what I wanted," she whispered. "Matt, no. You can't believe that. If you could have seen how you looked at me five years ago. Do you know what you said to me? How you destroyed me? I wasn't punishing you. I swear. I was trying to survive. I was so torn up inside, so hurt."

He wasn't impressed. He might have started with the idea of taking Gabe away from her as punishment, but now that he was realizing all that had been lost, he wanted her to feel what he was feeling now. The sense of knowing the past could never be recovered.

"You were wrong not to give me a chance," he told her. "Nothing I said justifies what you did."

Tears filled her eyes and spilled down her cheeks.

She started to speak, then stopped and shook her head. He felt her pain and did his best not to give a damn. She'd earned this.

"It wasn't what you think," she said.

"Does it matter? The end result is the same."

A truck pulled up behind his car. He barely noticed. Jesse wiped her face, turned at the sound of a door slamming, then stunned him by running past him and launching herself at the man who'd just climbed out of the truck.

Matt eyed the two of them, hugging. His irritation cranked up a notch when the other guy wiped her face, then kissed her forehead.

He crossed to them, prepared to do battle, only to come to a stop when they faced him.

"Are you responsible for making my best girl cry?" Jesse's friend asked.

Matt stared at him. This guy was old enough to be her grandfather, though tan, and still straight and tall. Under other circumstances, Matt would have instinctively liked him.

"She did that to herself," Matt told him.

Jesse wiped away the rest of her tears. "Matt, this is Bill. Bill, this is Gabe's father."

The old guy eyed Matt. "You've had a bit of a shock. How you taking it?"

"Not well."

"Jesse did the best she could."

She had a champion, he thought grimly, not lik´

the situation. "She had a responsibility to tell me the truth."

Bill looked at Jesse. "Is he an asshole? Do I need to beat the crap out of him?"

Matt was more than willing to take the old guy on. Except he couldn't, what with Bill being twice his age.

"He's okay," Jesse said. "We're working our way through it."

Bill studied him for a few seconds. "If you say so, darlin'."

Bill had his arm around her. She seemed very comfortable next to him. Yet looking at them, Matt *knew* there had never been anything between them. The old guy was just what she'd said. A friend.

Which should have made him feel better, but didn't.

Jesse knew she should probably be standing on her own two feet, but it felt good to be leaning on Bill, even for just a couple of minutes. He'd always been there for her and right now she needed a friend.

Matt's accusations still rang in her ears, making her feel small and petty.

He was wrong, of course. He had to be wrong. She hadn't been punishing him by keeping his son from him. Had she? While she'd never thought of that as her motive, was it possible that deep inside she'd wanted to hurt him back? Hurt him as much as he'd hurt her? Was she really that horrible a person?

It was too much to consider, so she focused on Bill. They walked up to the house, Matt coming with them.

She ushered Bill inside, only to have Gabe come running into the room, then launch himself at the older man.

"Uncle Bill! Uncle Bill!"

The boy's joy was impossible to miss. Jesse glanced at Matt. His face didn't show any emotion, but she saw the tightness in his jaw, the stiffness in his body. Bill had known Gabe all his life. He'd been a part of everything Matt had missed and it was possible that was her fault.

She touched his arm. "Matt, I'm sorry."

He looked at her, his eyes blazing with a rage she'd never seen before. "Do you think that comes close to being enough?" he asked, then turned and left.

CHAPTER FOURTEEN

Five years ago...

JESSE PUT THE LAST OF the plates in the cupboard, then stood back to look at the neat stacks of dishes. Matt hadn't had much in the way of housewares to move. Except for his clothes and a few personal items, everything in the town house was new. The flatware, the pots and pans, the sofa, the bedroom set, all of it. It was new and lovely and made what had been an empty space seem almost homey. Or it would when the furniture arrived.

She glanced at her watch. All the delivery appointments were between ten and one. She and Matt had decided to get them all over at once. She'd volunteered to take the day off work, because sitting in an empty place was better than dealing with Nicole at the bakery.

Now as she moved from room to room, she tried to imagine what it would look like when Matt really lived here. When *she* really lived here.

Just thinking the words made her both smile and

shiver. He'd asked her to move in with him shortly after he'd signed the paperwork to buy the place. They'd picked out all the furniture together, had argued about towel colors and who was going to do the cooking. They'd made love on the carpeted floor and he'd promised he would love her forever.

For all her sexual experience, Jesse had never had a real boyfriend before. Not one who called when he said, didn't explode for no reason, who seemed to love her as much as he said. It was wonderful…and terrifying. She couldn't stop wondering how long it would be until she totally screwed up everything.

That was her pattern. She'd done it all her life. Her sister kept telling her she took screwing up to a professional level. Jesse had never cared about it before because there hadn't been anything to lose. But now? Matt was everything to her. She didn't know if she would survive destroying what they had.

Which was why she hadn't yet agreed to move in with him. She was beyond scared. The love that burned inside of her was so strong, so real, it had become as much a part of her as her heartbeat. What if she did something wrong?

Matt understood why she was afraid and had told her to take her time. He'd been kind and loving and then had teased her into laughing. He was perfect, or as close as she needed a guy to be.

The doorbell rang. She hurried to the front door and let in the first of the delivery guys.

The next couple of hours passed quickly. The upstairs media room sofa came first, quickly followed by the kitchen table and chairs they'd ordered. The living room furniture was still being put into place when two guys showed up with the big bed he'd bought. A bed they'd giggled over in the showroom.

When she was finally alone, Jesse walked from room to room, seeing the town house as it was going to be. They still needed to get pictures and maybe some plants or books. Work was required to make the space lived-in, but they were getting closer.

Could she see herself here? Did she want to? She closed her eyes and imagined herself with Matt. In the living room, reading. Upstairs, watching a movie. In the shower, making love. Sleeping with him every night.

Her throat tightened as love washed over her. He was the best man she'd ever known. She would be crazy not to try to make it work, despite her fears. She could do this, couldn't she?

She was about to head upstairs to make the bed when the doorbell rang. She crossed the carpet. As far as she knew, everything had been delivered.

When she opened the door, she saw Paula standing there. The two women looked at each other.

Paula spoke first. "Matt said his furniture was being delivered today."

"It was. I let them in."

"Oh."

Obviously Paula had expected Matt to be the one waiting. She'd come by to see her son.

"Do you want to come in?" Jesse asked, hoping she would say no.

Paula nodded and stepped past her into the living room. Once there, she glanced at the leather sofa, shook her head, then faced Jesse.

"I've wanted to talk to you for a while," she said.

Inside, Jesse winced. Paula wanting to talk to her couldn't be good.

"This won't last," Paula said bluntly. "I know that sounds harsh, but it's true and the sooner you accept the truth, the easier it will be for you."

"Because you care so much about me," Jesse said bitterly, not surprised at the other woman's attack. "I'm who you're so concerned about."

"I am concerned," Paula told her. "Not that I expect you to believe that."

"Oh, good."

Paula ignored that. "Matthew is a very special man. I'm sure you've seen that in him. I'm sure that, and his money, are why you're together."

Jesse ignored the slam about the money. She hadn't known about it when she'd first met Matt and it had never mattered. But Paula wouldn't believe her so there was no point in trying to convince her.

"He is honorable and sees the best in people," the other woman continued. "What he wants them to be, rather than what they are." Paula walked over and glanced in the kitchen, then turned back to Jesse. "I'm a little like you. I have a past. Not one that we're going to discuss, but I've lived through things. I know what you are, Jesse. You're trying to be more than you were meant for and you see Matt as your way to get there. I'm sure you care about him, but you are completely out of your league with him and it's just a matter of time until he figures that out, too. Until he sees he can do better and moves on. You're simply not good enough and once he realizes that, it's going to be over."

Jesse told herself Paula was angry and bitter and her words didn't mean anything. Unfortunately, they still hurt to hear.

"You're wrong," she said quietly, holding herself still and straight. "About all of it."

"Am I? I don't think so. You won't last six months. I know you think I'm being an incredible bitch. Maybe I am. I'll admit to some anger about how you've turned Matt away from me. I wouldn't mind a little revenge. But I'm not going to bother. You know why? Because you'll be gone and I'll still be here. When he finds the right girl, he's going to marry her. That's what I'm waiting for."

Paula gave her a tight smile, then walked out of the town house.

Jesse sank onto the sofa and did her best not to cry.

"Stupid old cow," she muttered.

Paula was trying to push her away. Trying to make her doubt Matt so she would do something stupid.

That wasn't going to happen. She was stronger—stronger than Paula knew. She and Matt weren't going to break up. They loved each other. Jesse would do anything to protect their relationship.

That decided, she made her way upstairs where she went to work unpacking the boxes Matt had brought over from his mother's house. She put clothes in the new dresser and hung up shirts in the closet. The whole time she worked, she did her best to forget what Paula had said. Those words didn't matter.

Except they'd scared her because Matt's mother had said one thing that was true—she was in over her head. Being with someone like him, someone so good and loving and supportive, terrified her. She loved him so much and was desperate not to do anything wrong. If only she could shake the sense that she was going to mess it all up.

She reached for another box of stuff he'd brought over and pulled out a pile of T-shirts. As she lifted them to the bed, something fell onto the floor. She bent down to pick it up, only to gasp as she saw a small, pale blue box. A Tiffany's jewelry box.

Jesse's heart pounded in her chest. Her body went completely still just before her legs gave way and she sank to the carpet.

It was earrings, she told herself. Maybe a sort of thank-you present for helping him move. It could be for his mom, although she doubted that. Matt hadn't been getting along with Paula for weeks now. Or it could be something else. An engagement ring.

She should put it back in the box and stop unpacking, she told herself. She should pretend she never found it and just see what happened. That would make the most sense. Except she couldn't. She had to know.

Her fingers trembled as she picked up the box and opened it. Nestled on soft, white fabric sat a stunning solitaire diamond ring. The perfect engagement ring.

It was the most beautiful thing she'd ever seen, she thought, barely able to breathe. The diamond sparkled. It was probably a high-quality stone and expensive, but what reached inside and squeezed her heart was what it meant.

Matt wanted to marry her.

He loved her. He really *loved* her. He believed in her and trusted her and wanted to spend his life with her. He wanted to have children with her and grow old together. How was that possible? How had someone like him fallen for her?

"He loves me," she whispered, as she closed the box. "He loves me."

The wonder of the moment took her breath away. Her body felt light with hope, her future bright with possibilities. As long as Matt believed in her, she could believe in herself. Maybe she could go back to college and get her business degree. Maybe she could figure out a way to make it work with Nicole in the bakery.

Maybe her life didn't suck. Maybe she could be forgiven her past.

She stood and carefully tucked the ring back into the moving box and put the T-shirts on top. She moved that box back with the others in the closet and went downstairs. She would unpack the rest of the house, but leave the bedroom. She didn't want him to know she'd found the ring. She would wait until he gave it to her, until he asked her to marry him, and then she would tell him yes.

JESSE SAT ON HER BED in Nicole's house and sighed. "I'm so scared," she admitted to Drew, Nicole's husband. "He really loves me."

"Which is what you want."

"I know. It's hard to explain. I don't feel like I'm good enough. I'm terrified I'm going to mess everything up."

Jesse had never understood Nicole and Drew hooking up, let alone getting married, but it had happened. While Drew wasn't the brightest bulb in the chandelier, he was always willing to listen, which Jesse appreciated. Aside from Matt, she didn't have anyone else to talk to. Certainly not Nicole, who had an ongoing list of complaints about Jesse.

"He knows the worst about me," she continued. "He knows the worst and he's okay with it. Unbelievable but true."

"So be happy," Drew said. They were the right words, but there was something strange about him. His body language, maybe the intensity of his expression.

Jesse eyed him. "What's wrong with you tonight? You're acting, I don't know, kind of disconnected."

He moved from the chair to the side of the bed. "I want to be happy for you, Jess, but come on. You with one guy? You'll be bored in a week. You love the variety, the chase."

His words surprised her. "I *don't* love that. I love Matt."

"Or at least the idea of him."

"What? No. You're wrong. I love him."

"I don't think so." He shifted closer.

A little *too* close, she thought, moving away. Drew had been hanging out in her room and talking to her for months, but this was the first time she'd been uncomfortable.

"Maybe you should, um, go see what Nicole's doing," she said, trying to smile and not able to fake it. What was wrong with her? So Drew sat on her bed. He was Drew. They were friends. But there was something in his eyes...

"You're so pretty, Jess. Did I ever tell you that?"

Jesse couldn't move. She could barely breathe. Was he drunk? As far as she knew, Drew wasn't into drugs, but maybe that had changed. He shifted closer and put his hand on her arm.

"So pretty. You're a lot like Nicole. The long, blond hair, the blue eyes, but you're softer. Touchable. You're the kind of girl lots of guys fall for. Come on. Admit it. You like the attention."

Was he right? Sure, she'd used sex and men to feel good about herself, but not anymore. She had Matt. He loved her and wanted to marry her.

"One guy forever?" Drew asked as he leaned close and kissed her. "No way. It would be a waste."

Her mind exploded into a shrill scream, but she couldn't let out the sound. It was as if she'd actually left her body and was watching from a distance. She could see herself stiffening as his mouth pressed into hers, could feel his lips. Maybe he was right. Maybe she couldn't be faithful. Maybe...

Drew moved closer. "Oh, baby, I want you bad. I see you all the time, prancing around here in your shorts and T-shirts. You want it, too. I can tell."

He tugged at her T-shirt. Even though it was early, she'd already dressed for bed in an oversized shirt and shorts. So when he pulled it over her head and tossed it on the bed, she was nearly naked.

"Oh, yeah," he breathed as he kissed her neck. "I knew you'd have great tits."

Her eyes burned, but no tears fell. The shame was so powerful, she could taste it and still she couldn't move. Because she knew why this was happening. She knew why he had changed.

This was who she really was. All the other guys who hadn't mattered. All the times she'd used her body to hurt Nicole or to feel as if she belonged. She'd been little more than a whore and it was too late to change.

But the second Drew touched her breast, she came to her senses. She pushed his hands away.

"Stop," she told him. "You have to stop."

"What?" Drew said. "You've been practically begging for this for months."

She was just about to give him a firm shove when her bedroom door flew open.

Drew jumped up at once, leaving Jesse bare to the waist, staring into the horrified face of her sister.

"It wasn't me," Drew yelled. "It was her. She's been coming on to me for weeks, touching me, kissing me, begging me to take her. I couldn't stand it any more. I'm sorry, honey. I'm so sorry."

Jesse lay there exposed, trembling, ashamed. She pulled up the sheet to cover herself. "It wasn't like that," she whispered. "I never did that."

But it was too late. Her sister was gone and everything had changed forever.

JESSE STOOD ON THE doorstep of Matt's town house for a long time. She stared at the door, remembering how she'd first come here with him when he'd been looking for a place of his own. They'd been so happy then. So in love.

Not anymore. Not since he'd found out about that night with Drew.

Jesse didn't want to think about what had happened. How Nicole had thrown her out. She'd been so afraid, so ashamed, but Nicole hadn't wanted to listen to the truth and Drew had been plenty convincing.

That had been bad enough, but then Paula had gone looking for her again and had found Nicole instead. Her sister had been pleased to explain exactly why Jesse wasn't living there anymore, and Paula hadn't wasted any time in telling Matt.

Jesse had tried to get to him first, but he wasn't taking her calls. She'd waited for him at his work, but he'd managed to avoid her.

Her whole body hurt. She couldn't stop crying. How was it possible for one person to lose everything so fast? And yet she had.

She rang the bell and waited. She was here because she had something important to tell him. Something he would have to believe. Her stomach writhed from nerves and fear. She fought back tears. He *had* to listen to her. Somehow she would make him understand.

The door opened and Matt stood in front of her. She stared at him, feasting on seeing him for the first time in days.

He looked good. Tall and thin, but filling out from their regular visits to the gym. She'd been the one to introduce him to the idea of working out to build muscle and then he'd taken her to bed and rewarded her for her good ideas. He was very good at rewarding her, and telling her he loved her. He got this light in his eyes and what she called his special smile. Only he wasn't smiling now.

"I have nothing to say to you," he told her and started to close the door.

She threw herself against it and managed to squeeze inside. "We have to talk."

"You may have to talk but I don't have to listen."

God, he sounded so cold, she thought grimly. As if he hated her. Was that possible? Had hate replaced love this quickly?

She couldn't think about it because, if she did, she would fall apart. He was everything to her. She loved him. She who had vowed to never risk her heart had fallen for a geeky computer nerd with beautiful eyes and a smile that made her soul float.

"Matt, please," she whispered. "Please. Just hear me out. I love you."

His gaze narrowed. "Do you think your words mean anything to me? Do you think *you* do? I learn fast, Jesse. I always have. I trusted you. I gave you every part of me. I loved you. Hell, I wanted to marry you. I bought a ring. Which makes me an idiot, but it's not a mistake I'm going to make again."

She felt the tears on her cheeks and the slicing pain in her heart. "I love you, Matt."

"Bullshit. I was some fun project. Did you get a kick out of screwing the socially inept genius? Did you laugh about me with your friends?"

"It wasn't like that and you know it."

"I don't know shit about you. This was a game. You won, I lost, now get the hell away from me."

"No. I won't go until you listen. Until you understand."

"Understand what? That while you were sleeping with me, pretending to care about me, you were screwing Drew? Who else, Jess? How many other guys? I'm not asking for a total number. I doubt you can count that high. But, say, in the past two months. Less than a hundred? Less than twenty? Just give me a ballpark idea."

She cried harder, hating his words and the distance she saw in his eyes. "Stop. I'm not like that anymore."

"That's not what I heard."

"I didn't sleep with Drew," she screamed. "We used to talk. I could talk to him about stuff the way I could never talk to Nicole. That was it. Then that night he started kissing me and I freaked. I didn't know what to do."

"I'm not interested," Matt told her. "There's nothing you can say to make me care. Once a slut, always a slut. Everyone was right about you."

He was using her past against her, she thought in disbelief. She'd trusted him with her secrets, her shameful moments and now he was judging her.

"Matt, stop," she said, her voice breaking on a sob. "Don't do this. Don't take us to a place where we can't get back."

"Why not? You think you matter to me anymore? Just get out. I never want to see you again."

It hurt too much, she thought, using all her strength

to keep from sinking to the floor. She had to tell him. He had the right to know the truth, no matter what.

"I'm pregnant," she whispered.

"So what?"

She stared at him. What? He couldn't have understood her. "I told you. I didn't sleep with Drew. I'm having your baby."

"No, you're not." He spoke casually, as if he would never consider the possibility that the child might be his.

She grabbed his arm. "Matt, listen to me. This is *your* baby. Even if you hate me, you have to care about your child. I'm not lying. I can prove it. As soon as the baby's born, we'll take a DNA test."

He looked at her for a long time, then pulled free of her grip and walked to the door. "You don't get it, do you? I don't care, Jess. You're nothing to me but a regret. I don't believe that baby is mine and even if it is, I don't want a child with you. I don't want anything with you. Ever. I want you to go away. I never want to see you again. No matter what."

What scared her the most was how calmly he spoke. How easily he mouthed the words that ripped her soul apart.

She looked down, half expecting to see her body torn open and bleeding, but all the pain was on the inside.

"Matt, please," she begged.

He pulled open the door and stared outside. "Just go."

Walking took all her strength. Jesse barely made it

down the stairs to her car. She crawled into the front seat and cried until she couldn't breathe anymore. Until the emptiness threatened to swallow her. Until there was nothing left.

If he'd loved her, he would have believed her, she thought sadly, facing the truth for the first time. He hadn't loved her. They had just been words. All her dreams had meant nothing. All his promises had been meaningless. He'd sworn her past didn't matter, that no matter what, he would be there for her. And he'd lied, leaving her with an emptiness that would haunt her for the rest of her life.

CHAPTER FIFTEEN

Present Day...

JESSE TRIED TO SHAKE OFF Matt's obvious anger and hurt. The fact that Gabe had grown up with other people in his life had nothing to do with Matt being his father. Once Matt calmed down he would realize that having a great guy like Bill around had only been good for the boy.

While she could make a case for that, the guilt was harder to explain away, so she did her best to ignore it for the moment.

Paula came out of the kitchen. "I thought I heard you," she said, then stopped when she saw Bill. "Oh. Hello."

"Paula, this is Bill. He rescued me when I showed up in Spokane five years ago. He gave me a job, found me a place to live and was my friend as I tried to figure out how to be a mother to Gabe. Bill, this is Gabe's grandmother, Paula."

"Nice to meet you," Bill said, a twinkle in his eye.

"Are you sure you're that boy's grandmother? I could see his aunt."

Jesse stared at her friend. Was he flirting? It sounded like flirting, but it was behavior she'd never seen before.

Paula laughed. "Don't expect me to fall for that line, Bill. I'm past sixty."

"You don't look it." Bill turned to Gabe. "And look at you. You've grown. I barely recognized you."

Gabe giggled in delight. Bill picked him up and swung him in the air. Gabe squealed.

When Bill set Gabe down, he launched into an explanation of everything he'd done since arriving in Seattle.

"I met my daddy and he took me to see fish," Gabe said, gazing at Bill happily. "And Grandma and me made cookies a bunch of times. We go to the park every morning and there are puppies sometimes."

Bill crouched down so he was eye-level with the boy and listened attentively.

"I'm doin' math," Gabe continued. "Grandma's teaching me and she says I'm good at math, just like my daddy." He beamed with pride.

"I knew you were special," Bill told him and held him close. "I've missed you, Gabe."

Gabe hugged him back, squeezing hard. "I missed you, too."

Gabe took Bill off to see his room. Paula and Jesse went into the kitchen.

"I wondered how you made it by yourself in

Spokane," Paula said as she started a pot of coffee. "Now I know. You had friends."

"Bill was great," Jesse admitted. "Father, boss and someone to talk to all in one. I was so lucky to find him." She eyed Paula, who was a pretty woman with a giving heart. "You know, he's a widower. Has been for a while now."

Paula flushed slightly. "I don't see why that would be of interest to me. He's obviously crazy about you."

If Jesse had been drinking, she would have choked. "He's about forty years older than me."

"So?"

"I do love Bill, but like family." How could she have ever gotten interested in someone else when she'd been unable to get over Matt? "Besides, when we met, he made it clear I wasn't his type, so even if I'd had any ideas, nothing would have happened."

"It doesn't really matter," Paula murmured as she got out mugs and set them on the counter.

But Jesse wasn't so sure. Maybe it mattered a little.

An hour later she and Bill sat outside on the porch.

"I've been worried about you," Bill said. "Missing you, too. Both of you. That little boy grows on a man."

"I know. We've been thinking of you, as well."

"But you're doing okay?"

She smiled at him. "What you really want to know is if you were right to kick me out when you did. That's all you care about, but you're too polite to ask."

"You'll tell me," he said confidently.

She laughed. "Yes, I will and you were right."

"You were only living half a life, Jess. Hanging out with me and my friends. Not that we didn't appreciate your pretty face or the joy that boy brought to us, but you were hiding."

"I know." She rested her forearms on her thighs. "It's been good to be back, but hard. My sister hasn't accepted that I've changed. I think she believes me about Drew, but she's still angry."

She didn't have to explain about her past. Bill knew all her secrets.

"You've had five years to watch yourself change and grow and plenty of time to know you were coming back. Nicole got all this sprung on her. She has to adjust."

"I know that in my head. It's getting the rest of me to believe it that's taking some time. Besides, I think she secretly wants to be mad at me."

"She had a certain place in your family. Everyone has a role. You've changed yours. She's going to fight that."

Jesse had never considered that. Were family dynamics the real problem?

"If I'm different, then the balance of power, the rules, everything changes?" she asked, more to herself than him.

Bill, being Bill, didn't answer.

She was going to have to think about that some more.

"So Gabe's met his father," her friend said. "How did that go?"

"Not well. Matt's coming into his own with Gabe now, but the first couple of meetings were difficult. He didn't know how to relate to a four-year-old. Not that he's had a lot of experience." She hesitated. "We were fighting when you drove up."

"I noticed."

"He blames me for not knowing Gabe." She stared at the steps. "He says that telling him I was pregnant before I left wasn't enough. That I knew he wouldn't believe me. That I should have told him later, after Gabe was born. I should have given him a chance to be a father."

She didn't like talking about it. She felt awful inside, like she was a bad person. Like she'd been deliberately evil.

"It wasn't like that," she whispered. "I wanted him to care enough to believe me. I wanted him to come after me."

"Did you know he didn't believe you about the baby?"

She nodded. "What he said was so horrible." Once a slut, always a slut. Those words were burned into her brain.

"How would you feel if he'd kept Gabe from you?" Bill asked quietly.

Jesse felt pain rip through her body and had her answer. "Oh, God." To not have held him when he was born. To not have watched him grow. His first smile, his first step, the love in his eyes. The absolute trust. Thousands of perfect memories that would be with her always.

"He'll never forgive me," she whispered. "Why would he?"

Bill put his arm around her. "He's angry now, but he'll get over it."

"You don't know that."

"A man doesn't have that much emotion in himself without still caring."

"I don't know what he thinks about me," she admitted, letting herself lean on him again. Something she was going to have to stop doing. "Sometimes I think he really likes being with me and other times—" she sighed "—he's so different."

"You were gone a long time."

"I know. The Matt I knew loved me. At least I thought he did. That's what's confusing. I believed him when he said how important I was, how he would never leave. But the first time something went wrong, he turned his back on me."

"It was a big thing to go wrong."

She nodded. "I probably played into his worst fears. That it was just a game to me. That I didn't care about him at all."

"He reacted," Bill said. "If you'd stayed around, talked again, maybe things would have been different."

Would they? Jesse wasn't sure. "I couldn't have

stayed. I would only ever have been Nicole's screwup little sister. The useless girl who fell in love with a great guy. I needed to walk away to find out who I was."

She smiled. "That sounds so 'other dimension.' I should probably start chanting."

Bill chuckled.

"There's so much going on," she said. "The bakery burned down."

She told him about that and how they'd started up the business in a rented kitchen. "Nicole is hating the success. I know she is."

"You're only responsible for yourself, Jess. And that's the only person you can control. Other people will either get it or they won't but you can't define yourself by their opinions."

"You're just so rational. Have I mentioned that's annoying?"

"Once or twice."

She turned toward him. "I wouldn't have made it without you."

"You would have done just fine."

She knew that wasn't true, but why worry about it? She'd met Bill and she'd thrived. She glanced at the house.

"Paula is nice," she said. "An unexpected supporter. And pretty."

Bill looked at her. "What's your point, missy?"

"That you've been living alone long enough. Maybe it's time to consider the possibilities."

She'd teased Bill about other women before and he'd always politely dismissed her. This time he followed her gaze to the house and nodded slowly.

"Maybe it is."

HEATH TOSSED A FOLDER onto Matt's desk. "You'll want to look them over, make sure we're doing everything you want," he said.

Matt waved him into a seat, then opened the folder and flipped through the papers. Despite the legal language, the intent was clear. He was suing Jesse for full custody of his son.

"I'll study them tonight," he said.

Heath frowned. "You sure about this, Matt? I understand wanting Jesse punished, but taking the kid? That's a big responsibility."

Matt knew his lawyer meant well. If their circumstances were reversed, Heath would do all he could to avoid having a child in his life. When Matt had first started down this road, he'd only been out for revenge. Now he wanted more.

The good side of him wanted to make sure he had a relationship with his son. He wanted to get to know him, watch him grow, be there for him. But the dark side of him, the side that still raged against all he had lost, wanted Jesse to feel what he felt. He wanted her to know the bone-crushing sense of having lost something that could never be recovered.

"I can handle Gabe," he said.

"Okay. If she's not going to just hand him over, you're looking at a long court battle."

"She'll fight."

She would take him on and do everything she could to keep Gabe, but in the end he would win. He had the resources and he wanted revenge.

"I'll get these back to you by the end of the week," he said, touching the folder.

"That works. When do you want me to have her served?"

The first step in the battle. "I'll let you know."

ORDERS CAME IN AT an insane rate. *Good Morning America* had decided to go ahead with the story, despite the fire, changing the focus from how a small local business grows and changes with the times to how a small business can survive disaster. They'd turned it into a series, of which Keyes Bakery was just a small part, but those few minutes of airtime had tripled their already impressive Internet orders.

Jesse walked through the controlled chaos of the rented kitchen. At least here she could bury herself in work and forget the insanity that was her personal life. She'd come back to Seattle with a plan. While things hadn't worked out the way she'd thought they would, they'd still worked out for the better. She was getting the opportunity to show that her ideas were well-considered and successful. The fire, caused by a short in an aging electrical system, had given her an unexpected chance to shine.

She walked into the front of the restaurant, where all the shipping took place and where she and Nicole each had a desk with a computer. In the corner, two college girls answered the ever-ringing phone as people called in yet more orders. They had more business than they could handle. It was the best feeling in the world.

She crossed to Nicole's desk and pulled up a chair. "I talked to Ralph yesterday."

Nicole looked confused. "Who's Ralph?"

"The guy who owns the sandwich shop across the street."

Nicole's face immediately scrunched up. "Jesse, honestly, you're looking for ways to complicate our lives. We're a little busy now, but things will calm down. We're fine."

Jesse felt the familiar frustration building inside of her. "We're not fine. We're late on more than fifty percent of our Internet orders because we can't keep up with volume. We're drowning in potential success and if we're not careful, we're going to go under. Ralph bakes his own bread. He has specialty ovens that would be perfect for the brownies. We could bake eight triple batches at a time. He's willing to rent the space to us from eleven at night until eight in the morning. That's plenty of time to get out all the brownies we'll need, freeing up the ovens here for the cakes."

Jesse handed over the information she'd printed out that morning. "The rent is incredibly reasonable. He's excited to have the extra cash. We pay for the increase in electricity and that's it. Our only start-up costs will be extra pans for the brownies and a few more bodies."

Nicole shook her head. "I just don't know," she began.

Because she didn't want to know, Jesse thought, frustrated and annoyed.

She stood and grabbed her sister by the arm. "Okay, that's it. Come with me."

Nicole jerked free. "What are you doing?"

"You and me. Outside. We're going to have this out. I'm tired of almost fighting with you every single day. Let's get this settled."

For a second she thought Nicole was going to refuse, but then her sister followed her out into the parking lot where they faced each other in the light morning rain.

They stared at each other, arms folded, both glaring. Jesse figured she was the one who had called the meeting so she got to go first. She thought about all the rational things she and Bill had discussed, then spoke from her gut.

"You're seriously pissed off because I'm making this work," she said. "You're angry that I came back and you resent that I know what I'm doing. You can't stand not being the good sister anymore. You want me to go back to being the screwup, because that's the world you know and it's a lot more comfortable than facing me as an equal."

Nicole stiffened. "You want to be honest? Fine. I'll be honest. Who the hell are you to waltz back into my life and try to take over? Where have you been for the past decade while I was struggling to hold it all together? I took care of you your entire life, Jesse. I was the one who was always there for you, who handled things and grew up too fast so you still got to be a kid. But does that matter? Of course not. It has to be about you. So you're back. Let's hold a parade. Jesse got her life together and is willing to work with me now. I'm all quivery inside. Yes, you got it together, but you know what? I never lost it. I never had to go off and find myself. I was too busy being here, running the business on my own."

They were hard words to hear, probably because they were the truth, Jesse thought sadly. "I'm sorry," she said quietly.

"Sorry?" Nicole's voice was shrill. "Sorry isn't good enough. Who the hell are you to show up and make it better? I've busted my ass here for years and you're the one who will reap all the rewards. Do you think I like that? Do you think I'm proud of how I'm acting? I don't know how to fix it. I don't trust the new you. I keep waiting for the mistake, because I believe it's coming and I wonder how big it's going to be this time."

"You don't trust me?" Jesse asked, stunned.

"Why should I? You've been home five minutes.

You won't even acknowledge what you did last time. No one else knows the reason we're doing so well on the Internet is that you have practice."

She was bringing that up now? "You do realize it's been five years," Jesse said.

"You stole the family recipe for chocolate cakes, baked them yourself and sold them on the Internet."

Jesse couldn't argue with that. She had. "You fired me from the bakery."

"I thought you'd slept with Drew."

"Yeah, and I hadn't. You fired me for something I didn't do. I had to earn a living."

"You could have gotten a job."

"The bakery was all I knew. Besides, I'm half owner, remember? So I owned that recipe, too. How could I steal what was already mine?"

They stared at each other, the tension practically pulsing between them.

Nicole looked away first. "At least admit you showed bad judgment."

"I did," Jesse said easily, knowing it was true. "You'd hurt me and I wanted to hurt you back. So I sold the cakes. I knew that would make you crazy."

Nicole nodded. "Thanks for saying that. For what it's worth, you did make me crazy." She looked at the ground, then back at Jesse. "I'm sorry I didn't believe you about Drew. There are a lot of reasons I didn't. Your past, how you were always being so difficult. But mostly I wanted you to be the bad guy because then I didn't have to look at myself. Like you said before, if you slept with him, I wasn't the reason the marriage failed."

Jesse absorbed the words, letting them fill her with peace. Finally, she thought. That had been a long time coming.

"You weren't the reason your marriage failed," she said, able to be generous now. "He was. Drew was a jerk."

Nicole gave a half laugh, half sob. "Yeah, and I picked him. I know I shouldn't have married him. I knew it was a mistake when I said yes. I guess I was afraid no one else would ask."

Jesse moved to her sister and held her. "That's crazy. You're beautiful and smart and funny. Guys love that. Look at the guy you're married to now. Hawk is a total hottie."

"I know. Sometimes I look at him and wonder how I got so lucky."

Jesse stepped back. "As long as he thinks the same thing about you."

"He does. Who would have thought."

They looked at each other. Jesse knew the harmony was tentative at best, but there was more to be said.

"We need to rent the space across the street. It's cheap, it's close and it's short-term, so the risk is minimal. If we don't keep up with orders, we'll lose everything."

Nicole gritted her teeth, then nodded. "I know you're right. I don't like it, but I know it."

"I'm sorry I came back with an attitude," Jesse continued. "I didn't mean to imply I'm better because I've changed. But you're not better because you didn't have to change. Because you *do* need to be different. We can't keep the old roles we had before. I'll always be your sister, but I'm not the person you knew. Everything is different. We have to get to know each other all over again and figure out how we fit. I want us to be family, but if you can't get over the past, that's not going to happen."

"I know," Nicole said softly. "I see what's wrong, but I'm not sure how to change it. We've each lived such different lives."

Meaning what? They had nothing in common anymore? They couldn't be close? Had their connection been lost to hurt feelings and time?

The front door opened and Sid stuck out his head. "Nicole, you got a call. Walker Buchanan. He runs the Buchanan restaurants. He says he's interested in stocking our cakes. Want me to take a message?"

Jesse smiled at her. "Buchanan's, huh? That's the big time."

"I know. I should take the call."

Jesse watched her walk away. She felt both better and worse. Some of the problem between her and Nicole had been solved, but new roadblocks were now in place. Was her sister willing to accept who she was today? Was the past really, if not forgotten, then forgiven? And if it wasn't, how would Jesse ever be able to make things right and prove herself?

CHAPTER SIXTEEN

MATT WOKE UP RESTLESS after a bad night's sleep. He couldn't stop thinking about how Gabe had run to Bill, like the old man was the kid's father. Just as bad, he couldn't shake thoughts of Jesse either.

His plan was working. They were getting closer. Soon he would be in the right place; he would win everything. So why didn't he feel better about the situation? Why didn't he have that powerful sense of victory that came when he was about to launch a great new game? He had everything he'd ever wanted and he couldn't shake the feeling of "So what?"

He drove to the office where Diane watched him as he greeted her.

"What's wrong?" she asked, following him into his office.

"Nothing."

"You look like something's wrong. Is it Jesse?"

She knew too much, he thought, reminding himself to tell her less. He'd made the mistake of talking about Gabe and Jesse when they'd first arrived.

"It's not Jesse."

"Of course it is. What else would it be? It's been five years since she left town. Is having her back better or worse?"

"Both," he admitted.

"So you still have feelings for her."

"No." He didn't have feelings for anyone. He knew better. Jesse had taught him that. Except she'd never betrayed him. She'd been caught up in circumstances that had conspired to make her look bad. Because of her past, he'd believed her sister rather than her.

No, he told himself. Not because of her past. Because a part of him had never thought he could win someone like her. Someone smart and funny and beautiful and totally into him. She'd been his fantasy and what guy got to keep his fantasy?

It was different today. *He* was different. He knew he could get any woman he wanted. It made other men envy him. But the price of that was there weren't any more fantasies. There was only the women who came and went in his life, interchangeable beauties who offered all they had and left him completely unmoved.

"Matt?" Diane watched him. "Are you all right?"

She was concerned because that was her nature. She worried about him. For the past few years, she'd been the closest thing to a connection he'd allowed himself. His assistant. A hell of a legacy, he thought.

"I have to go," he told her. "I'll check in later."

He drove around the city and found himself parked in front of his mother's house. It was early, so he called before walking up to the door.

"You up?" he asked when she answered.

"Sure. Want some coffee?"

He joined her inside, sitting in the renovated kitchen, following her movements as she made a fresh pot, then offered him breakfast.

"Coffee's fine," he told her.

She looked good. Older. He liked her new shorter hairstyle. He studied the wrinkles around her eyes, then did the math. She was in her sixties now. While he'd always had Diane send flowers for her birthday, he hadn't called or done anything to celebrate. He'd never forgiven her for being happy about Jesse's infidelity. Never forgiven her for not wanting to lose him.

He knew all about her past, about why she'd held on so tight. When he'd been younger, he'd appreciated her support. If that was her biggest flaw, he'd gotten off very lucky.

He swore under his breath, walked around the high counter and pulled her against him.

"I'm sorry, Mom," he said. "I've been gone too long."

She was stiff with surprise, then softened in his embrace and hung on to him with a fierceness that spoke of pain and love.

"You had to be yourself," she said.

He rubbed her back, feeling how small she was. "You're giving me too much credit. I wanted to hurt you. I was a selfish bastard, thinking staying away was the worst thing I could do. What I didn't see was how I was punishing myself."

"Oh, Matthew," she breathed, her voice muffled as she clung to him.

"I hope you'll be able to forgive me and give me another chance."

She stepped back and smiled at him, her eyes bright with tears and love. "There's nothing to forgive."

He thought about Gabe, his growing feelings for the boy. How he wrestled with a fierce protectiveness that was unlike anything he'd experienced before. How much bigger would that feeling be if he'd known him longer, had been with him since birth? Is that what his mother felt for him?

He returned to his seat while she poured coffee. She kept looking at him, as if checking to see he was real. She smiled as she handed him his mug.

"Normally Gabe would be in here, making a mess, but Bill took him out for breakfast."

"Not someone I want to talk about," Matt grumbled. "He knows Gabe better than I do."

"He's known him longer, but that will change. You should be happy. Jesse and Gabe had someone special to care for them while they were gone. Bill's a good man."

There was something in her voice. He looked at her. "How do you know him so well?"

"I don't. We just met a couple of days ago. But

there's a strength about him, a steadiness. I'm glad Jesse wasn't completely on her own."

Matt knew he should be glad, too, but he wasn't. He resented everything about the other man, especially the look on Gabe's face when he'd run to him.

"Being alone with a baby is a frightening thing," his mother said. "I was alone with you and I was terrified. You were so small and it was all up to me. But having you changed me. I finally grew up." She sighed. "It only took me thirty-plus years."

He wasn't sure where she was going with this. "You were always there for me," he said. "No matter what."

"I loved you with every part of me," she said as she leaned on the counter and held her coffee. "You were so different from me. So smart. Scary smart. You were eight when you took apart your first computer. You were ten when you learned how to put them back together."

He remembered that. He'd been far more interested in the insides of a computer than what it could do. Once he understood the basics, fixing them, making them better, was easy.

"You were right about me," she said quietly, not meeting his gaze. "Before. I resented your relationship with Jesse. I could see it was different. *You* were different with her. You'd never had a lot of girls around. I knew you'd grow into yourself and figure it out. I just didn't think it would happen when it did. I wanted to keep you with me forever and she showed me that wasn't going to happen."

She looked up and gave a sad smile. "I turned into someone I didn't like. A clinging, horrible person who cared more about herself than her child. I knew you were in love with her and I was thrilled when Nicole said she'd been cheating on you. I couldn't wait to tell you. What I didn't think through was how much you would be hurt or how you would see my actions for what they were. I never thought I'd lose you."

"Mom," he began, but she shook her head.

"No. Let me say this. I was wrong, Matthew. Very wrong. I was selfish and I hurt you. I'm sorry."

They were the words he'd been waiting to hear. For the second time that morning, he walked around the high counter and held her. She set down her coffee and hugged him, then began to cry.

"I'm sorry," she said again.

"I understand," he told her. "It's all right. I love you. I'll always love you. I shouldn't have waited this long to come back to see you. I was a thoughtless bastard and I'm sorry."

A part of him, a cold empty place, filled a little.

She pulled back and brushed her face with her fingers. "I'm a mess."

"You're fine."

"I'm a cliché, but I can live with that." She smiled at him through her tears. "I've missed you."

"I've missed you, too." He hadn't allowed himself

to feel it, but it had been there. "I didn't get the parent thing before, but I do now."

She nodded. "You're doing better with Gabe. He's wonderful."

The angry surge caught him off guard. "I shouldn't have to be doing better. I should have known him all this time. Yes, Jesse told me she was pregnant, but she knew I didn't think the baby was mine. She should have tried again. She should have tried harder."

Paula shifted uncomfortably. "I understand your frustration and I agree."

He narrowed his gaze. "But?"

"But she was young and scared and hurt. No one believed her. No one would listen. Not even the man she loved most in the world."

Matt didn't want to think of it that way. He didn't want to see her side. "She could have picked up the phone. How hard would that be? I can't get back what I lost."

"I know." She touched his arm. "Believe me, I know what we've all lost. I keep thinking if I'd acted differently, if I'd welcomed Jesse instead of pushing her away, none of this would have happened. I wouldn't have gone to Nicole's that day and heard about Drew. You two probably would have gotten married. We would have been a family all this time."

He remembered the diamond solitaire he'd bought at Tiffany's. How excited and in love he'd been. He'd wanted to give Jesse something as perfect as possible, something to show how much he loved her. He'd wanted her to know she was his world.

What would have been different if he hadn't learned about Drew the way he had? If she'd calmly told him about that night. He probably would have gone over and beaten the crap out of the bastard. Based on what he knew about Drew, that might have helped out everyone.

Then he pushed the thoughts from his mind. What did he care about what ifs? There was only the now. Jesse had gone away, taking his child with her. She'd shown him he was a fool to ever love, to ever trust. She'd returned and handed him the perfect means for revenge. It was the cycle of life.

"I need to get back to work," he said, kissing his mom's forehead. "I'll call you soon."

"We can all have dinner."

Like a family. Like everything was perfectly all right. It was a battle strategy any general would be proud of. Lull the enemy into a false sense of security, then attack.

Except Jesse wasn't the enemy. She was the mother of his child and the woman he had once loved.

He reminded himself this wasn't the time to get soft. Didn't he want her punished for what she'd done?

He remembered the look on Gabe's face as his son had gleefully run toward another man who was very much the father Matt should have been, then hardened himself against any weakness. Victory was close. He could feel it. He would claim it and move on.

NICOLE SAT ON THE REAR deck of her house, coffee cup in hand. Eric was at a friend's house and the twins were, for once, sleeping at the same time. She told herself she should enjoy her rare moment of solitude, but she couldn't. She couldn't stop thinking about Jesse and their most recent fight.

They were both right and both wrong, she thought sadly. Both so determined to come out on top, in terms of righteous anger. Maybe her a little more than her sister. Jesse wanted her to see all the changes she'd made, acknowledge how she'd grown. Nicole wanted proof that everything was different. Once she got that in writing, she might be willing to believe.

She took a sip of coffee, then nearly choked when a familiar male voice said, "You get more beautiful every year. I'm never going to find someone who measures up to you."

She turned, shrieked, set her coffee cup on the deck and raced toward the tall, good-looking man standing on the stairs.

"Raoul! You're here! What are you doing here? You didn't call. Does Hawk know about this? Are you okay?"

She threw herself at him and he caught her and held her just as tight. "You look good," she said, taking in the strong, handsome face, the well-cut clothes.

"Thank you. I've been working out."

She laughed at the joke, then motioned for him to follow her inside.

Raoul did more than work out. He'd just signed with the Dallas Cowboys after graduating from Oklahoma, where Hawk had gone.

"Did you get that investment material I e-mailed you?" she asked as they entered the kitchen. "You can only spend so much of your signing bonus. You need to think of your future. You won't be in the NFL forever."

Raoul hugged her again and then kissed her cheek. "You always worry about me. If not about my grades, then who I'm dating and if she's good enough for me. You're—"

"Do *not* say I'm like your mother. I'll be forced to kill you." There were only ten years between them. Nicole didn't need any more help feeling old. The current state of her life was enough to leave her exhausted.

"You were born to nurture," he said instead.

"An average save. Not a great one, and I expect greatness from you."

"I know."

They smiled at each other.

Nicole had met Raoul five years ago, the same day she'd met Hawk. Raoul had been a senior in high school, dating Hawk's daughter and living on the streets. It had been weeks after Jesse had left. Nicole had offered Raoul a place to stay and they'd been family ever since. In many ways she thought of him as a replacement for Jesse…only he'd managed not to screw up his life.

Except Jesse hadn't screwed up hers, either. Not for the past five years.

"What's wrong?" he asked.

"Nothing. Everything. You don't want to hear about it."

He led her to the kitchen table and pulled out a chair. "Sit. Tell me what's happening."

She sat. "Jesse's back."

He settled across from her. His lack of surprise made her think Hawk had probably already told him that.

"And?" he asked.

"And I just don't know anything."

She began slowly, telling him about her sister's unexpected arrival. The words came faster and faster, the confusion about what to think, Jesse's business plan, the fire, how she, Nicole, seemed to have turned into a bitch.

"She's my sister. Of course I love her. Why am I doing this?"

"Because you're afraid of getting hurt again."

Nicole stared at him. "What?"

"She hurt you before by leaving. What if she leaves again? So you hold back. You've always had a giving heart, Nicole. That's why you love so much. But you're afraid."

Was that it? As simple as that? Fear of being rejected by Jesse again?

Tears filled her eyes. "When did you get so smart?"

"About eighteen months ago. It was a Thursday."

She laughed, which helped her control the tears. "I miss having you around. Now you're moving to Dallas. What's up with that?"

"You know how much they paid me."

"So you're saying you can be bought?"

He grinned. "Absolutely."

"I'm so proud of you, Raoul."

He squeezed her hand.

She wiped her face. "Okay, enough about my problems. Are you seeing anyone? Because that last girl you brought home was way too snotty for my taste. Can't you find a nice girl?"

"You don't think any of them are good enough for me."

"You're right about that. But we can always hope for a miracle."

JESSE WALKED THROUGH THE kitchen, pointing as she went. "We're mostly doing the cakes here. They take a lot of work and these ovens are better."

Claire glanced across the street at the small sandwich shop. "You're really baking the brownies over there?"

Jesse grinned. "The bread ovens are perfect. The heat's even, the racks are close together, which isn't a problem because brownies are flat. We bake them there, cool them, then run them across traffic at six in the morning."

Claire winced. "Tell me everyone is crossing at the corner."

Jesse laughed and patted her arm. "You're such a worrier."

"I can't help it."

They moved into the front of the rented restaurant where controlled chaos ruled. "All the shipping and order-taking happens here. Most of our orders come in online which is much easier than answering the phone. We have our specialized boxes, our packing material. We stack the ready-to-go packages over there."

Claire turned in a slow circle. "Very impressive. I can't believe how fast you've pulled this all together."

"I know. It's been great. Normally after a fire like we had, we'd need to shut down or at least lay people off. We've hired more. Business is great. Specializing in just a couple of items has cut down on our inventory needs. We can get bigger discounts because we're buying a few items in larger bulk."

She drew in a breath. Claire nodded, but there was a slight glaze to her expression. "I've lost you," Jesse teased. "You're so not into this."

"No, it's great." Claire shrugged. "Okay. Maybe not. I guess I don't have the bakery in my veins as much as I thought."

"You're forgiven. I've never been able to play the piano."

Jesse frequently wondered what quirk of DNA had allowed her sister to be such a brilliant pianist. How did that happen? Was it deliberate or just one of those things?

Claire picked up an order form. "I can't believe you pulled all this together so fast."

"You're not alone in that." Jesse held up both hands. "Sorry. Pretend I didn't say that. I'm trying to work on my attitude."

"Still frustrated by Nicole?"

"Yes. And myself for letting her get to me." Jesse crossed her arms over her chest. "I keep playing the same conversation over and over in my head. She didn't trust me. She still doesn't trust me. She wants me to fail. Then I tell myself that she needs more time, that we're slowly working things out. Blah, blah, blah. I want to move on."

"You want things back the way they were," Claire said softly. "You want the bad stuff to have never happened."

"That, too," Jesse admitted. "But there's a fantasy that will never be fulfilled. The situation exists. It can't be changed."

"She never stopped loving you," Claire told her. "She missed you all the time."

Jesse tried to find comfort in that. "Then why didn't she get in touch with me? You did. I wasn't that hard to find."

"Nicole is different."

"Stubborn. The Queen of Stubborn."

"You share that title."

Jesse didn't say anything because she thought Claire might be right.

"She could have sent a postcard," she grumbled.

"So could you." Claire sighed. "She wanted to reconnect, but I don't think she knew how."

"Because she wasn't ready to forgive me for something I didn't do."

"She didn't know that."

"I tried to tell her and she wouldn't listen. She thought she knew everything. She thought I was the kind of person who would sleep with my sister's husband."

That's what hurt the most. That Nicole had believed the worst about her.

"So Nicole isn't the only one who has to think about offering forgiveness."

Jesse opened her mouth and closed it. Was that the next step? Forgiving Nicole for thinking badly of her? Was Jesse ready for that?

"I'm very comfortable being right," she admitted.

"We all are. But sometimes it's a lonely place."

JESSE'S DAY OF self-exploration and humility continued when Matt showed up that evening to spend some time with his son. She kept to the background as he and Gabe discovered the thrill of the remote car he'd brought over.

It had big wheels and a sturdy control that was easy to learn. Gabe made the car go forward and back, then giggled as he tipped it on a turn and it automatically righted itself.

"Excellent choice," she murmured as Gabe went chasing after the car down the hallway. "He loves it."

"I did a lot of research online," Matt told her. "This had the highest rating."

She wasn't surprised he'd taken the time to find the toy, then buy it. The Matt she knew had always been thorough and thoughtful. When they'd been together, he'd taken care of her.

While he played with his son, she allowed herself to think about what Paula had said a few days before. How everything would have been different if Matt hadn't found out about Nicole's accusations the way he did. If she, Jesse, had been able to tell him herself.

Would they have made it? Would he have offered her that diamond ring? She knew she would have accepted his proposal. She would have been terrified of screwing up everything, but she'd loved him too much not to try.

She tried to imagine what their life would have been like, if only things had gone differently. Gabe would have grown up knowing his father. There might even be other children. She and Matt would have been together over five years now. An old married couple.

Happy, she thought wistfully. They could have been happy.

Later, Matt helped put Gabe to bed. He supervised the ritual of him brushing his teeth, then tucked him in bed and read him a story. Jesse sat curled up in a corner chair, watching the two of them together, feeling heartsick over all Gabe and Matt had missed.

Because she hadn't just cheated the man she'd loved, she'd also cheated her child.

When Gabe had fallen asleep, she and Matt crept out of his room. She shut the door, then led the way back into the family room.

"He goes to bed early," Matt said, glancing at the clock.

"He still needs a lot of sleep. He was taking naps until his last birthday."

Matt nodded without saying anything. She had a feeling he was thinking he should know that.

"How late will my mom be out?" he asked.

"They're going to dinner, then catching a late movie." This was the first time Paula and Bill had gone out together. Jesse was excited for them but Matt didn't seem that thrilled.

"You okay here on your own?"

She nodded. Being by herself with Gabe wasn't anything new. She'd lived it for years.

Guilt flared up inside of her and made her hate herself. She looked at the man she'd wanted to love forever and wished everything could have been different.

"I'm sorry," she said quickly, wanting to get it all out at once. "I'm really sorry I kept Gabe from you. You were right about all that. I knew you didn't believe me and I couldn't seem to see past that. I kept waiting for you to come after me, to find me and tell me you were wrong or at least that you were willing to listen to me. I never thought about it from your perspective. That you hadn't believed me when I said the baby was yours. I should have given you another chance to know him. I should have called when he was born."

She paused because her throat hurt and it was hard to get out the words. She felt awful inside.

"I was wrong," she said quietly. "I'm sorry."

Matt stood there, looking at her, judging her, she knew. "I can't get that time back."

It was like he'd stabbed her. "I know."

"You didn't have the right."

If only she could go back in time and undo all her mistakes.

He reached out and grabbed her, then pulled her close. "Dammit, Jesse, what am I going to do with you?"

Before she could figure out what he meant, his mouth was on hers.

The kiss was hot and tempting, an unexpected reaction to their conversation. He held her against him as if he would never let go.

Wouldn't that be wonderful? she thought as she gave in to the sweet, erotic pressure of his lips on hers. She kissed him back, pressing against him, trying to let her body speak for her. Trying to let it say how much he mattered, how sorry she was, how she wanted things to be different.

She wrapped her arms around him, holding on as if she would never let go. When his tongue swept across her lower lip, she parted for him and groaned when he pushed inside.

They teased each other, touching, brushing, circling. He ran his hands up and down her back, then raised them and cupped her face.

"I want you, Jess," he breathed.

Magic words, she thought as her blood heated and need made her insides quiver. Words she'd waited a long time to hear.

CHAPTER SEVENTEEN

WITHOUT SPEAKING, JESSE took Matt's hand and led him down the hall, to her room. Once inside, he shut the door, then drew her close and kissed her. At the same time, he cupped her butt, causing her to arch against him. He was already hard.

Liquid heat settled between her legs, making her long for more than just standing and kissing. She wanted them naked, touching, pleasuring each other. Somehow this wasn't like the last time. Maybe because the emotional connection had returned.

He nudged her backward until she felt the bed behind her thighs, then he gently lowered her down on the mattress, with her legs dangling to the floor. He bent over her and pulled up her T-shirt, then kissed her belly.

He tickled and teased, kissing, licking, blowing on her skin. It was just her stomach—it shouldn't have done much more than tickle. Yet her breasts swelled and she squirmed, wanting him to touch her lower.

She grabbed the hem of her shirt and pulled it off. Matt smiled. "That's my girl."

He slid a hand under her and unfastened her bra, then removed it. She was bare to the waist and breathless in anticipation.

Her nipples ached for his touch. She wanted him kissing her there, licking and sucking. Wanting grew as she imagined the sensation. Her hips pulsed slightly. He bent down and pressed his mouth to hers. At the same time, he lightly stroked her breasts, exploring the curves, circling around, getting close but never actually touching her nipples.

She felt them getting hard. An ache began, low in her belly. She was hot and wet and more than ready. She wanted to push off her jeans and panties and beg him to fill her.

Sure the kissing was great. She loved closing her lips around his tongue and sucking so that he stiffened and groaned. She enjoyed the feel of his hard muscles, the thudding of his heart, the anticipation, but could he get to it already?

He pulled back slightly and trailed his mouth down the side of her neck. She held her breath as he got closer and closer to her breasts, then he moved between them and back to her belly.

She gasped in disappointment.

He raised his head. She saw the teasing light in his eyes. "What?" he asked innocently.

"You know what."

His expression turned both passionate and knowing. "This?" he asked, flicking his tongue against her nipple. "Is this it?"

She groaned. Warmth and need poured through her, settling between her legs.

He did all that she'd imagined and more. He made love to her breasts until she was both tense and ready to explode. It was as if there was a direct connection between her chest and that spot between her thighs.

He sucked hard enough to make her groan and nearly come, all the while running his hands up and down her arms. Then he reached for the waistband of her jeans and unfastened the button. He lowered the zipper, then pulled off the rest of her clothes.

When she was naked, he knelt on the floor, parted her and kissed her between her legs. She was exposed and had nothing to brace herself on, nothing to do but enjoy the moment and give in to him.

He relearned all of her, finding familiar places that made her tremble and lose control. As he zeroed in on that one spot, she found herself racing toward her climax and did her best to hold back. Not yet, she thought. Not so fast.

She clutched at the bed, then when he withdrew slightly, pushed herself toward him. He couldn't stop, she thought as her muscles tensed and the inevitable pleasure loomed closer. Not yet.

He licked her over and over again, then slipped a finger inside of her, imitating the final act of lovemaking. She felt the exact second he curled up his finger, so he touched her clit from the inside as well as with his tongue.

The pleasure was exquisite. Every muscle in her body tightened. She wanted to lose herself in the moment, but just as much she wanted to give herself to him…to this. She wanted him to make her come, as if that act would somehow heal them both.

Then she couldn't think because it felt too good. There was too much, the touching, the rubbing. Tension grew until it was easy to simply give in to the pressure and let the thunder shake her into her release.

She writhed as her body surrendered to his touch. She groaned and gasped, then rode the climax as he drew it out, moving just as quickly but more gently, exactly the way she liked. As if he'd remembered what pleased her.

When she was done, she opened her eyes and found him staring at her intently. His eyes were dark with need and his mouth twisted slightly.

"What?" she asked, suddenly worried. "Are you okay?"

"No." He stood up and swore, then began ripping at his clothes. "I nearly lost it while you were coming. I'm too old for that. What the hell are you doing to me?"

His shirt went flying. He kicked off his shoes, ripped off his socks, then pulled a condom out of his pocket and dropped his pants. He was already hard and, judging from his breathing, more than ready to be inside of her.

Delighted beyond words, she scrambled back on the bed, ready to welcome him. He knelt on the mattress, put on the condom, then moved between her legs.

"I'm better than this," he growled as he braced himself. "I have learned a thing or two. I'm good, dammit."

"Of course you are," she soothed, trying not to giggle. "Matt, it's okay. I like that you're out of control. Just go for it."

He kissed her once, then took her at her word, filling her in one fast, deep thrust. She held on to him, riding him as he took her hard.

There was nothing he could do she wouldn't like, no way he could touch her that didn't bring her pleasure. They were meant to be together, she thought as he pushed in again and, seconds later, gave in to his orgasm.

They held on to each other, joined. Maybe the past couldn't be undone, but the present could be healed, she thought as hope filled her chest and made her believe in possibilities. Because her heart had only ever belonged to one man and she would do anything to win him back.

JESSE FLOATED INTO THE bakery. After last night, she felt so amazing that she thought she might actually be glowing. It wasn't just the sex, either. The last time they'd done it, technically she'd had no complaints. But the previous evening had been different—she'd been with the man she remembered. The man she loved. Not some guy with something to prove and that made all the difference in the world.

She was hopeful that she and Matt could find their way back together. Okay, it was a long shot, but she knew there were still feelings there. Still a connection. She was willing to be patient, but wouldn't it be amazing if they could fall in love again? He was the only man who had ever touched her heart. To be with him, the father of her child, the man who owned her heart, would be beyond extraordinary.

But first there was a bakery to run, she thought as she forced herself to concentrate on reviewing the orders that had come in during the night. The fresh brownies sat on trays on the tables lining one side of the front of the store. Sid and Jasper had the second batch of cakes in the oven. Everything was going smoothly. It was nearly eight in the morning when Nicole showed up, her serious expression making Jesse's good mood start to fizzle.

No, she thought as she stood and looked at her sister. She wasn't going to let Nicole ruin what was a perfectly excellent morning.

"Just so we're clear," she said. "I'm not fighting with you. There's nothing you can say or do to make me angry."

Nicole nodded, then surprised her by starting to cry. "Is that really what you think of me?" her sister asked. "That I only want to fight with you? I know it is and it's my fault. I'm sorry."

The unexpected confession nearly brought Jesse to her knees. She crossed to Nicole and hugged her. "No. I don't think that. I don't. I'm sorry. I just reacted."

"Because we've been fighting." Nicole hugged her back, then moved away and wiped her face. "It's all right. I deserve what you said. Probably more. It's been such a shock having you here. I was barely getting used to that when the bakery burned down."

"I know. It's okay." Jesse felt awful.

Nicole ignored her. "It's not okay. I've been thinking a lot about what you said and I don't like the truth, even though I can't escape it. The reality is I wanted you to be the guilty party with Drew. I wanted you to be the reason he cheated on me because if it wasn't you, it was him. It was me. I needed to blame you, so I took the easy way out. That was wrong of me and I'm really, really sorry."

"Nicole, don't blame yourself."

"Why not? I did it all. I threw you out. You're my baby sister and I love you and I sacrificed you because I was hurt and angry and I wouldn't see the truth. I sent you away when you were pregnant. How could I have done that?"

"You didn't send me away," Jesse told her firmly. "I left on my own and it's the best thing I could have done."

"What if it wasn't? What if you hadn't found a job and somewhere to live? What if something awful had happened?"

Jesse noticed Jasper and Sid had disappeared into

the kitchen, not that she could blame them. They wouldn't want to be a part of this emotional moment. Even as she and Nicole talked it out, they were probably in the back, covering their ears and humming.

Jesse touched her shoulder. "If something awful had happened, I would have come home."

Nicole stared at her. Her skin was blotchy, her eyes swollen. "Are you sure? Do you swear?"

"I swear. I was mad and hurt, but not suicidal. I wouldn't have risked myself or Gabe."

More tears filled Nicole's eyes. "You had a baby all on your own. How did you do that? I was so scared when I had Eric and Hawk was with me."

"I had friends." Bill had been with her every second except for the actual birth.

"You should have had family. I'm sorry. I've been holding back because I'm scared of losing you again. But that's wrong. You are wonderful and amazing and you deserved my support. I don't know why I couldn't give that to you."

"Maybe because you were forced to raise your baby sister from the time you were twelve years old. Maybe because you never got to be a kid yourself."

Nicole hugged her. "You're not supposed to be so understanding. I have a whole speech prepared."

They clung to each other.

"I'm so proud of you," Nicole whispered fiercely. "Look at all you've done. You have great ideas. You've saved the business. I would have just shut down. All these people are working because of you. I can never thank you enough."

Simple words strung together, Jesse thought. But so powerful. She felt the tear in her heart mend and the last of the resentment fade away.

"I love you," she told her sister.

"I love you, too," Nicole said, then straightened. "Which is why I'm giving you this. Because money talks, right?"

Jesse stared down at the check. It was for one hundred and fifty thousand dollars. Her breath got caught in her chest.

"What is this?"

"Half the insurance money. There will be more. They're paying it out as we need it. Half the business is yours. It's always been yours. I was wrong to keep it from you. So take it. You can start something of your own, or put a big chunk down on a house, whatever you want. It's enough to fund a dream."

It was more money than Jesse had ever seen in her life. Way more. It offered possibilities and home and the chance to...

To what? Start another business? She wanted to make the bakery work. She wasn't ready to buy a house. Not until everything was settled. Besides, she already had plans for the money.

She handed the check back to her sister. "I don't think so," she said.

Nicole blinked at her. "Why not?"

"Because if I take half the insurance money, we won't have enough left to build the bakery."

"I don't understand."

Jesse smiled, then raised her arm toward the trays of brownies. "This is temporary. I want a real store, too. The fire means we can modernize, get new, more efficient equipment, redesign the space better. I have some ideas."

Nicole stared at her, then started to laugh. "Just like that?"

"My last name is Keyes, too. The bakery is in my blood. But we'll have to talk about a few things. I have some thoughts about changes we can make in how we do things."

Nicole grinned. "Of course you do."

JESSE WAS STILL UP when Paula came home that night after yet another date with Bill. Jesse took one look at her flushed face and bright eyes and said, "This is getting serious. Should I be worried about you?"

Paula ducked her head. "Don't be silly. Bill is a very nice man. We're just having fun together."

"Oh, I think it's more than fun," Jesse teased. "You're remembering to practice safe sex, right?"

"I'm ignoring you," Paula said as she set down her purse on the kitchen counter. "I do like him."

"He likes you." Jesse had a feeling it was beyond simple "like" for both of them. Bill and Paula seemed to have fallen hard for each other.

"He lives in Spokane," Paula said. "That's a bit of a problem, but not one we have to deal with right now. It's just—interesting."

"Sometimes interesting is a really good time."

"I know." Paula settled on one of the stools by the counter. "How are orders at the bakery? Still piling in?"

"We have more than we can fill, but we're working the program. Nicole and I have finally reached an understanding." She filled Paula in on the conversation she'd had with her sister earlier that day. "I didn't realize what a knot I had in my stomach until it was gone. I've missed Nicole. I'm sure we'll fight, we've always fought, but it feels different now. Like we've cleared the air. I like that."

"I'm glad. Any other air being cleared?"

Jesse grinned. "You're not subtle."

"I know. I just wish you and Matt could get back together. I have selfish reasons. Not only would it keep you and Gabe close by, I could probably let go of some of the guilt I've been carrying. Not all of it, but even a little would be good."

Jesse touched the other woman's hand. "Don't feel guilty. You reacted to a situation. But you didn't force Matt to turn his back on me and you're not the reason I left town."

"Easy for you to say. I keep thinking about how much better things would have gone if I'd just stayed out of everything." Paula squeezed Jesse's fingers. "I can't undo that, but I can hope for the best."

"There's nothing for you to undo. You were looking out for your son. I have Gabe, now. I get it. I would do the same thing."

Paula smiled. "Well, maybe not the same thing."

"Something close."

"Okay, thanks for saying that. Matt was over the other night. How was that?"

Jesse thought about the lovemaking, the connection, how she'd finally felt right with him. "Good. Better than good. He's great with Gabe and that's wonderful. I think—" She swallowed, barely able to think the words, let alone speak them. "I'm hoping we have a chance. I think he still has feelings for me. I'm not sure."

"I think he does, too," Paula told her. "From what I've heard, there have been a lot of women in his life, but no one has gotten close. I can't helping wondering if it's because he never stopped loving you."

A wonderful, thrilling, terrifying thought. Terrifying because if he *had* forgotten what they had together, she would be crushed.

"I want that to be true, but I don't know," Jesse said honestly. "I'm afraid I'm reading too much into his actions. Wishful thinking."

Paula looked at her. "Because you never stopped loving him."

Jesse nodded slowly. "I guess I can only give my heart once. He has it. The question is, does he still want it?"

MATT AND GABE WALKED to the front door of the house. Matt paused before knocking, wanting to enjoy these last few minutes alone with his son.

"I had fun," he told his four-year-old.

Gabe grinned up at him, then leaned against him. A slight weight, but so special. "I love you, Daddy."

Gabe had said that before. He expressed his feelings easily. Was that because of his age? Was it due to Jesse? Matt wasn't sure. He'd always been wary of sharing his heart and after Jesse he'd vowed never to love again.

But this was different. His connection with his child transcended ordinary love. It was beyond anything he'd known and it mattered more than he would ever be able to explain.

He crouched on the porch and stared into Gabe's big blue eyes. "I love you, son."

Gabe threw himself into his arms and hung on as if he would never let go. "For always?" he asked in a whisper.

"For always. No matter what. No matter what happens. I love you. I'm your dad."

Gabe squeezed harder.

Such small arms, Matt thought, holding him equally tight. Such a small body to hold so much life.

They released each other and went into the house. Gabe went running off to find Jesse and his grandmother. Matt moved more slowly, still feeling the emotion of the moment. Jesse found him in the formal living room no one ever used.

"Are you all right?" she asked as she approached. "Did you have a good time?"

"Yeah," he said, looking at her move, remembering her naked. "We did great."

"Gabe's excited. He loves spending time with you." She winced. "Sorry. Just had a guilt flash."

One she'd earned, he thought grimly, trying not to get caught up in all he'd missed. The flicker of passion died as if it had never been.

"I grew up without a father," he said. "I didn't know anything about him and my mom wouldn't say much except he wasn't interested in the fact that she was pregnant. She wasn't all that interested in having him be a part of our lives and me asking about him made her cry, so I stopped."

Jesse nodded, looking uncomfortable. "Gabe asked about you more and more. It's one of the reasons I came back. I knew he had to have the chance to get to know you."

He shouldn't have had to "get to know" his son. He should have been there from the start. "I looked him up a few years ago. My father. I had an investigator find him and let him know I was looking for him. I didn't use my name. I didn't want him interested for money."

Jesse's expression softened. "Oh, Matt. You shouldn't have to worry about that."

He didn't let himself respond to her. "He wasn't interested in me. He said he hadn't cared about his bastard before and he didn't care now. He told me to go away and never bother him again."

She crossed the room and held him. He let her, absorbing her concern without feeling it. "Today, with Gabe at the park, he tripped and fell. It was like I was falling, but worse because I didn't care if I got hurt but I didn't want anything to happen to him. I reached for him and caught him, but in that second, I died a thousand times."

She raised her head and stared at him, her eyes bright with tears. "I know," she whispered. "I know exactly how that feels. It's horrible to be so afraid and so unable to control everything that's going on. Sometimes I can barely breathe for worrying. But he's tough and strong and he'll make you proud. You'll see."

Gabe didn't have to make him proud. Matt's love wasn't conditional.

Emotions welled up inside of him. The feelings for Gabe, his rage and anger at Jesse, anger she apparently couldn't sense. He wanted to shake her for stealing all this time from him. He wanted her punished. He wanted her to suffer as he'd suffered.

She smiled then. It was a little shaky around the corners, but happy. "Matt, this probably isn't the time or the place. But—I love you. I probably never stopped loving you." She laughed and stepped back. "Please don't say anything. I just want to get this out. I'm so sorry about what happened with Gabe. I hate what you lost and if I could change it, I would. But we can't make the past different. So we have to deal with where we are. I hope—"

She cleared her throat. Color rose on her cheeks. "I hope you can forgive me. I know it's going to take a while, but I'll wait. I hope you can understand why I did what I did. I hope we can come to some agreement about Gabe. Sharing him or whatever."

Whatever? She wanted more. She wanted it all, he thought contemptuously. If she thought that was possible after what she'd done, she'd never known him at all.

She raised herself on tiptoe and kissed him. He let her, even helped by bending slightly. Then she smiled at him and left.

He watched her go. When he was alone in the room, he pulled out his cell phone and scrolled through the names until he found the one he needed.

"Heath," he said when his attorney picked up. "It's time. I want Jesse served."

CHAPTER EIGHTEEN

MATT DIDN'T SLEEP THAT night. He kept tossing and turning, thinking about Gabe and Jesse and what was going to happen when Jesse was served with the papers. As he lay in the dark, he told himself he should be pleased. He'd won. His victory would be her broken heart and shattered life. She would pay for what she'd done to him.

He thought about how he and Gabe would hang out together. How his son would run to greet him when he got home from work. How they'd take trips on weekends and do guy stuff together. Maybe he'd get a boat and they could go out on the lake. But instead of his son's smiling face, he saw Gabe in tears, crying for his mother. He saw a faceless nanny spending her days with the boy because he, Matt, was busy at work. He saw the pain in Jesse's eyes.

He gave up pretending to sleep around four in the morning, got up and went into his study. There he researched schools online. Only the best for *his* son. He visited college Web sites and told himself he was doing what had to be done. That Jesse had earned her suffering, even as a voice in his head whispered that Jesse had run because she'd been hurt. That she hadn't deliberately set out to keep him from Gabe.

"Does it matter?" he asked aloud. "The end result is the same."

He didn't want to be reasonable. He didn't want to see her side of things. He wanted retribution and payback. He wanted her to know the loss he'd experienced.

But he didn't want to hurt Gabe. And somewhere, deep inside, he wasn't sure he wanted to hurt Jesse, either.

He swore loudly in the silence of his study. If he didn't do this, how was he ever supposed to forgive her for what had happened? How was he supposed to get over what he'd lost? Wasn't this the only way?

After a sleepless night, he got to his office shortly after six and cleared out his e-mail in-box. Diane arrived at eight.

"Want to talk about it?" she asked as she carried in a mug of coffee.

"No."

"So you're in a crappy mood."

He glared at her without speaking.

"You sure have that body language thing down," she murmured, standing her ground. "Talking about it will help."

He narrowed his gaze.

She ignored his obvious annoyance. "What have you done?"

"What makes you think I've done anything?"

"You're a man, you're dealing with the sudden appearance of a child you didn't know about. You're not sure how you feel about Jesse. Men don't deal well with emotion. When in doubt, you try to fix things. That's usually a bad idea."

He'd told her the basics of what had happened when Jesse had come back and Diane had met her once or twice. Still, he hadn't been that specific with the details, so how had she figured it all out? Was it a woman thing or was Diane just better than most?

"I'm doing what has to be done," he told her.

She sighed. "That doesn't give me a lot of confidence. Matt, I've known you a long time. I'm going to presume on that and say something that goes beyond the confines of our boss-secretary relationship. I'm only going to say it once and I'll never refer to it again."

"You sure you want to do that?" he asked, confident he didn't want to hear what she had to stay but unsure how to stop her without giving away too much.

"Yes, because I care about you. You're basically a good guy, but you've been burned when it comes to love. You hold back, you don't trust and you never put yourself out there. You can't accept what you don't offer. You can't keep what you aren't willing to give away." She paused, her expression kind. "You still love her. Hurting her is only going to hurt you more. And you have a child to think about. How do you think Gabe is going to feel about the man who made his mother cry?"

She turned and left.

Matt stared after her, unnerved by how easily she'd read him. She couldn't know the specifics, but she'd obviously guessed he'd set some kind of plan in motion.

He told himself her words didn't matter and for the most part they didn't. Except the part about Gabe. He'd come too far to lose his son again.

Yes, the boy would be upset for a while, but he'd get over it. Children dealt with moving from parent to parent all the time. They managed. Except he wanted more than for Gabe to manage. He wanted him to thrive.

"I have to do this," he muttered as he turned back to his computer. But the graph on the screen no longer held his attention.

He stood and paced the length of his office, then sat back down and flipped through his phone book. He dialed.

"Hello?" The voice was calm, cool and very sultry.

"Jade, it's Matt."

"Matt? I haven't heard from you in a while. How are things?"

"Good. I wondered if you were free for lunch."

"I should be coy and say I have to check my schedule, but I happen to know I'm free. Buchanan's at noon?"

"I'll be there."

When he hung up, he leaned back in his chair. Lunch with Jade would be good for him. She was a beautiful, brilliant attorney who enjoyed sex as long as there were no strings attached. She was the sexy centerfold version of a man. She hated emotion, played it straight and asked for what she wanted. In other words, she was perfect.

JADE WAS ALREADY AT the restaurant when Matt arrived. She was a slender, dark-haired beauty in a power suit and high heels.

"You look better than I remember," she murmured as he kissed her cheek. "And that's saying something."

Her perfume was familiar, as was her quick smile. They'd been lovers a few months back, until work commitments had pulled them apart. He'd been meaning to call for a while but he'd never gotten around to it.

He put his hand on the small of her back as they were led to a booth and handed menus. He set his down and stared into her dark eyes.

"We should have done this a long time ago," he said, wondering why he hadn't made the effort.

"We've been busy." She shrugged. "I haven't been sitting around waiting for you."

"No. You've been out raising hell."

She laughed. "A little. Work has been keeping me busy." She started talking about a twist of corporate law that had nearly doubled her billable hours.

Matt watched more than listened. He admired the play of light on her perfect skin, the way she moved her hands as she spoke. She was elegant and amusing, telling her story with just the right combination of confidence and humor. They would have been the perfect couple. Neither overly interested in romantic love, finding contentment in good sex and the occasional dinner.

Then he thought about his son, how Gabe looked when he smiled. He thought about the games and toys scattered around the house. How the kid was always sticky and happy and pure joy.

"Do you ever think about having kids?" he asked.

Jade's eyes widened. "Dear God, no. Children? Why?"

"I like kids."

"Since when?"

A woman with long, blond hair walked by. Thinking she looked a lot like Jesse, he turned, but it wasn't her. Why would she be here in the middle of the day? She was at the bakery, making her brownies. He could see her there, flour on her nose, her blue eyes dancing with amusement.

"Matt?" Jade asked, her voice sharp.

What the hell was he doing? Not just here, having lunch, but with the lawsuit? He didn't want to take Gabe away from his mother and he sure as hell didn't want Jesse destroyed.

"I'm sorry," he said as he stood. "I have to go."

She glared at him. "You're leaving? Let me be clear. You won't get another chance with me."

Matt didn't even respond as pulled out his cell phone and dialed Heath's office. His lawyer's assistant said he was in court and couldn't be reached.

Matt swore and hung up, then made his way to his car and drove the few blocks to Heath's office. He had to stop Jesse from being served. He had to destroy the papers, make sure she never knew. He had to make this right.

What had he been thinking? That by punishing her now, he could change the past? He couldn't. It was done. Yeah, what she'd done had been shitty and he had every right to be pissed at her, but he had to deal with that head-on. Not take away her kid. He didn't want to lose her or Gabe. He wanted them both in his life.

Diane had been right. He'd never stopped loving her.

The realization crashed into him. He loved Jesse. He'd always loved her. Maybe from that first moment, when she'd called his name on a sidewalk outside of a Starbucks and changed his life forever.

He drove faster than he should, raced through a yellow light and parked illegally outside of his lawyer's office. The elevator seemed to take forever. What if they'd already been sent out? What if he couldn't take it back? Finally he hurried into the office and found Heath's assistant.

"I need to find out the status of some papers," he

said, telling himself he was in time. He *had* to be. "It's urgent. They should not be served."

She took a couple of steps back and nodded, looking wary. "Um, sure, Mr. Fenner. Let me check."

"They were going to Jesse Keyes and they're about our son. I don't want her served. Do you get that? I want every copy of those papers given to me personally."

She went on her computer and typed for a couple of seconds. "They're still here."

Relief washed through him. "Good. Collect all the copies and give them to me."

"I can't give them to you without speaking to Heath and that won't be for a couple of hours. Can I have them messengered to your office?"

He didn't want to wait. He wanted to hold them in his hands and know that he was safe. That he had a chance to make everything right.

"Fine," he said, knowing his only alternative was to take them by force. "I want them today."

"Of course, Mr. Fenner." She smiled tightly, as if eager for him to leave.

Matt nodded and headed out. He reached for his cell phone again, then decided to go straight to the Eastside. He could pick up Gabe from his mom's and take him over to the bakery. He didn't know exactly what he was going to say to Jesse, but he would figure it out. She loved him. She'd told him that and if she loved him, everything was going to be fine.

JESSE KNEW SHE WAS going to throw up. Not that it mattered. Vomiting was the least of it. The horror and fear were so big, she couldn't feel much of her body. She was mostly numb and maybe that was a good thing.

She'd come home for lunch on a whim only to be met in the driveway by a small man wearing a suit. He'd asked if she was Jesse Keyes and then had handed her an envelope. Inside were words that made her heart stop beating.

Now she stood in the center of Paula's kitchen, re-reading, hoping she'd misunderstood. She had to. He couldn't have done this to her.

"Jesse?"

She looked up and saw Paula looking very worried. Without saying anything, Jesse handed over the paper-work. Paula skimmed it, gasped and swayed, then passed it to Bill.

Jesse walked to the stool at the counter and sat down. She couldn't think, couldn't breathe. This wasn't happening. There had to be a mistake.

In the background, she heard the happy music from a DVD Gabe was watching. He would be busy with that for at least a half-hour, which gave her time to pull herself together. Assuming that was possible.

She hurt everywhere. There was panic, as well, but she couldn't give in to the fear. She had to stay strong. No matter what it cost, no matter how she had to fight, she wasn't going to let Matt take away her son.

Strong arms wrapped around her shoulders as Bill offered physical support.

"We'll get the bastard," he told her, his voice low and firm. "We'll take him down."

"Can we?" she asked, barely able to speak. "I don't know what to think, what to feel. This isn't the Matt I know. He could never do that. Never hurt me and Gabe that way. Oh, God, Gabe."

She fought tears even as her eyes began to burn. "He loves his dad. He can't get caught between us and I won't give him up." She couldn't imagine life without her son. "I don't understand. How could Matt do this? I'd always thought we'd come to some agreement. That we'd talk and figure things out together. I thought he wanted that, too." She'd been wrong.

She knew he was angry, that he blamed her for keeping Gabe from him and…

Her brain slowly cleared. "He's doing this to punish me," she whispered. "He wants me to miss out the way he did. He wants me to suffer."

"No," Paula said, from Jesse's other side. "He wouldn't." But she didn't sound convinced.

Jesse covered her face with her hands. Of course, she thought. Everything made sense now. He'd been playing her from the beginning. All of it was a lie. Every second of their time together had been part of his plan. He'd done a hell of a job, she thought grimly.

"I trusted him. I encouraged him to get to know Gabe. I helped him and all the time he's been setting this up. He put me through all that crap about how I'd taken his son away from him. He made me feel horrible. He made me crawl, all while he *knew* he was going to try to take Gabe from me."

There was only silence around her. It was enough to let her know that Bill and Paula feared she was right.

The sense of betrayal was nearly as great as her fear of losing her son. She'd gone to Matt with the incredibly stupid thought that he deserved to get to know his child. She'd been open and giving and honest. She'd exposed her soul to him. She'd confessed her deepest secrets, shown the worst side of herself and, for the second time, he'd turned on her.

"It was just a game," she murmured. "A game of revenge. He made me believe in him, then he ripped out my heart."

They'd made love, she thought, humiliated beyond words. She remembered the last time they'd been together. How perfect it had been, how connected she'd felt. Then she remembered how he'd had a condom in his pocket. An amazing coincidence she hadn't noticed before. He'd planned everything, down to the last detail. From pretending to be her friend to seducing her until she trusted him.

She stood up and brushed the tears from her cheeks. "No! He's not going to win. I didn't deliberately do anything wrong and he's doing this on purpose. He's not going to get Gabe. I can't let him."

"No, you can't," Paula said sadly. "I don't know

what to say. This isn't my son. Matt isn't like this."
Only she didn't sound sure.

Jesse didn't bother pointing out that Matt had obviously changed a lot in the past five years.

"You have us," Bill told her. "We'll fight this. He
won't win."

She appreciated the support and knew she was
going to need it. Matt would be a formidable oppo-
nent. But what neither of them understood was that
he'd already claimed a good part of his victory. He'd
stolen her heart for a second time, then returned it
broken and bleeding.

He might have done his best to destroy her emotionally, but he wasn't the only one who had changed. She
was stronger than he could imagine. He could do what
he wanted to her but Matt was never, ever taking Gabe
from her. She would fight him to the death if she had to.

The difference between them was that while he
would revel in his thoughts of triumph, hers only made
her sad. Defeating her son's father wasn't going to be
a victory for anyone, especially not Gabe.

MATT ARRIVED AT HIS mother's house, only to find no
one home. He went by the bakery, but Nicole hadn't
seen her sister since lunch. He returned to his office
with a vague feeling of unease. Jesse wasn't answering her cell phone.

He told himself that he would catch up with her later,
only he had a gnawing sense he had to talk to her now.

It was nearly two when the door to his office burst open and Bill walked in.

Matt saw past him to Diane's empty desk. Had the old guy timed his visit when his assistant was out of the way or had he just gotten lucky? Did it matter? One look at Bill's face told him there was a big problem and Matt could easily guess what it was.

He stood to face the other man, cursing the disaster that couldn't be undone. Jesse had been served. She'd read the papers, she knew what he'd had planned. She was hurt, confused and probably terrified.

"Let me be clear," Bill said. "I'll do whatever is necessary to take you down. When I'm done with you, just lying in the gutter will seem like a step up."

Matt had to respect the other man's balls, even as he knew it was all just talk. There was nothing Bill could do to hurt him.

"She got the papers," he said, ignoring the threat. "She wasn't supposed to."

"So it's a clerical error," Bill said sarcastically. "Great. I'll tell her that, because that will make everything just fine. She can sure ignore the fact that you planned all this, that you set her up. What the hell were you thinking, boy? Trying to take away Gabe? Why not just take a lung or a kidney? You've seen them together. You've seen how much they love each other. They're a family. You don't mess with that. Who the hell are you to hurt Jesse this way?"

Matt felt every one of those words as if they were

individual punches. They hit him hard in the gut and the chest and the heart.

"I can explain," he started, knowing it was a feeble attempt at best.

"Explain what? That you didn't lie? To Jesse? To all of us? It's too late for that. Whatever it takes, Jesse will win. Your mom and I will make sure that happens."

Because they were on Jesse's side. He was oddly comforted to know that she wasn't in this alone.

"You're right. I lied to her. I was angry when she first came to see me. No, more than angry. She'd kept my son from me for four years, then she showed up with no warning. She didn't even seem to understand what she'd done. Telling me she was pregnant, then taking off, wasn't enough."

"You think anyone cares about that argument? You think that comes close to being enough?"

"No," Matt said quietly. "It's not anything. It's why I did it. I wanted her punished. I wanted her to feel what I felt. I wanted her to suffer and I was wrong."

Bill's gaze never wavered. "I hope you're not expecting points for that."

"I don't. I'm telling you what I was thinking. As I got to know Gabe, as he became more real to me, I was even more angry at what I'd missed. All that time, all those firsts I didn't get to see. They can never be recovered. They're lost forever."

"Jesse should have tried harder to tell you about him," Bill told him. "She's admitted that. She made an honest mistake, but that doesn't justify you sneaking around, pretending to be one thing while waiting to destroy her."

"I know. I need to talk to Jesse. I need to tell her she doesn't have to worry. I can fix this."

"Now that's the first thing you've said that makes me feel sorry for you," Bill told him. "There's no fixing this."

Matt hadn't actually been worried until that minute. He knew he'd hurt Jesse, that she would be scared and angry and upset, but he believed he could make it right. That he could explain in a way she would understand.

What if he was wrong?

He pushed away the thought. He could get through to her. He'd always had the ability, because he knew her.

"She loves me," Matt said, more to himself than Bill. "She's loved me all this time."

"That makes the situation worse. It sure doesn't help you. Jesse is never going to forgive you. Just as bad, eventually Gabe's going to figure out you're the reason you've made his mother sad. A boy doesn't forget that sort of thing."

Without wanting to, Matt remembered a time years ago. He'd been maybe seven or eight and had found his mother crying. She'd been stretched out on the bed sobbing that she couldn't do this alone, that it was too much. He'd been scared and wondered who she was talking to. His father was the only person he could think of.

He'd hated him then, had vowed never to forgive him. It had been nearly twenty years before he'd been willing to try and get in touch with the man.

Matt sat heavily in his chair. The reality of the situation, the potential disaster, weighed on him like the side of a mountain.

"He's my son," he muttered. He'd just discovered Gabe. He couldn't lose him now.

"You should have thought of that before," Bill said contemptuously. "You had it all, you stupid bastard. Everything you could have wanted. It was all there for the taking. The love of a good woman, a son who only wanted to be with you, a happy family. Everything that matters. But you would rather be right. You'd rather get your revenge. How does it feel now?"

Matt didn't have an answer. He was too focused on everything that had gone wrong.

"Jesse isn't alone," Bill continued. "She has a whole lot of people on her side. People who aren't afraid of you. People who have resources. I, for one, plan to enjoy every minute of your fall."

With that, he turned and left. Matt watched him go. When the door closed, he was left alone in silence. He hadn't felt this alone for a long time. Not since before he and Jesse had first met and she'd changed everything.

He could fix this, he told himself. He'd never found a problem he couldn't handle. It was just a matter of figuring out the best strategy.

Only, he found it hard to think with the burning emptiness in his gut and the voice that whispered it was possible he'd gone too far.

CHAPTER NINETEEN

JESSE PULLED THE MORNING orders from the computer and scanned the report. Thank goodness the software they used provided a list of products ordered by type. It meant they didn't have to scan each individual order to figure out what to bake. She compared that list to the inventory being baked and noted how many extra batches of brownies and cakes they'd need to finish that day.

As she worked, she was aware of Nicole and Claire whispering in the corner. They weren't subtle, she thought, both exasperated and touched by their constant hovering. They were worried about her, which meant they loved her. That was the good news. The bad news was every look of concern, every shared knowing glance, reminded her of what Matt had done and caused her to emotionally crash yet again.

At least she was getting good at picking up the pieces and moving forward.

She started toward the kitchen. Claire stopped her. "Can I help?" she asked.

"I'm going to tell Sid how many more batches of brownies we need."

"I can do that." Claire took the paperwork from her and glanced at it. She frowned. "Just tell me how to read this Sanskrit."

Jesse retrieved her printouts. "I appreciate that you're trying to help, but the truth is, I'm okay. I'm getting through this. I can do my job and still be sad. I'm great at multitasking that way."

"I want to help," Claire said.

"I know."

Nicole sighed. "Hawk keeps offering to beat the crap out of Matt. Should I let him?"

"It's not going to be as easy as Hawk thinks. Matt works out." Jesse happened to know, having seen Matt naked. Something she didn't want to think about. Although Hawk was the professional athlete.

"Would it make you feel better?" Nicole asked, obviously serious about the question.

Jesse made herself smile. "Look, this is great, but you're making me insane. Let's just act normal, okay? That's best for me. Which means you shouldn't even be here, Claire. You should be at home practicing for a concert or something. And, Nicole, you have babies waiting for you. I can totally handle this. I would prefer to lose myself in work."

The twins glanced at each other, then at her.

"All right," Claire said slowly. "Wyatt is looking

around for the perfect lawyer to take on Matt. As soon as he has names, I'll pass them along."

"Thanks."

"And I meant what I said about the money. I don't want you to worry about it. Whatever the lawyer costs isn't a problem."

Jesse nodded. Claire had offered to give her what she needed to hire the best lawyer on the West Coast. Nicole had told her the resources of the bakery were hers to use. While she hated the idea of accepting money from either of them, she didn't have a choice. She had to be able to fight Matt on his own terms.

Her sisters finally left. She sat in the small corner that was her office and tried to think about work. At the moment, it was impossible. All she could think about was how much Matt had hurt her. Last time he'd broken her heart she'd been crushed, but this time she wasn't sure she was going to survive. She had so much more to lose. Her child was on the line.

Bill had told her about his visit to Matt. That Matt had said he'd never meant for her to be served. The problem was he'd still had the papers drawn up. He'd manipulated everything between them.

The front door opened and a woman walked in. She looked at Jesse. "Is this where the Keyes Bakery moved to?" she asked.

"Yes." Jesse stood and approached her. "We're not really open to retail right now. Our building burned down."

"I know. I just went there and was horrified." She smiled. "I'm sorry. Let me introduce myself. I'm Cathy. My in-laws are celebrating their fiftieth wedding anniversary this weekend. It's going to be a huge party. Everything is taken care of, or it was. My mother-in-law just told me that when they got married, the groom's cake was one of your famous chocolate cakes and that she would like to surprise my father-in-law with that cake again. Is there any way I can order one?"

The woman looked both frazzled and desperate. Jesse smiled. "Sure. You want to pick it up sometime Friday?"

"Yes. That would be wonderful. Thank you."

Jesse took the information. They settled on a time, the woman paid for the cake, then left.

When she was gone, Jesse wondered what it would be like to be married to someone for that long. Fifty years seemed like a lifetime. Once, when she'd been young and foolish, she'd thought she and Matt might get that lucky, but she'd been wrong.

The front door opened again. This time Hawk, Nicole's husband, entered. He was big and muscled, just like the football player he used to be. He was so not anyone she could imagine with her sister. Too bad she'd missed the courtship—that would have been amazing to see.

"Where's Nicole?" Hawk asked by way of greeting.

"I sent her home. She was hovering. I can't take that right now."

"And she listened?" Hawk looked impressed. "You're going to have to teach me that."

"You do fine on your own." Nicole was crazy about her husband. It showed in everything she did and said.

Hawk led her to her desk and motioned for her to sit. He took the visitor's chair by her computer. "I'll get right to the point. I'm rich."

Despite everything, she laughed. "You're not subtle, are you?"

"Why would I be? I made millions when I played football. I've tried to convince Nicole to let me pay for the new bakery, but she won't let me. She wants to do it on her own."

Jesse liked the combination of exasperation and love in his voice. "She's very stubborn."

"Tell me about it." Hawk shook his head. "I hope you're not like her in that respect. You're going to need money for the lawyer you hire."

Unexpected tears filled her eyes. First Claire, then Nicole and now Hawk, all offering her money. She was sure she would soon be hearing from Bill and maybe even Paula. They all cared about her and wanted to protect her. As far as her heart went, the damage had been done, but there was still hope for the rest of her problems.

He leaned toward her. "I'm not kidding about the millions. Say the word and whatever you need is yours. I mean it, Jesse. I want to help."

She believed him and because she didn't share the

same past with him as she did with her sisters, she was more inclined to say yes.

"Let me get some information on retainers and estimated costs," she said slowly. "Then I'll know an approximate amount."

He grinned. "You're saying yes?"

She laughed. "Most people aren't so happy to be loaning money."

"You have no idea how hard it is to do something for the women in your family. They're stubborn."

"Nicole in particular."

"You got that right."

He was a good man. She was glad her sister had found him. "I'll want this to be a loan," she said firmly. "I *will* be paying you back."

"Whatever. What we need to strategize is how you're going to take Matt down."

"Sure," she said, not wanting to think about that. Despite everything, she still loved him. She didn't trust him, she would probably never forgive him, but she loved him. Which made her the biggest fool around.

JESSE LEFT THE BAKERY close to four. She was beyond exhausted, but knew that might not translate into sleeping that night. She'd barely been able to close her eyes since she'd been served. Every time she tried to relax, she panicked and worried that she could lose Gabe.

As she headed toward her car, she saw someone standing in the parking lot. Matt.

She stopped, not sure what to do. Part of her wanted to run away. Part of her wanted to run toward him so he could hold her and tell her everything was going to be all right. Neither was possible. She wasn't going to show weakness and she wasn't going to wish for the impossible. Matt wasn't a place of refuge anymore—he was the enemy and she was going to defeat him.

She squared her shoulders and walked toward him, telling herself he wasn't the man she'd fallen in love with. Maybe that man had never existed—maybe she'd created him in her mind.

He waited without saying anything. As she got closer, she saw the shadows under his eyes. He looked bad, which probably should have made her feel better, but it didn't. In the end, there wouldn't be any winners in this battle. Victory would come at a price that would require payment forever.

"I'm sorry," he said when she reached her car. "Jesse, I'm more sorry than I can say. You shouldn't have been served. I know what you went through when you read those papers. I didn't want that."

"Starting when?" she asked, steeling herself against being close to him. "You obviously saw a lawyer more than once about this. You had the papers drawn up. You set everything in motion and then what? You changed your mind at the last minute? Big deal. It's done, Matt. It can't be undone."

"I was pissed," he told her. "Beyond pissed, beyond

angry. I hated that you'd kept Gabe from me. You took something that can never be made right."

"So you're going to do the same and then we're even? You're right—I can't change the past. But at least I've admitted I was wrong. I'll do everything I can to make up for my mistake. Because it was a mistake. Nothing more. Not deliberate. Not a plan. Not cruel. You're so big on not getting played, but you played the hell out of me. You thought this all through and then you watched the events unfold. How do you think that makes me feel?"

"Like shit," he said bluntly. "The same way I felt when you left."

"I left because you rejected me and our child. I'll accept that you could believe I slept with Drew. But even if I had been sleeping with my sister's husband, there was still a chance the baby was yours. You ignored that. You let me walk away because thinking the worst about me was what you needed to do."

"What else was there?" he demanded, his voice rising. "Do you know what it was like to find out you'd betrayed everything we'd had together?"

She stared into his eyes. "I know exactly how that feels."

He stiffened.

"It's better being right, isn't it?" she taunted. "It's much more uncomfortable to be the bad guy. You don't get to win this one, Matt. There's nothing you can do or say to make anyone believe you weren't the bastard. You wanted me to care about you. You used everything you remembered about me to make me fall in love with you."

She'd been over everything so many times in her head. "You were just waiting for me to fall in love with you. You wanted the words. The second I said them, you called your lawyer and told him to get the papers ready."

"Yes."

"I meant what I said. I loved you and I trusted you and you used that. You set out to destroy me, but you've done far more than that. You've threatened my child. I may not seem very formidable to you, but I'm not alone. I will do whatever is necessary to keep Gabe safe. You're not going to win by default. Every member of my family has offered me money and I'm taking them up on it. I will annihilate you in court. You have no idea what you're up against."

He could have at least pretended to look frightened. Instead his expression turned sad. "I'm sorry," he told her.

Jesse hadn't expected that. "So what? You're sorry. That's meaningless."

"I know, but it's true. You're right about all of it. I wanted revenge, so I played the game. Only everything changed once I got to know Gabe and spent time with you. I never saw the flaw in my plan—that I would lose everything important to me, including you. If I could take it back, I would. All of it. Not just serving you, but getting a lawyer involved at all."

The truly pathetic moment in all this was how desperately she wanted to believe him. "I'm not falling for that again," she told him, hurting as she said the words.

"I know. I've screwed it all up, Jess. I get that." He shoved his hands into the front pockets in his jeans. "You don't need a lawyer. I'm not going to try to take Gabe away. I don't want to hurt you. I want us to try again."

She stared at him. "Try what? Being together? After this? There's no way in hell."

He ignored that. "I want a real relationship with you. I want to be Gabe's father. I want us to be a family."

She wished she could hit him hard enough for it to really hurt. "That's crap. Total crap. Someone who wants a relationship doesn't plan the other person's emotional destruction. If you really cared about me you would have let go of your plan, but you didn't. You walked away from me telling you I loved you and called your lawyer. You care a whole lot more about revenge than anything else. I would never want to be with someone like you."

For the first time he didn't look as if he was confident he was going to win. His shoulders slumped a little and his mouth straightened. "You don't mean that."

"I mean every word."

"You can't." He drew in a breath. "I love you, Jesse."

The words were meaningless, she told herself, even as they searched for a way into her heart. No! She wouldn't give in, wouldn't be weak again. If it was just her, maybe. But Gabe was on the line here.

"You don't love anyone but yourself. You don't know how to love. You're not sorry about what happened, you're sorry you got caught."

"Jesse, no. That's not true. You can't walk away from me."

She stared at him. "Five years ago I *begged* you to believe me when I said I hadn't done anything wrong. But you wouldn't listen. You only cared that you'd been hurt. The irony is, I didn't do anything wrong. But did you bother to find out the truth? You believed what you wanted to believe, not based on my actions, but on my past. Something you were never a part of."

She sucked in a breath, determined to stay strong. "I came back with the idea of us being a family. I didn't expect to still have feelings for you. I thought we'd be friends and you'd be Gabe's father. I did everything I could think of to make up for you not being a part of his life. I didn't judge you on anything but your actions. You're still Gabe's dad and I won't stand in your way as far as seeing him, but what we had, what we felt is dead. I will never forgive you, I will never trust you and if it wasn't for the fact that your son would miss you, I would honestly tell you to go to hell and mean every word."

She pushed him aside, unlocked her car, got in and drove away. She was proud of herself for not completely losing it until nearly a mile later when she had to pull over because she couldn't see through all the tears.

CHAPTER TWENTY

JESSE KNEW SHE'D MADE a mistake as soon as she walked into the Starbucks. It was in Woodinville, by the Top Foods, a warm, cheerful place with plenty of seating. She'd never actually been to that one before, although she'd driven by it a thousand times. The problem wasn't the location, it was the memories. She and Matt had first met at a Starbucks. Five years might have passed, but she could recall everything perfectly. The way he'd looked, what he'd said, how she'd followed him and had boldly offered to change his life. As if she had the magic answer to anyone's problems.

Now she knew better. She knew that she was more than capable of making a mistake, of misjudging a situation. There was no magic—only the potential to have her heart ripped out and kicked to the side of the road.

"Dramatic much?" she murmured to herself as she climbed out of her car and approached the Starbucks. Okay, maybe a slightly more rational frame of mind would help.

She stepped into the store and looked around. She didn't see Matt at first, but knew he had to be there.

She'd noticed his car in the parking lot. She spotted him sitting at a table outside. She ordered an iced tea then walked out to join him.

There was a second or two before he looked up. A moment when the breeze played with his hair and the sunlight illuminated his profile. A moment when he was just the man she'd always loved, not her enemy.

Her heart thudded faster in her chest. How much of that was from anticipation and how much from terror? She didn't think he could really take Gabe from her—she believed in the end she would win. But what would the battle cost all of them?

She straightened her spine and steeled her nerves. She had asked for this meeting. It was her moment to play, her game to lose. Only it wasn't a game…not when Gabe was at the heart of all of it.

Matt looked up and saw her. There were shadows under his eyes and a tightness to his expression that spoke of loss and sadness. She could almost feel badly for him. Except *he* was the problem. She had to keep reminding herself of that. She had to remember how *she* felt every minute of every day as she remembered what she'd thought she had and what had been lost.

"Jesse." He stood and pulled out a chair for her. "Thanks for agreeing to see me."

"We have a lot to talk about."

He waited until she was seated to sit himself. He'd always had good manners, she thought. That was Paula's doing.

"You heard I had lunch with Gabe?" he asked.

"Your mom told me. That's what made me set this up. We need to work out some kind of visitation schedule. Gabe enjoys spending time with you and consistency is important."

"I agree."

His gaze was steady, his voice low. She couldn't let herself look at him for too long. It was like staring at the sun—she could get hurt, perhaps permanently.

"I'll go along with whatever schedule you want," he told her. "I'll make myself available."

The expression in his eyes seemed more sad than angry. "Jesse, I'm more sorry than you can know. I took what you gave me and threw it away. That was the stupidest thing I've ever done in my life. I want to make it up to you and to Gabe."

"How?" she asked, feeling tired beyond words. "You can't undo what happened, Matt. Look, Gabe wants a dad and you want to be one. Great. So we'll move forward from that. You'll see him and have a relationship with him."

"But not with you."

"No. Not with me." She clutched her tea. "I wish it could be different." More than he knew. Despite everything, she still loved him. The problem was she no longer had any hope where they were concerned.

"It can." He leaned toward her. "Everything can be different. You got the paperwork, right? Withdrawing the custody petition? Just give me a chance. Let me prove myself to you. Let me show you who I am."

Unexpectedly, her eyes began to burn. She stood quickly. "I already know who you are. What you are. I can never let myself trust you or believe in you. You've shown me that in the clearest way possible. So stop trying. Let me know what schedule works best for you with Gabe. Then we can finalize the details of your visitation."

He rose at the same time that she did. "This isn't the end. I'm not giving up. I love you."

The words hurt more than anything else he'd said—mostly because she desperately wanted to believe him. "People in love don't do what you did, Matt. E-mail me a schedule that works for you and I'll get back to you within a day or so."

"Jesse, no. Stop. Talk to me. There has to be more."

She looked at him. "There should be, but this is all we have now."

Then she left, doing her best not to run, not to show weakness. But it was hard to go, with her eyes filled with tears and her heart begging her to listen and given him one more chance.

MATT'S SUGGESTED DATES and times for seeing his son arrived in Jesse's e-mail, along with a notice from her bank about an automatic deposit. Jesse stared at the large amount and suspected it would appear at the same time every month. It was child support. Matt had found a way to get her the money.

She didn't bother wondering how he'd found out her bank account number. A man like him could do that easily. Computers were his thing. And he had near unlimited resources.

No doubt her bank would be stunned by her new balance. She'd always been one of those customers who sometimes had to ride her balance down to the last couple of pennies. She'd never bounced a check, but it had been close a few times. She'd struggled for so long and now there was more than enough.

Her first thought was to put most of it aside to pay for Gabe's college, but to what end? Matt would take care of that. She could offer Paula rent, again, but doubted she would take it. Eventually she would move out and get her own place, but Paula had made it clear she didn't want that to happen anytime soon. Jesse wasn't in a hurry, either. Paula loved being with her grandson and Gabe thrived under her attention. Jesse appreciated having another adult around. So for now, she would stay.

Gabe ran into her bedroom and stood next to the bed where she sat with her computer on her lap. His eyes were big, his expression hopeful.

"It's Grandma's birthday on Saturday," he said in a loud whisper. "I heard Uncle Bill say that. Grandma needs a party."

Paula's birthday? Jesse had never known the date. She pushed her computer aside and scrambled off the bed. "You're right," she told her son. "We need to have a big party for Grandma." She had a feeling Bill would want to take Paula somewhere nice for dinner. "What about lunch? We could have balloons and presents and a cake."

"And ice cream," her son said, clapping his hands together. "And presents."

"Lots of presents." Paula might not be willing to accept rent money, but she wouldn't turn down a few gifts. Jesse knew it was the least she could do. Plus it would be fun. "I'm going to go tell Uncle Bill our plan. I think the party should be a surprise."

Gabe grinned. "A secret?"

"Uh-huh. So you can't tell."

"I won't."

She had her doubts. Excitement usually won out in the four-year-old consciousness, but either way, Paula would know she was loved and appreciated.

"Can Daddy go shopping with us?" Gabe asked.

Jesse hesitated. "He'll buy his own presents for his mom."

Gabe's chin came up—a sure sign he was about to be stubborn. "I want Daddy to go shopping with us."

Refusing would be so easy. She could say that Matt was busy and Gabe would never know the difference. Except that would be lying and she'd done her best to never lie to her son. But spending time with Matt?

She hurt every time she thought of him. Her heart ached and her body burned. She missed being around him, missed his touch, his laugh, the way he knew her, understood her. Telling herself that knowledge had allowed him to devastate her didn't take away the fact that she still loved him.

"I'll ask him," she promised, knowing it was the right thing to do. Knowing she would get through it

SWEET TROUBLE

and hey, maybe even be stronger for it. She would ignore the fact that every time she was with him, another piece of her heart withered and died.

GABE SNIFFED ONCE, then sneezed. Matt laughed. "Not that one, huh?"

His son wrinkled his nose. "It doesn't smell like Grandma."

Jesse bent down and touched Gabe's cheek. "Are you sure you want to get perfume? Grandma might like a nice sweater, or some gloves to keep her warm this winter."

Their four-year-old shook his head. "I want 'fume. But it has to smell like Grandma."

Matt glanced at the sales associate who had patiently sprayed scents on half a dozen paper sticks and handed them to Gabe. "Sorry about this," he said. "We should have headed him off earlier."

She smiled. "That's fine. The right scent is important."

She was pretty enough, and smiling in a way that let Matt know she was more than interested. Not that he cared. His attention was solely on Jesse, who had been polite and emotionally distant ever since he'd picked both her and Gabe up an hour ago at his mom's place.

He'd been surprised when she'd called him about his mother's birthday and pleased when she'd suggested the three of them go shopping. Even her making it clear that the idea had been Gabe's didn't detract from his pleasure in her company. However he got to spend time with her was fine with him. He would use every minute to his advantage.

"You don't like any of these?" Jesse asked.

Gabe shook his head.

"Not even this one?" She picked up the sample of the first fragrance.

"Uh-uh."

"Maybe we should take a break from perfume shopping," Jesse told the boy. "I want to get Grandma a sweater, so let's do that and we'll try somewhere else."

"Okay." He slipped his hand in hers. "Grandma likes red."

"Yes, she does." Jesse glanced at Matt. "Is this making you crazy?"

"Not yet."

She smiled. It was an easy smile that told him, at least for the moment, she'd forgotten to be on her guard. Then the smile faded and she looked away.

"We should go upstairs," she said. "I saw sweaters there."

Matt hesitated. "I'm going to grab a coffee. You want one?"

"No, thanks."

He waited until they'd gone up the escalator, then returned to the perfume counter. The girl was waiting.

"You're back," she said, her tone suggestive.

He ignored that. "The first perfume we tried. What was it?"

"Shi by Alfred Sung. It's lovely. One of my favorites." All he cared about was that Jesse had liked it.

"Give me a bottle. Or a set. Do you have a set?"

She showed him a box with perfume and lotion.

"I'll take that." Maybe showing Jesse that he paid attention would help.

He caught up with them over a table of sweaters. She glanced at his package. "What happened to the coffee?"

"I changed my mind."

She held up a dark red sweater. "I think Paula would look great in this. What do you think?"

"I agree."

She glanced at the price and winced, then shrugged. "She's worth it."

He wanted to point out that the money he'd deposited in her bank account would keep her comfortable, but guessed that was the wrong tack to take. He also didn't offer to pay for the sweater. She would take that as an insult.

"Now we're getting 'fume?" Gabe asked as they stood in line to pay.

Jesse nodded. "There's a Sephora store here. Let's try there. You might like the Philosophy scents." She looked at Matt. "They're really clean and appealing."

"Then we'll go there next."

She paid for the sweater. Matt took the bag from the clerk. "I can carry this."

Jesse hesitated. "Thanks."

They walked toward the escalator. As they paused at the top, waiting for a couple of women to go in front of them, he put his hand on the small of her back.

He felt the heat of her body through the fabric of her long-sleeved T-shirt. She didn't react at all. Was she aware of his touch? Enduring for the sake of Gabe? What did she think when she looked at him? Did she allow any possibility of forgiveness?

One step at a time, he reminded himself. He'd worked his plan before and it had turned into a disaster. This time he was going to live the moment, doing the best he could to prove himself to her.

They left Nordstrom's. Matt motioned to the Ben Bridge Jewelry store. "I need to stop here."

Jesse raised her eyebrows. "Really?"

"I want to get my mom a pair of earrings." He didn't mention that for the past five years he hadn't bothered with a gift at all. He'd been too angry, then too lazy to bother. Another relationship that needed mending, he thought. Although Paula had been completely open to his apologies.

Jesse followed Matt inside the jewelry store. The beautiful pieces glittered and winked from behind their protective cases. At least everything was locked up so she didn't have to worry about Gabe bumping into a display or picking up something breakable. She relaxed her death grip on his hand, although still kept him close.

Matt walked up to the salesman behind one of the counters. "I'd like to see what you have in black Tahitian pearls," he said firmly.

Jesse blinked. Okay, so he was a man who knew what he wanted. She wasn't sure she even knew what Tahitian pearls were.

"Right over here, sir," the man said and moved to his left. He opened the back of the case and brought out several pairs of earrings.

She stared at the deeply colored pearls. They were lovely and sophisticated. Some dangled, some had diamonds. Matt pointed at the pair with the largest pearl, each set off by a sizeable diamond.

"What do you think?" he asked.

"They're exquisite," she told him. "The dark pearls will be beautiful with Paula's coloring."

"Good. I'll take these."

Jesse noticed he didn't bother asking the price. She knew he could afford whatever they were. Five years ago he would have writhed and hesitated. Not because he was cheap but because he'd never spent the money he earned. He'd been too busy being a computer nerd. He'd been sweet and honorable and he'd made her feel safe. If she had to say what she'd missed the most when she'd left, she would have to admit it was how right she'd felt in his arms. Like she belonged. As if nothing bad would ever happen.

"Mommy, look."

Gabe pointed to a display of diamond bracelets. Several of them looked expensive enough to cost the same as a small car.

"They're pretty."

"I like that one."

She looked at the white-gold bangle with graduated diamonds.

"It's very nice."

Matt moved next to her. "Which one do you like?" he asked Gabe.

The boy pointed.

"You should try it on, Jess."

She took a step back. "No, thanks."

"Not your style?"

It was too beautiful for her to say that. "I don't have anywhere to wear it."

The salesman pulled the bracelet out of the case. "Today women wear bracelets like this all the time."

Not in her world, she thought, releasing Gabe and tucking her hands behind her back. "I'm okay. Thanks."

"Just try it on," Matt told her. "See how it looks."

As if it could look bad. "I'm—" All three of them were staring at her. She sighed. "Fine. I'll try it on."

"This is a Journey bracelet. Two carats of diamonds set in white gold." He put it around her wrist.

It fit perfectly and looked amazing. Jesse had never tried on anything this lovely before. The diamonds seemed perfect, so bright and practically casting a rainbow when they caught the light.

"We'll take it," Matt said.

She gasped. "No, we won't."

"Why not? You like it. It looks good on you."

"It's insane. I can't take this."

"Your bracelet is pretty, Mommy," Gabe said.

It was too much. It implied…she wasn't sure what, but something. It had to.

Matt leaned toward her. "A man giving the mother of his child a gift is traditional."

"There's a stretch," she muttered. "I can't. And even if I could, this is too extravagant."

"Your gift with interest. Please, Jesse. I want you to have this."

"It doesn't prove anything," she whispered. "It's not going to make me like you more."

The words sounded more harsh than she'd intended, but before she could apologize, he nodded.

"I know you well enough to believe that. Take the bracelet. Because it's nearly as beautiful as you are. Please."

His dark gaze seemed to see inside of her, to the place that still wanted to believe in him.

"Matt, I—" She nodded. "Thank you."

"You're welcome."

He looked pleased. Not victorious, but happy. Which shouldn't have made her feel better, but it did.

SATURDAY MORNING, BILL took Paula out to run some errands so the rest of them could get ready for the party. Matt arrived right at ten-thirty, his arms filled with bags and packages.

"I still have the cake in the car," he said as he put everything on the kitchen table. Then he grabbed Gabe and swung him in his arms. "How's my best boy?" he asked.

Gabe laughed. "We bought ice cream."

"I had to hide it in the back of the freezer," Jesse told him, trying to keep things light, trying not to show how good it was to see him. "Why don't you go get the cake and I'll get this unpacked?"

"Sure."

He ruffled Gabe's hair then went back out to his car. Jesse unpacked the various bags. He'd bought everything she'd asked him to. The three-foot sub sandwich she'd ordered, the matching paper napkins and cake plates. There were two sprays of flowers from the florist in Woodinville, a small wrapped package that was his mother's present and a bag full of cheesy birthday banners and party favors.

She set out the latter and had Gabe separate them into piles so they could fill goodie bags. Matt returned with the cake.

They worked together, setting the table, then slicing the sandwich. Matt blew up balloons and hung the banner. Gabe mostly got in the way, but Matt was patient.

Together they loaded the dozen or so goodie bags for all the guests. Matt held them open while Gabe dropped in the silly prizes. Jesse watched them, seeing the similarities in their eyes, the way they moved. Love filled her, for the boy and the man. Then she reminded herself what the man had done and turned away.

Paula and Bill got back at noon. Jesse, Gabe and Matt, joined by neighbors and Paula's friends, hid in the kitchen, then jumped out, yelling, "Surprise!"

She actually looked startled, then delighted. "A party for me? I haven't had one in years." She gave them all a hug before they sat down to lunch.

Afterward, before Paula opened her presents, Bill took Jesse aside.

"How you doing?" he asked.

"Better."

"Still hurting?"

She shrugged. No one wanted to hear the truth. She didn't want to live it, but it was impossible to escape.

He put a hand on her arm. "I don't know if this is the time or not, but I'm going to ask Paula to marry me tonight. When I take her to dinner."

Jesse laughed. "Seriously? That's fast."

He looked both pleased and chagrined. "I knew it was right the second I met her. We're old enough to know what we want and that's each other. I talked to Matt about it. Not to ask his permission, exactly, but to let him know my intentions."

"What did he say?"

"That he was happy for us both." Bill squeezed her arm. "I'm going to sell the bar. Paula and I have talked about getting a big RV and driving around the country for a couple of years. We'll come back here to see you and Gabe every couple of months, then settle here permanently when we're done seeing what we want to see."

Jesse didn't want to think about them being gone, then reminded herself they were her friends and of course she wanted them to be happy.

"I told Matt," Bill continued. "He wants to buy the house and give it to you. So you'll always have somewhere of your own. Paula and I will get our own place later."

She didn't know what to think. "He can't buy me a house." She'd thought the bracelet was too much.

"It's about making things right. He wants to take care of you and Gabe."

Jesse couldn't believe it. "He got to you?"

"There's no getting. He made a mistake. It's going to be a long time before I trust him with your heart, but that doesn't mean he can't try to do the right thing."

Was it doing the right thing or was it just for show? "I can't believe in him again," she whispered. "I just— I need a second."

She pushed past him and walked outside.

The air was quiet, the temperature warm. It was still summer, but soon the days would shorten and it would be fall. She'd already signed Gabe up for preschool. Time continued to flow, no matter how much she wanted to turn it back.

She heard footsteps behind her, then strong hands settled on her shoulders.

"You all right?" Matt asked.

He was so close, she thought longingly. All she had to do was relax and she could lean on him. Just let him take over and manage her life. The thought was tempting and very foolish.

"Bill told me that he's going to ask Paula to marry him," she said.

"You're not out here because of that. You're upset about the house."

She turned to face him. His hands fell to his sides and she desperately wanted them back on her. "You can't do that. You can't buy me things and expect it to be okay. It's not."

"I want you to be taken care of. My mom will want to sell the house and you need a place to live. It's not like you're going to come and live with me."

No, she wasn't going to do that. "Matt," she began.

"I'll put the house in Gabe's name, if that will make you happy," he said, cutting her off. "It can be in a trust fund until he's twenty-five. I want you to know you always have a place to go." He cupped her cheek. "I can't take back what I did, but I'll do whatever I have to so I can prove myself to you. All I need from you is a chance. You still love me. I'm the father of your child. We belong together, Jesse. I'm not going anywhere. I'll prove it to you."

She desperately wanted to believe him, but she couldn't. She knew that he would get tired of trying to win her and move on.

She turned away, but he grabbed her and pulled her close. Then his mouth was on hers, so hot and sweet she couldn't help but give in. She closed her eyes as his lips pressed against hers, claiming her, making her want him more than she wanted to breathe. Passion flared, then grew. She trembled with need and hope and finally with despair.

She drew back.

His eyes were dark with fire. His breathing was as fast and ragged as her own.

"You used up all your second chances already," she whispered. "There's nothing you can say or do to make me trust you ever again."

"I won't give up. I've spent the past five years

missing you. I did my best to distract myself, but it didn't work. I love you, Jesse. I'd rather spend the rest of my life trying to change your mind than be with anyone else. I'm not going away. You'd better get used to that."

She was too surprised by his words to move, so he got to be the one to walk away. She watched him return to the house, then closed her eyes and prayed that he meant everything he said and that she could one day forgive him.

CHAPTER TWENTY-ONE

"MATT'S MEETING US TOMORROW morning," Jesse said as she loaded the last of the dinner dishes in the dishwasher.

Paula stored the leftovers in the refrigerator. "Are you sure?"

"He called earlier and said he'd be there. He said he bought a new digital camcorder, so he can capture the whole event." He'd also offered to make her a copy so they would both have Gabe's first day at his new preschool to view in the future.

Paula straightened, then frowned. "But the world-wide launch of his company's latest game is at eight in the morning. There's a simultaneous release around the world. They've been planning the event for months. It's been on the news."

Jesse didn't know what to say. She'd known there was a new game in the works, but there was always a new game. "Why is this launch so special?"

"It's the sequel to some game from a few years ago. Apparently it's a big deal. People have been waiting for months. There are going to be launch parties all over the world and the ones sponsored by his company are being televised to each other. So if you're at the Seattle party, you can see people in London and Tokyo. According to *Business Week,* this game is supposed to increase profits at least thirty percent over last year. I can't believe Matt would miss all that."

Jesse couldn't either. "He never mentioned anything to me," she said slowly. "He's the president of the company. He should be there for that."

"I guess he wants to prove a point," Paula told her. "That family is more important than anything."

He'd been doing a lot of proving lately, she thought. Showing up exactly on time for his days with Gabe, never returning him a second late. In the past few weeks, Matt had been attentive, caring and friendly, without pushing. There'd been no repeat of the kiss, a fact that should make her happy. She didn't trust him, right? But she sure missed his kisses, along with other things.

Jesse excused herself and went into her bedroom. Gabe was already in bed, probably dreaming about his first day of preschool. He was excited about starting school, about his teacher and making new friends. She was lucky—he'd always been a social kid, which meant she didn't have to worry about him not fitting in.

She booted up her computer, then went online and did a search for recent articles on Matt's company. There were a few press releases about the new game launch and the party. It seemed to be as big a deal as

Paula claimed. There were also mentions of a recent stockholder meeting where Matt had arrived late. A few of the stockholders had taken issue with that and complained publicly.

Jesse checked the date, then compared it to her calendar. The afternoon Matt should have been at that meeting, he'd been with her and Gabe, buying their son new shoes for preschool. Now he was missing the launch of his company's biggest product all year because of Gabe's first day at school?

She picked up the phone and dialed his number.

"Hello?"

"Are you crazy?" she began. "You can't keep doing this. You can't miss important meetings at your company because of me and Gabe. I know we have a schedule for visitation and you want to be a part of things, but you're being ridiculous. Honestly, Matt, we could have rescheduled shoe shopping. I can't help the start of preschool, but I can take the camcorder and it will be just like you were there. As for the other stuff, we can always change the schedule. Or do you think I'm such a bitch, I can't be reasoned with?"

He was quiet for a second before saying, "I don't think you're a bitch at all. I'm not doing anything I don't want to do."

"You missed your stockholder's meeting."

"I was late, there's a difference."

"This is your career. Your company. Your life."

"It's not my life," he told her. "Not the part that

matters most. I want you and Gabe to know how much you matter to me. There may come a time when I feel comfortable moving things around, but for now, that's not going to happen."

Was he insane or just plain stupid? "You have to be at the launch party."

"I will be. I'll get there an hour late."

"Everyone will notice. They'll write it up in the press."

"No one who plays my games gives a damn about me being at the launch party."

He might have a point about that. "You're making some really bad choices here."

"Not from my perspective. I'm making the choices I should have made before."

What was she supposed to say to that? "Okay, but don't linger tomorrow. You can stay until he's in his classroom, then take off."

"I thought parents got to hang around for the first hour or so."

"They do."

"Then I'll be there."

"You're a very stubborn man," she grumbled.

"If you're saying I don't give up, you're right. I don't. I still miss you, Jess. And I love you. That hasn't changed."

She clutched the phone tightly in her hand. Magic words. Words she desperately wanted to hear. But could she believe them? Trust them? Trust him? "Matt—"

"I know," he said. "You want me to let it go. Only I won't. I won't stop telling you how I feel. I want us to be together, as a family. I'll wait as long as I have to—until you're willing to give me another chance."

"And if that never happens?" she asked, her voice a whisper.

"Then I'm going to spend a lot of time missing you. See you in the morning."

He hung up, leaving her alone in her room, listening to silence and wondering if she was doing the right thing or turning her back on the best offer she'd ever had.

AFTER GABE HAD CHARMED his new teacher and made friends with nearly every kid in his class, Jesse drove to the construction site where she was meeting Nicole so they could review the new bakery's progress.

In the nearly three months since the fire, the rubble had been cleared, new plans drawn up, permits approved and a foundation poured. Rebuilding had moved at lightning speed, mostly due to the publicity the bakery had received. Every agency had cooperated, the insurance money had flowed freely and now they were only a few months away from a grand opening.

She parked beside a couple of construction trucks, next to Nicole's luxury SUV. When she got out, she saw both her sisters were there.

"How did it go?" Claire asked. "How was Gabe? Robby starts tomorrow. I don't know if he's going to cry, but I think I will."

"He did better than me," Jesse admitted. "He just sailed into the classroom and started talking to all the other kids. He doesn't get that from me. Or Matt. Somewhere in our past is a very chatty, outgoing relative."

"Eric was only a little clingy," Nicole said. "I thought Hawk was going to lose it, though."

"I have everything on DVD," Jesse said. "Or I will. Matt recorded everything and will make copies. If you're interested."

"I am," Nicole said. "We have Eric's big day recorded, too."

"We'll do the same," Claire said. "So maybe this weekend, we should all get together and relive the moment?"

Jesse laughed. "Sounds like a plan." Who would have thought, after all this time, she and her sisters would finally find their ways back to each other? "So what's going on with the construction?"

Nicole groaned. "It's going fine, but the equipment is going to kill me. Do you know how much those new ovens you want are costing us?"

"Yes, but they're energy-efficient and they'll make back the difference in a year."

"They'd better. For that price I also expect them to fluff and fold my laundry."

"You're getting those fancy display cases," Jesse reminded her. "I get my big specialty ovens."

"And mixers." Nicole turned to Claire. "They have enough horsepower to moonlight as Jet Skis. Plus there's custom packaging and a new logo. She's sucking up money faster than it's coming in."

"We'll make it back," Jesse said, confident in her decisions. "You'll see."

"I'd better. At least the construction is going well. On time and under budget. It's like a miracle from God."

"More money for equipment then," Jesse teased.

"No and no. Did I mention no?" Nicole glared at her. "I swear, Jesse."

"Yes? You swear what?"

Nicole groaned. "Talk to her," she told Claire. "Make her see sense or hit her or something."

Jesse grinned. "You love me."

"I do, but some days—"

Jesse continued to smile. Oh, yeah. It was good to be home.

"How's Matt?" Claire asked.

Jesse's smile faded. "That was a subtle subject change. He's fine."

"It's been over two months," Claire said. "How long are you going to punish him?"

Jesse glanced longingly at her car. If she made a run for it, would her sisters follow? "I'm not punishing him. I'm being smart."

"About what?" Nicole asked. The twins exchanged a look.

That wasn't good, Jesse thought. Obviously they'd been talking about her behind her back.

"We aren't trying to interfere," Claire began.

"Yes, you are." Jesse was clear on that. She just didn't know how to stop it.

"Fine. We're interfering," Nicole said. "Matt screwed up. He more than screwed up. He was a total asshole. But he's obviously sorry and he's doing whatever you say. He's hung in there when most guys would have walked away."

"That's it?" she asked, outraged. "He's already won you over? You don't care about what he tried to do?"

"Of course we care," Claire said. "He was awful and stupid and he totally didn't think things through. But when he realized what he'd done, he took it back. We all make mistakes. We all screw up. We shouldn't be judged on the ways we mess up, but on how we try to make things right. Isn't that the true measure of who we are?"

Jesse didn't want to think about that. "Fine. He's sorry. He's trying. But for how long? It's been a couple of months. So what? He'll get bored eventually and go away."

"Is that what you're waiting for?" Claire asked. "Is that what you think is going to happen?"

"I don't know." Jesse just knew she didn't trust him. "He wanted me to fall in love with him so he could rip out my heart. Now he claims he loves me. How am I supposed to ever trust him?"

"You take a leap of faith," Claire said. "You give him a chance. Jesse, you love him. Even after all this. You're trying to punish him, but the person you're hurting most is yourself."

"I'm very comfortable with that," Jesse muttered. "I won't risk it. I need to be sure about him."

"Which is the real problem," Nicole said. "Because the person you really don't trust in all this isn't Matt. It's you."

Jesse opened her mouth, then closed it. "That's just crap."

"No, it's not. You're terrified that if you give your heart to him again and he tramples all over it, you won't survive. You don't think you're strong enough to handle the rejection, so you take the safe way out. You don't bother trying. But by doing that, you may be cheating yourself out of the best thing that ever happened to you. You love him, Jess. It's been five years and you never stopped loving him. He's Gabe's father—he's not going away. So your choices are simple. You accept that every relationship comes with risks or you turn your back on him. You walk away and spend the rest of your life regretting all the things you weren't brave enough to go for."

Nicole stared at her. "You're not a quitter and you're not a coward. Giving up isn't like you. You take risks and to hell with the consequences."

"Look where that got me," Jesse said.

"Yeah, look." Nicole shook her head. "You raised a great kid totally on your own. You came up with a business plan, a killer brownie, you got your AA degree. You thrived. I'm so proud of the person you've become. Look what my baby sister did all by herself."

Jesse's eyes burned with unexpected tears. "Don't you dare get all mushy on me," she whispered.

"Why not? You earned it. I love you, Jess, but you're going to hate yourself forever if you don't give Matt another chance."

Jesse wasn't sure who moved first, but suddenly she and Nicole were hugging.

"I love you," she whispered fiercely.

"Not as much as I love you," Nicole told her.

"Group hug," Claire said, throwing herself at both of them. "I just love having sisters."

"Me, too," Jesse said, feeling their affection wash over her.

They held on to each other for a few more seconds, then disentangled, each wiping away tears.

Jesse looked at both of them. "If you're wrong, this is going to all be your fault," she said. "I'll never let you guys forget that."

Claire and Nicole glanced at each other, then back at her.

"A risk I'm willing to take," Nicole said.

Easy for her to say, Jesse thought. She had a whole lot less to lose. But by not trying, Jesse knew she did, as well. Nicole had been right about a lot of things. Especially Jesse having loved Matt for the past five years.

What he'd done was horrible and mean. But what did loving someone mean if not understanding that mistakes could be made and regret might be genuine?

She didn't know if Matt deserved another chance, but she knew *she* did. A chance to be with the only man she'd ever loved.

WHEN THE STEADY pounding of the rock band at the launch party started sounding as if the beat was hammering inside his head, Matt knew it was time to escape back to his office. He collected his leather briefcase and walked toward the exit.

Diane stopped him before he was halfway there. "You are *not* leaving," she said loudly enough to be heard over the music. "You said I had to stay to the end."

"I take it back."

She grinned. "Feeling a little old for this sort of thing?"

"I guess. I don't know when that happened."

Her expression turned knowing. He had a feeling she was thinking that becoming a father had changed everything for him. She was right.

"You can head back to the office now," he told her. "I have to swing by the house, then I'll be in." He wanted to make copies of Gabe's first day of school for Jesse and his mom. Maybe he could drop the disks off later, which was nothing more than an excuse to see Jesse again. Not that he had any reason to hope. She wasn't acting any differently than she had a month ago. But he wasn't giving up. Somehow he would win her over.

He left the party and made his way to the parking lot. His car was off to the side, a familiar red Subaru next to it. Jesse stood between their vehicles, watching him approach. There was something different about her expression, about the way she was hugging her arms to her chest. Something that made him walk more quickly.

"What's wrong?" he asked as he approached. "Is it Gabe?"

"It's not Gabe," she said, her eyes bright with an emotion he couldn't read. "Everything is fine. I wanted to talk to you."

He set down his briefcase. "About what?"

She moved closer, then put her hands on his chest. "I still remember the first time I saw you. I thought you had a lot of potential."

He'd been a total geek without a clue. "Not my favorite memory." The girl he'd wanted to ask out had blown him off, then Jesse had shown up. "Until you came along."

She was staring at him as if trying to figure out something. As if…as if she still cared. As if he had a chance.

Relief and hope ripped through him, making him want to pull her close, kiss her, take her home and make love to her until she was too weak to resist. But he held back, knowing she had to take the first step. He'd been saying the words over and over. Now it was her turn. If they were going to make this work, she would have to commit.

Except standing there was torture. Waiting for her to see that they belonged together made his chest ache.

"I'd never been in love before," she told him, her blue eyes gazing into his. "I didn't know what to expect and I didn't think it would be so powerful or last so long. Moving away didn't change anything. I still loved you. And I love you now."

He sensed she wasn't done, that there was more to say. So he stood there, trying to be patient, knowing the prize was worth the effort.

"I know you were angry and hurt and that you wanted revenge," she told him. "I understand that you got caught up in your plan and didn't think it through. I believe you're genuinely sorry and that you love me and Gabe. I can keep punishing you or I can take a leap of faith. You've said you want us to be together. I want that, too."

He didn't know if she had more and he didn't care. He grabbed her and hauled her close, then kissed her until they both couldn't breathe.

"I love you," he murmured against her mouth. "I'll love you forever."

"Good. Because the women in my family live a long time."

He chuckled, then kissed her again. "I can't wait." He straightened. "Marry me, Jess. Marry me and have more babies with me. I want to spend the rest of my life convincing you that you made the right choice."

"I already know that." She smiled at him. "And yes, I'll marry you."

"Soon?"

"Let's take it one step at a time."

"I LIKE THE BLACK," Claire said as she stepped in front of the full-length mirror.

"Me, too." Nicole stood next to her twin and brushed her hands against the sleek, sophisticated black dress.

Jesse grinned as she remembered their terror the first time they'd gone shopping for bridesmaid dresses. She'd tortured her sisters with pink-and-sea-foam tulle before showing them the dozen or so black cocktail dresses she'd picked out.

The black and white color scheme fit the New Year's Eve theme. With the wedding at six and dinner and dancing to follow, their guests would party through midnight, then spend the night safely at the hotel.

Gabe leaned against her. "You look pretty, Mommy."

"Thank you."

"You do make a beautiful bride," Nicole told her.

Jesse smiled. "It takes a village." Or in her case, someone to put up her hair while her sisters had laced her into her strapless white gown. She loved the beaded bodice and flowing skirt, but she hadn't thought the whole lace-up back through. She would never be able to get out of the dress herself. Not that Matt would mind helping.

Paula entered the suite. "You girls about ready? All the guests are here and Matt is pacing, poor guy."

Jesse hugged her soon-to-be mother-in-law. "You

look fabulous." Paula's dress was a flattering black-and-white floor-length gown. She eyed the black pearl necklace that matched the earrings Matt had given her for her birthday. "That looks new."

Paula touched it and smiled. "From my son. Isn't it nice?"

"Very. This is fun. You and Bill should have a wedding."

Paula laughed. "I don't think so. We're going to stop in Vegas and get married there. We'll send back pictures."

The two of them were heading off in February for their two-year trip around America in their big RV. For now, they were spending time in both Seattle and Spokane as Bill sold the bar and settled things there, before they put Paula's house up for sale.

For the next two weeks, though, they would be taking care of Gabe while Jesse and Matt honeymooned in Hawaii.

"I have a couple of things for you," Paula said. "Matt said paperwork before toys, so here you go."

The envelope was slim. Jesse frowned. "What on earth?"

"I have no idea."

She opened it. Nicole and Claire moved close to read over her shoulder.

"It looks like a deed," Nicole said. "For a house. His house."

Jesse blinked. That big, massive, multimillion-dollar estate on the lake?

She opened the handwritten note in the envelope. "Because I love you."

She felt tears in her eyes and did her best to blink them away. "He's put the house in my name." Because he knew how much she wanted a home. And so that she would always feel safe.

"He turned out right," Paula said, sniffing slightly. "I'm going to cry."

"Don't," Jesse said, still blinking. "You'll have to redo your makeup. I can't believe he did that." But it was so like him. He'd gone out of his way to make her feel special and loved. How had she gotten so lucky?

"There's more," Paula said and handed her a large, flat velvet box. "I know what's in there, so I'm going to warn you against fainting."

Jesse opened the box and felt her heart leap. Inside was a necklace made of graduated diamonds. The largest stones, in the front, had to be at least a couple of carats each.

Behind her, both Claire and Nicole gasped.

"I think that might be worth more than the house," Claire whispered. "At the very least, it's a tie."

"I thought the big engagement ring was going to be the jewelry highlight," Nicole murmured. "I guess I was wrong."

Jesse grabbed the necklace and left the suite. She went down the hall to where she knew Matt waited, and walked in.

He stood in the center of the room, looking handsome and perfect in his black tux. When he saw her, he grinned.

"See, I knew you'd freak about the necklace. The house would make sense to you but all those diamonds would really bug you."

She felt her lips twitch. "You bought me a present because you knew it would piss me off?"

"That's not the only reason. I saw it and knew it would look beautiful on you. I like buying you things."

"You make me crazy."

"You look amazing. I really like the dress."

"You should see me in the veil."

"I will in about twenty minutes."

Love filled her, warming every part of her. She shook the necklace at him. "Don't do stuff like this anymore. Try buying stuff on sale."

"Not my style."

"It used to be."

"You changed me."

"Not this much."

He moved close and took her hands in his. "You changed everything about me, Jesse. You made me the man I am today."

"I love the man you are today."

"So it worked out." He stared into her eyes. "If I try to kiss you, are you going to complain about your makeup getting messed up?"

"I can fix it later."

"Good." He bent his head and brushed her lips. "Still want to marry me?"

"More than anything."

"Then let's go get it done."

He took the necklace from her and turned her around, fastening it around her neck. They were facing a mirror and she supposed her attention should have been riveted on the extravagant jewelry, but all she saw was Matt and how he gazed at her. Love burned in his eyes. Love she'd waited her whole life to find.

"I need to walk down the aisle," she said.

"I'll be the guy waiting at the other end."

"Thanks for not giving up on me."

"Thanks for coming home."

She smiled. "I belong here. With you."

"You're the best thing that ever happened to me, Jesse. I want you to know that."

"Oh, Matt."

Minutes later, Paula was led down the aisle and seated. Claire and Nicole lined up to start the procession. Gabe stood behind them and held a satin pillow with the two rings resting on it.

He looked at Jesse. "Now I have a real daddy," he said happily. "We're a family."

"Yes, we are. For always."

Jesse's sisters began to walk down the aisle. Gabe followed, moving slowly as he'd been taught. He carried the pillow carefully and took his place next to Matt.

Jesse waited until the music changed to the wedding march, then it was her turn. She held her bouquet in front of her. While there were dozens of people in the room, she only saw one.

When she reached Matt, he smiled. "What took you so long?" he asked in a quiet voice.

Despite the significance of the moment, she laughed. "I got held up." For five years. "But I'm here now."

"That's what matters. Oh, just so you know. I'm not letting you get away again."

"Is that a promise?" she asked, already confident of the answer.

"Yes, and you can hold me to it."

"I will."

He squeezed her hand. "You mean 'I do.'"

"That, too."

* * * * *

*For those who can't get enough of
SUSAN MALLERY'S sizzling romance and
gripping family dramas, HQN is proud to
introduce Susan's brand-new series,
LONE STAR SISTERS.
Every family has secrets....*

*Turn the page for your
sneak preview of the first book,
on sale in January 2009!*

"IT'S ONLY TWO MILLION. Is that going to be a problem?"

Lexi Titan forced herself to smile. "Not at all," she lied, wondering if John, her banker, had lost his mind. Two million *dollars?* She had to come up with two million dollars in twenty-one days? Oh, sure. She would just go home and dig around for loose change in her sofa. There had to be a million-dollar bill or two stashed under the cushions.

"You could always ask your father," John said, studying the papers on his desk as if they were the most interesting thing in the world.

Lexi smiled. "Thanks so much for the information," she said as she rose. Ask her father? Not likely. Even if Jed Titan was willing to bail her out, having to go to him would destroy everything she'd worked for. "I'll get back to you."

"Soon, Lexi," John told her, standing and shaking her hand. "You only have three weeks to come up with the money or you lose everything."

Having the ability to sum up the disaster of her life

in a single sentence was quite the gift. She hoped John appreciated it.

"I'll figure it out," she told her banker. "Talk to you soon."

With that she picked up her purse and walked out of the elegant office.

Frustration and annoyance hurried her along the carpeted hallway. She ducked out at the nearest exit and found her car in the parking lot. Once inside it was all she could do not to bang her head against the steering wheel. She could accept that bad things happened. What she hated was when they were her fault.

"You gotta be tough if you're gonna be stupid."

The familiar phrase, spoken in her head by a voice from the past, made her groan. She was in really big trouble—and she had no one to blame but herself.

CRUZ RODRIGUEZ HAD never believed that cars and women had much in common. He loved cars—they were his life. But they couldn't keep him warm at night...or in the morning. And even brand-new, they never smelled as good as a beautiful woman about to surrender.

He climbed out of his silver Bugatti Veyron and tossed the keys to the valet. The kid stood there, staring at his car.

"J-jeez. You're gonna let me drive that?"

Cruz looked at the car. "You going to damage it?" he asked.

"No, sir!" The kid walked closer, reached out a

hand to touch the side then pulled it back. "It's the most beautiful thing I've ever seen."

Cruz grinned, then moved toward the massive house. Now it was his turn to stare at the most beautiful thing *he'd* ever seen.

Lexi Titan stood on the porch of Glory's Gate, talking to a couple he didn't recognize. Even from this distance he could make out her long blond hair piled on her head, the delicate, classic features of her perfect face. She laughed at something the woman said. The sound carried to him on the warm night air. It was a sound he remembered, just as he remembered everything about her.

He knew all about Lexi—statistics were easy to come by. But he knew other things. Like the way her skin felt in the shadows and how her breath caught when she couldn't help herself. He knew pride was both her greatest strength and her greatest weakness, that she played to win and, unless her back was against the wall, she lost with a graciousness he'd never mastered.

He also knew she resented the hell out of him and would not be pleased he'd been invited to her sister's charity event....

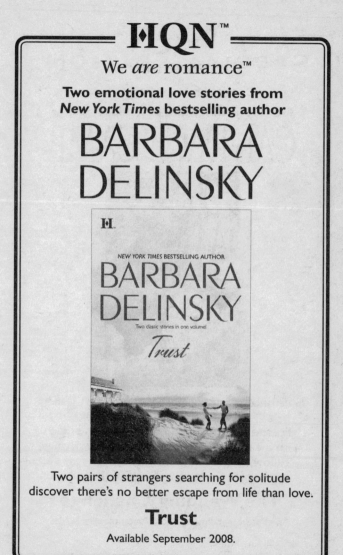

Silhouette®

SPECIAL EDITION™

NEW YORK TIMES BESTSELLING AUTHOR

DIANA PALMER

A brand-new Long, Tall Texans novel

HEART OF STONE

Feeling unwanted and unloved, Keely returns to Jacobsville and to Boone Sinclair, a rancher troubled by his own past. Boone has always seemed reserved, but now Keely discovers a sensuality with him that quickly turns to love. Can they each see past their own scars to let love in?

Available September 2008 wherever you buy books.

SUSAN
MALLERY

77314	SWEET SPOT	___ $6.99 U.S.	___ $6.99 CAN.
77297	SWEET TALK	___ $6.99 U.S.	___ $6.99 CAN.
77205	ACCIDENTALLY YOURS	___ $6.99 U.S.	___ $8.50 CAN.
77210	TEMPTING	___ $6.99 U.S.	___ $8.50 CAN.
77176	SIZZLING	___ $6.99 U.S.	___ $8.50 CAN
77117	IRRESISTIBLE	___ $6.99 U.S.	___ $8.50 CAN
77056	DELICIOUS	___ $6.99 U.S.	___ $8.50 CAN..

(limited quantities available)

TOTAL AMOUNT	$ _____
POSTAGE & HANDLING	$ _____
($1.00 FOR 1 BOOK, 50¢ for each additional)	
APPLICABLE TAXES*	$ _____
TOTAL PAYABLE	$ _____

(check or money order—please do not send cash)

To order, complete this form and send it, along with a check or money order for the total above, payable to HQN Books, to: **In the U.S.:** 3010 Walden Avenue, P.O. Box 9077, Buffalo, NY 14269-9077; **In Canada:** P.O. Box 636, Fort Erie, Ontario, L2A 5X3.

Name: _____

Address: _____ City: _____

State/Prov.: _____ Zip/Postal Code: _____

Account Number (if applicable): _____

075 CSAS

*New York residents remit applicable sales taxes.
*Canadian residents remit applicable GST and provincial taxes.

HQN™

We *are* romance™

www.HQNBooks.com

PHSM0908BL